Praise for Elaine Wolf's *Danny's Mom*:

"Brutally honest, no-holds-barred narrative . . . expertly blends the account of [the protagonist's] personal loss into the story. Wolf writes with insight and authority about an issue that society cannot afford to ignore as she points out that, even though many schools have implemented effective programs to deal with bullying and intolerance, recent cases serve as proof that institutions like [the high school in *Danny's Mom*] do, indeed, exist and that more needs to be done."

—*Kirkus Reviews*

"Once you start, it's hard to put down."

—*Instinct Magazine*

"*Danny's Mom* is an eye-opening novel about what really goes on in schools and with the people in charge. This is an excellent read."

—*Coming Out Journal*

"An excellent and essential read for mothers, adults who work in schools, and the LGBTQ community."

—*Advocate.com*

"Wonderful book . . . very inspiring. *Danny's Mom* made me sit up and take notice. . . . I truly enjoyed this book and believe it will give many something to think about."

—*MoonShine Art Spot*

"With its themes of grief, rage, school bullying, sexual orientation, hate crimes, and how much educators can and should do to protect students and themselves, this novel seems ideal for reading groups."

—Jefferson Cour ʳ   ᵖ ᵇ ˡⁱᶜ ᴸⁱᵇʳᵃʳʸ, Alabama

"*Danny's Mom* is engrossing. I didn't wa
have ripple effects and contribute to impro
—Jerryl Lynn Rubin, MI

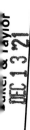

Awards and Recognition for *Danny's Mom*:

Book of the Month: Holocaust Memorial & Tolerance Center of Nassau County (New York)

AbOUT-Online's "Summer's Hottest LGBT Titles"

WellRead Westhampton's "Hot Books for Cool Moms"

DANNY'S MOM

Also by Elaine Wolf

Camp

a novel

DANNY'S MOM

ELAINE WOLF

ARCADE PUBLISHING
NEW YORK

Copyright © 2012 by Elaine Wolf
First paperback edition, 2015

Arcade Publishing books may be purchased in bulk at special discounts for sales promotion, corporate gifts, fund-raising, or educational purposes. Special editions can also be created to specifications. For details, contact the Special Sales Department, Arcade Publishing, 307 West 36th Street, 11th Floor, New York, NY 10018 or arcade@skyhorsepublishing.com.

Arcade Publishing® is a registered trademark of Skyhorse Publishing, Inc.®, a Delaware corporation.

Visit our website at www.arcadepub.com.

10 9 8 7 6 5 4 3 2 1

The Library of Congress has cataloged the hardcover edition as follows:
Wolf, Elaine.

Danny's mom : a novel / Elaine Wolf.
p. cm.
ISBN 978-1-61145-694-3 (hardcover : alk. paper) 1. Mothers and sons--Fiction. 2. Teenagers--Death--Fiction. 3. Life change events--Fiction. 4. Grief--Fiction. 5. Student counselors--Fiction. 6. Bullying--Fiction. I. Title.
PS3623.O5445D36 2012
813'.6--dc23
2012027381

Cover design by Rain Saukas
Cover photo credit Thinkstock

Paperback ISBN: 978-1-62872-513-1
Ebook ISBN: 978-1-62872-563-6

Printed in the United States of America

To Ira, my remarkable husband.
And to Adam, my wonderful son.

And to all those teachers who go above and beyond.

A Note from the Author

It has been years since I completed the manuscript that became *Danny's Mom*, and bullying still exists in our schools, summer camps, and places of business. Yes, we now have anti-bullying legislation, anti-bullying policies, and anti-bullying workshops. Nonetheless, too many children skip school for fear of being victimized. And bullying in the workplace continues to traumatize many adults. As a reviewer for *The Denver Post* wrote about the hardcover edition of this book, "You think only students have to deal with bullying and backstabbing in high school? Think again. Wolf's heroine, a guidance counselor, fights back."

Fortunately, most schools are so much better than the fictitious Meadow Brook High School in *Danny's Mom*. But, sadly, what happens in Meadow Brook could really happen anywhere. Although most school administrators truly care about the well-being of students, some don't. As in any workplace, some administrators become jaded and power-hungry, and when they do, their schools may turn into dysfunctional communities in which students and teachers are victimized.

I think parents believe (or want to believe) that everyone who works in their children's schools are compassionate, knowledgeable adults who always look out for the students' best interests. And most of the time, most of the adults to whom we entrust our children's safety do a good job, or a terrific job. But sometimes they don't.

I think of *Danny's Mom* as an admonition: know what goes on in your children's schools; stay involved—even when your children are older, when they're in high school; speak up and speak out; and always be a fierce advocate for your children. When parents such as Mary Grant in *Danny's Mom* ignore warning signs and refuse to acknowledge the difficulties their children face, then, yes, schools may become horrific places.

Many teachers who read *Danny's Mom* tell me that I got it right: that, sadly, what happens in this book can, and sometimes does, happen in their schools. Infrequently, though, I hear from a teacher who says this could never go on in a school, that school administrators could never be as bad as those in *Danny's Mom*. I look forward to the day when that's true, when no adults in our schools get away with treating students and colleagues the way Peter Stone does in this novel. And I look forward to the day when no students get away with victimizing others the way Tina Roland does in this book.

I didn't set out to become "the anti-bullying novelist"; my books led me to that mission. I'm glad that *Camp* (my young adult novel) and *Danny's Mom* are springboards for important conversations about bullying. I hope that someday all of our children and grandchildren can go to school without fear, that someday bullying will no longer be part of our culture.

Let's work together to make our schools and summer camps kinder, gentler, more inclusive places for everyone. I invite you to visit my website, **authorelainewolf.com**, for information about my novels and author visits, as well as for anti-bullying resources.

The present changes the past. Looking back
you do not find what you left behind.
—Kiran Desai,
The Inheritance of Loss

Woman must come of age by herself.
She must find her true center alone.
—Anne Morrow Lindbergh,
Gift from the Sea

Chapter One

People would say it began with the snow. Yet in the end, I could see it started long before last winter.

Danny was in his room while Joe and I argued about letting him drive that night.

"Jesus Christ, Beth!" Joe said as he stepped from the bathroom. "You've got to let him grow up already. We've been through this a hundred times."

"Please, Joe." I spoke softly, anxious to hide our quarrel from Danny. "I know you told him he could go to Noah's, but another storm's coming. It's not safe for him to drive."

Joe leaned into the doorframe and sucked in a long breath. His citrus shaving cream perfumed the hallway.

"If it wasn't safe, do you think I'd let him go? You have to stop babying him."

My stomach twisted. *What's the matter with you, Joe?* I wanted to say. *I'm not babying him. I'm only treating him like a seventeen-year-old who just got his license.* But my mouth filled with cotton; I couldn't push the words out.

"And don't change our plans with Tom and Callie," he went on. "I've been thinking of that steak all week. I'm not staying home to play chauffeur tonight. Danny doesn't need us to drive him anymore."

That's when Danny came out of his room.

"Please, Mom." His eyes found mine. "Dad said I could go. I already told Noah. And all the other parents said yes. Even the girls'. Please, Mom."

"Danny, I don't know—"

"Come on. You gotta let me. I won't take Dad's car. I'll take the Buick. Airbags and anti-lock brakes, right?"

"But—"

"I'll wear my seatbelt. Promise. And anyhow, it's not even snowing yet."

Then Danny hugged me—just like that. Standing there in the hallway, in the summer scent, in the dead of winter, my son wrapped his arms around me. I felt the muscles he'd been working on since September.

"Please, Mom."

Joe and I were at The Bay View Steakhouse with Callie and Tom Harris, our closest friends, when it happened. We had taken Tom's Jeep because Tom knows storms brew quickly in the Northeast.

That's why I should have said no. *No, Danny. You can't drive to Noah's later. It's gonna snow again.*

That's what my father would have urged me to say if only I'd have called him. *Joe's wrong on this one, honey. Just tell Danny he can't take the car tonight. How long do you think he'll stay mad at you?* Dad would have told me what I already knew: A teenager's resentment melts faster than snow.

Before the accident, I hadn't seen my father cry since the first time he heard me sing to my newborn son:

Hush, little baby. Don't say a word.
Mama's gonna buy you a mockingbird.

"Your mother used to sing that to you, Beth," Dad said, stroking Danny's tiny hand. "She would've been so happy and so very proud of you."

Then my father reminded me—as he always did—that after my mother died, I began biting my lower lip, chewing on it until a frayed, bloody rim outlined its edge. What I remember is that when I was seven and eight, toothpaste burned when I brushed.

After the accident, Dad came to see me every day for three weeks. Then I went back to work. Joe had headed off to JM Construction after only a week. Now everyone said I had to get back to Meadow Brook High School: Joe, Callie, even Bob Andrews, my principal, who had paid a visit and called a couple of times.

"Take as long as you need," Bob told me. "You've got plenty of unused sick days. But you know, Beth, the counseling center isn't the same without you, kiddo. So . . . well . . . maybe it's time to come back. Nobody else in Meadow Brook appreciates my ties."

I pictured my principal strumming his mustache and showing off his Beatles collection. Bob owns every Beatles CD and an assortment of Beatles ties, each illustrating a song. Whenever Bob wore one, he would find an excuse to come to the counseling center, where I'd guess the title and sing a line or two.

I don't know why, but I never forget lyrics. Tell me a phone number, it's gone in a second. Lyrics, though, live in my head forever.

But not in Joe's; he rarely remembers the words. Yet he loved to sing. He even signed us up for a song contest when Danny was in fourth grade. Winter vacation, 1993. We had gone to one of those old-fashioned family hotels with a never-ending agenda of silly games—bingo, charades, Name That Tune. In this particular contest, the activities director shouted a word and family teams had just one minute to call out songs with that word in the lyrics. We won GRAND

CATSKILL RESORT T-shirts when I came up with eleven tunes for *star*. Danny high-fived me that whole afternoon.

He was good with lyrics too, even at that age. He loved music, though he never took up an instrument—unless you count his three-week stint with the trumpet, which he begged for when he was nine. That ended when the teacher told us Danny had to practice more, and Danny pleaded with me to let him quit.

So I admit Joe was right when he used to say Danny had two speeds: *no interest* and *passion*. The summer after tenth grade, Danny went to the British Virgin Islands with a student group of volunteers and came back a do-goodnik craving spicy chicken and reggae.

Joe smiled whenever he told anyone Danny helped build a house in Tortola. And to Danny he said, "Building's good, son. It's like I always say: If you can build a house, you can do anything."

When I heard that, it made me think of what Joe had said when we were dating: "Good fences don't make good neighbors, Beth. People who can *build* good fences make good neighbors."

After Danny came back from Tortola, reggae seeped through our house, filling the air with sad tales trapped in happy beats. Danny taught me to dance to it, to let the music pull my hips while my feet stayed still. We sang along with Bob Marley: "Buffalo Soldier"; "Get Up, Stand Up"; "I Shot the Sheriff." Sometimes Joe sang with us. And though he mangled the words, he tried all the same.

But Joe stopped singing after the accident. I noticed the silence when he showered. No reggae or pop classics booming through the spray. No humming my wake-up call while he dressed for work.

It didn't matter, though, that morning I went back to Meadow Brook High School. I didn't need help getting up; a nightmare jolted me awake.

I see it still, this dream in which I race to the tennis courts for Danny's match. Noah's on Court 1. He's playing without a partner.

"Hey, Noah!" I call. "Where's Dan?"

Noah bounces a ball before serving. "Don't know. Can't help you."

I spot Eric's mother in the parents' line up. "Joan, have you seen Dan?"

"Nope. Not here."

Coach Roberts stands behind Court 5.

"Coach!" I scream. "Where's Dan?"

"Gone, ma'am. So sorry."

That dream clung to me as I pulled myself out of bed. And though hot sweat soaked my nightgown, my icy bones didn't thaw. I wrapped myself in my navy flannel robe and worked my way downstairs.

The coffee maker hissed as I called Callie. Tom answered the phone.

"Hey, Tom. It's Beth. Didn't wake you, did I?"

"No way. It would take a miracle to sleep around here on a school day." Tom hesitated, as if deciding what to say next. "You okay?" he finally asked.

I battled tears. "Sure. I just need to talk to Callie."

"She's in the kitchen, I think. Hang on a sec."

I didn't hear Tom call Callie, but I did hear Ellen, their older daughter: "Dad, it's not fair! Mom said *I* could borrow her sweater, and stupid Mollie won't take it off!"

When Callie picked up, I cried.

"Another dream?" she asked.

"Yes. And Cal, I don't think . . . I don't think I can go back yet. It's only three weeks since . . . since the accident." As I said those words, I didn't know that everything had already changed for me—even Meadow Brook High.

"So here's the deal," Callie said, knowing I wasn't ready for before-school hall traffic, well-wishers at my office door, and teens who have problems and futures. "I already spoke to Bob. He's arranging first period coverage for me. It's just my photo class. They can have a study hall. So get yourself together. I'm picking you up at eight."

"Cal, I can't." My voice came slow and thick.

"Sure you can. You have to go back to work. You can't just sit around and cry all day. That doesn't do anyone any good."

I couldn't think of what to say, so I poured a cup of coffee and waited for Callie to tell me what to do next.

"Beth, you hear me? You have to get ready now."

Silently, I took a swig from my favorite mug, the one with MOM written on it.

"Just put on your gray dress with that scarf I gave you for your birthday," Callie instructed. "And don't worry about make-up or anything. I'll be there soon. Bob'll have my head if I'm not in by second period."

"Callie?" I took a moment, but all I could say was, "Thank you."

Then I called Dad to check in—despite the early hour. I needed his familiar *Hey, honey. How's my girl?* In the last few weeks, I had come to count on him as a bellows for my lungs, as if I couldn't get enough air until I'd hear my father's voice.

I lied and told him I was fine.

"Callie's picking me up. I don't know what I'd do without her." I swallowed hard. "And without you, Dad. Thanks."

"Oh, honey, I'll always be here for you. And please eat something before you go. Not just coffee. You're getting awfully thin."

I lied again when I said I would. Instead, I refilled my mug and took it upstairs, where I sat on the floor outside the closed door to Danny's room. As I warmed my hands on the word MOM, the memory of my dream stabbed me. And with the pain, I felt the truth: Danny is dead. He is never coming back.

Joe knocked into me when he dashed from the hall bathroom. I didn't feel the splash of coffee, didn't feel the burn. A few days later, I would notice the blister above my knee.

"Beth?" Joe said, studying me as if I were a ghost. "What are you doing on the floor?"

I couldn't answer, but in my head I screamed *Fuck you, Joe! Fuck you! You killed my son!*

Chapter Two

The crash came minutes later. I hopped to my feet, flew down the steps. "Joe? What was that?"

In the kitchen, a shattered vase. Orange marigolds, red tulips, and slivers of glass on the wet tile floor by Joe's feet. "What happened?" I asked again.

Joe said nothing as he moved to the coffee pot.

Without a word, I picked up the flowers: remnants of arrangements from the teachers' union, Joe's business associates, friends, neighbors, people we scarcely knew. Every day my father had mixed fresh flowers and old in blended condolence. By the time I went back to work, a strange assortment crowded the vase on the kitchen table.

Joe topped off his thermos. "I couldn't look at those stinking flowers anymore," he finally said, focusing on turning the lid as if that took full concentration. "I just couldn't look at them."

Then sidestepping fragments, Joe came toward me. "Sorry," he said, his voice softer now. "That must have scared Moose."

I stayed quiet, avoiding conversation, avoiding Joe's touch, as I sopped up water and glass.

Back upstairs, I fiddled with the scarf around the neck of the lady in the mirror and noticed that her dress hung like a poor hand-me-down. Moose nuzzled my thigh.

"I know, old boy. The noise scared you, didn't it?" I stroked his golden head. "Wanna go out?"

I blinked, and there was Danny, just six years old and begging for a dog. Joe had begged too, after one of the guys on his construction crew told him about a yellow Lab with a litter of pups.

"Come on, Red. Please," Joe had said, calling me by my hair color as he did when he wanted something.

"It's not the right time, Joe. I'm starting a new job in September, and you're never home anymore. Who's gonna take care of a dog?"

"But you know what they say. Man's best friend and all? Don't you want Danny to have a best pal?"

Moose followed me downstairs after I gave up on fixing the scarf. I let him out the kitchen door, picked up a condolence card from the pile on the table, and tried to recall who Donna, Sam, and Jordan Rogers were. It came to me when I looked out the window and saw Moose circle the basketball post. Jordan and Danny had played on the same team in the sixth-grade basketball league.

Moose licked my hand on his way in and trudged to the stairway, leaving huge, muddy paw prints on the blond oak floor in the hall. I watched him lumber up the steps, his rear legs buckling as he reached the top, and waited for the creak of floorboards when he'd plop down outside Danny's room.

The doorbell made me jump. I opened the front door, and Callie hugged me as if we hadn't seen each other in a year.

"I'm okay. Really, Cal." She wouldn't let go. "Why didn't you just honk?"

"I did. A zillion times. Your neighbors must think I'm nuts, bangin' on the horn like that. Guess you were upstairs, huh?"

"I was getting dressed." My voice sounded flat. I knew I'd have to lie my way through the day. Time had evaporated. Fifteen minutes maybe. I couldn't explain it.

"Let's just do something with that scarf," Callie said, placing me at arm's length. She unknotted the silk. "Wouldn't want anyone to think you've lost your touch. You know what they say at school."

"No. What?" I tried to sound as if I cared.

"That you're one classy lady. A regular fashion plate." Callie slid the scarf from my neck and folded it lengthwise. In an instant, she fastened it around me like a tie. "That's better. All set."

A bubble of acid burst in my chest. All set, with a hole in my center.

We pulled into the teachers' parking lot three minutes before second period. Thinking in minutes meant back to work. Forty-two minutes per class. Three minutes in between. Sign in at least ten minutes before the first bell. Leave no earlier than thirty minutes after the last. Only the principal's buddies, the teachers who partied with him and the assistant principal, didn't watch the clock. They came in late, left early. Danny's death had promoted me, temporarily, to that higher caste. Callie must have bargained with Bob, I thought. She'd get me back to work if she could have extra time that morning.

We ran from the far end of the lot toward the entrance near the art room. I slowed down as we approached the building.

"Sorry," Callie called over her shoulder.

"Go ahead, Cal. I'll let Bob know we're here."

Callie stopped. She turned to face me. "You can do this. You have to. Any problems, just come to the art room."

I nodded and tried to smile. "Go on. I'm fine." My list of lies grew.

"I'll come by your office, Beth. Fifth period, for lunch." The door banged as Callie zipped into school.

I stood outside and listened for the bell, the start of second period classes. The building hushed. I pulled in a slow breath and opened the door. "I love you, Danny," I whispered. Then I walked into Meadow Brook High.

My first thought was that I should have gone around front. From there I could make it to the main office in seconds, then slip into the counseling center. Instead, I now had to weave through the art and music hallways, where a student's poster screamed: LIFE WITHOUT ART IS DETH. The missing *A* didn't bother me nearly as much as it would have only a month before, when I'd bolted into the art room after Callie had posted another student's misspelled announcement: SMOKEING CAN KILL YOU.

Peter Stone, the assistant principal, cornered me before I was able to duck into the office.

"Well, well. If it isn't Beth Maller. It's about time, I'd say. Oh, and welcome back."

"It's good to be back." Another lie.

"You know, when Marie's husband died, she came back to work the next week," Peter went on. "And the counseling center doesn't run right when we're short a counselor. Debra and Steve had to divide your caseload." Peter moved closer, looking down at me. "But I'm sure you know that. It's just a good thing all the college applications got out in January."

I stepped back, eager to distance myself from his odor of sweat and Marlboros.

"I'll let Bob know I'm here."

"Bob's in a meeting with the superintendent. Just tell the secretaries you're back." Peter checked his watch. "Better late than never, I suppose."

I hoped he would let me go then, but Peter's eyes narrowed, holding me in their glare. "And I don't know why Bob told Mrs. Harris she could come in late too. Wasn't easy getting coverage for her this morning. But hey, that's why they pay me the big bucks."

Peter chuckled as he walked down the hall. I wasn't surprised he hadn't said anything about Danny. I had worked with Peter Stone long enough to know that there's a rock where his heart should be—and a grudge like a boulder when it comes to me.

Callie used to say Peter was allergic to work. But, in fact, Peter and I were allergic to each other. Callie once asked what I'd do if someone held a gun to my head and made me choose: sleep with Charles Manson or sleep with Peter Stone. "That's simple," I told her. "I'd say *Pull the trigger.*"

Back then, I didn't know why Peter disagreed with me about everything from students' schedules to before-school clubs. I was the Honor Society adviser the year that group decided it wanted breakfast meetings. Peter fought me. "If those kids are so damn smart," he said, "they're smart enough to eat *before* they come to school. I won't have them hanging out in the counseling center, munching bagels and missing homeroom."

Bob, however, sided with me on breakfast meetings—one of the few times he and Peter didn't play their authority as a duet. But the next fall they chose Alan, a science teacher, for the Honor Society position.

A few years later, when Danny was in middle school, I applied for the junior class advisership. "It's a good thing there're only a couple of chairs in your office, Beth," Bob said. "'Cause if I gave you more, we'd just have groups of kids jammed in to chat with you. But . . ." Bob paused and fingered his mustache, ". . . but you see, Lana asked for an advisership this year." Lana, a math teacher, has long legs and short skirts. And she drinks with Bob and Peter on New Year's and Super Bowl Sunday. "So . . . well, Peter and I think Lana would do a good job with the juniors. Not that you wouldn't, of course. But we've decided to give Lana a shot at it."

By that time, Joe and I had started a college fund for Danny. I planned to add the adviser's stipend to that account. Dad wanted to contribute too. When he had something left at the end of the month, he'd insist we take it.

"Don't you think we can afford to educate our own son?" Joe asked my father one Sunday when the three of us brunched on the bagels and tuna Dad had brought. Danny, who'd slept at Noah's, had just called for a ride home.

"By the time Danny graduates," Joe said, "we'll have enough so he can go to any college he wants. Even without your help."

"Dad, what Joe means," I blurted out, "is that we're really grateful. You're always so generous with us, but we—"

"Your father knows what I mean, Beth. And I'd bet he's real glad we'll be able to do this by ourselves. Aren't you, Al?" Joe pushed back from the table. "I'm gonna get Danny."

"Honey, is everything okay?" Dad asked as I opened a box of Earl Grey.

"Sure." I handed him a mug, the tea bag bobbing near the top. "But I guess maybe Joe feels you don't believe he can take care of us. And he can, Dad. Really. He's doing well now. And he's proud of having his own company."

"I know. He should be. And I don't mean to step on his pride. It's just that . . ." my father started, dunking the tea bag with a spoon, ". . . it just makes me feel good to help with Danny's future, is all."

As he did that morning, Joe always set the tone in our house. The next time Dad came for brunch, Joe made pancakes. Danny, already dressed for his Little League pitching debut, drenched his with syrup—then claimed he wasn't hungry—while Joe showed my father the blueprints for a project he had bid on. When Moose buried his head in the mixing bowl Joe had given him to lick, Danny laughed so hard chocolate milk flew from his mouth to a corner of the building plans. And Joe didn't get angry. Had I won a contest that day, gotten to choose a vacation anywhere, I'd have said *No thanks.* There wasn't a place I would rather have been.

On the day I went back to work, Meadow Brook High School looked different than it had back then, different even than just a month earlier. It seemed dingier. Grayer, somehow. Yet the details in the main office hadn't changed: a clutter of pink discipline forms; copy for the next day's homeroom announcements; yellow plastic flowers in a dime-store vase. I thanked Lucille and Carol, the secretarial duo, for the fruit basket they'd sent from the office staff. My thank-you note, anchored with a green push pin, decorated the staff bulletin board.

Bob's door was closed. His secretary, Mary Grant, hugged me. "This must be so hard for you. Let me know if there's anything I can do."

"Thanks, Mary. And thank you for coming to see me after the funeral and for bringing Liz. I was glad she visited."

"Well, you know how much my daughter likes you." Mary took my hands in her cool, slender fingers. "Beth . . ." She held me at arm's length and caught my eyes. Tears welled in hers as she swallowed what she was about to say. "Umm . . . I guess you want to see Bob, but the superintendent's in with him."

"Could you just tell him I came by to thank him for letting Callie come in late today too? I don't know how I'd have gotten here without her."

"You bet. And Beth . . ." Mary paused, as if rehearsing the next line in her head. My eyes fixed on the strand of pearls that brushed the neckline of her dress. I used to wonder how she achieved her high-maintenance look on a school secretary's salary. Her husband had moved out years ago.

"Beth," Mary continued, "I'm glad you're back. I know Liz missed seeing you around here."

Though Liz Grant wasn't my student, we'd often chat in the cafeteria before school. In the months before Danny died, Liz seemed to appear for a container of orange juice whenever I bought my coffee. Once, she walked me back to the counseling center, said she had to see her counselor about adding an elective during lunch period. Debra Greene, who had the sophomores A through L, wasn't in yet, so I invited Liz to wait with me. She studied a photo of Danny, one I kept on the low metal bookcase in my office. "Wow! He's a hunk, Mrs. Maller! Think I could meet him someday?"

Liz was the first student to welcome me back to Meadow Brook. She sat, ramrod straight, at the round worktable in the counseling center. Her blond hair, ponytailed in a red scrunci, swayed as she turned toward me.

"Mrs. Maller, hi! I've been waiting for you." Ann Richardson had excused her from gym, Liz told me. The class was at the end of a fitness cycle, boys pumping iron in the weight room and girls pumping up the volume in aerobics. Liz said she knew the routine so well she could even lead it.

Everyone assumed Liz worked on her tight body; she barely feathered the ground when she walked. And she favored small things: skimpy skirts, dainty jewelry, miniature dogs. She once showed me a picture of her toy poodle. A black fuzz ball, he looked like something you'd pick off the floor and wonder where it came from.

"Isn't he the cutest, Mrs. Maller? His name's Cori, short for Licorice, which I think is the world's grossest candy, don't you? But it's a great name for a dog, don't you think?" I'd smiled, having learned not to answer once Liz got going. Her train of thought derailed easily. If I interrupted, she'd labor to get back on track—repeating the story, adding details, building speed.

I didn't feel ready for Liz Grant that day I returned to Meadow Brook. But there she was. I took a deep breath and recited my line: "It's good to see you, Liz." She followed me into my office. "But this isn't the best time, sweetie. I have so much to catch up on. How about right after school?"

"Please, Mrs. Maller." Liz curled into one of the brown chairs that faced my desk and braided her ponytail as she talked. "I've missed you so much, and this is my only free time, well, not free, actually, but I don't really need gym, right? I mean, I work out every day at home, and Ms. Richardson said it was okay for me to miss today so I didn't even change into gym clothes, and if I go back now it'll be such a waste. So please, don't make me go." Liz paused for only a split second. "And I have select chorus after school so I can't see you then, and I just want to talk 'cause I'm so used to seeing you and it's different when you're not here. But wow! You look great. You've lost weight."

I stopped thumbing the mail on my desk, looked at Liz, and realized I hadn't forgotten how to smile.

Sue, the counselors' secretary, waved as she came in from her break, then shrugged as if to say *Sorry I wasn't here to run interference* when she saw Liz in my office. The strange thing was, though, once I realized I couldn't escape, I didn't mind the chatter. Maybe I needed this respite from grief, this role in which I pretended to be the same as before.

A steady flow of students followed Liz. And although I'd thought the kids would rub my grief raw, in a strange sort of way they lessened the pain.

But in the moments when no one waited to see me, I felt as if I were sleepwalking in a once-familiar place. I looked at the two posters that brightened the beige walls of my office. WHEN THE GOING GETS TOUGH, THE TOUGH GET GOING masked a crack behind my desk. The other poster hung to the left of the door: WHAT'S POPULAR IS NOT ALWAYS RIGHT; WHAT'S RIGHT IS NOT ALWAYS POPULAR. And in smaller letters across the bottom: MAKE A DIFFERENCE! DO THE RIGHT THING.

That poster, which I used with students in the peer leadership program, always reminded me of how I'd met Callie. She had introduced herself ten-and-a-half years earlier, on my first day in Meadow Brook. "Great poster," she'd said. "If you want, I can laminate it for you. Just bring it by the art room." Later, she admitted the introduction had been secondary. What Callie had really wanted was for me to get two seniors out of her studio art class.

Now, on my first day back, I studied my office—a dull, ugly space I used to think was funky and sweet. Hodgepodge furnishings crammed the small room: a gray desk rimmed in dented chrome; a tan, vinyl armchair with a cross of black tape in the corner; two fabric chairs, the color of Hershey bars; and a matching low bookcase for supplies, PSAT and SAT materials, and family pictures in plain Lucite frames. Danny and my father at Shea Stadium—Danny in a Mets sweatshirt too large for his twelve-year-old body. Joe and me the following year in the parking lot of the Clam Shack in Maine, where we'd stopped on the way to visit Danny at camp. Danny just last year. I wiped dust from the close-up of his face: backward baseball cap, smiling eyes, corny grin.

A whirlpool of longing churned inside me. I stared at my mail: faculty meetings, conferences, a note from a science teacher asking me to down-level a student in honors biology. Things that used to seem important. How could I work in this place teeming with teenagers who laughed and shouted, took tests, played sports?

Between visitors, I touched base with the other counselors. Steve, who had come to the district a few years before I had, enjoyed his reputation as guidance chairperson and winning soccer coach. Debra Greene was the newest addition to the counseling center—and a kid herself. After her interview the year before, when Bob had said she was "adorable," I knew I'd be working with her.

Steve met with Debra and me during fourth period, when student traffic lulled. I tried to seem interested in who was failing what class, who already heard from which college, and who had in-school suspension. I thanked Steve and Debra for filling in for me, for "pitch-hitting" I must have said, because Steve chuckled when he corrected me. "You mean *pinch*-hitting, Beth. Thought the guys taught you better."

The guys. Those words cracked me open. I held back tears—or tried to, at least—as Bob entered the counseling center. He ushered in Dr. Sullivan, the superintendent of schools.

"Beth," Dr. Sullivan said, "I'm so sorry about your loss." I dabbed my eyes as I stood to greet him. "The Board asked that I extend their condolences." I struggled to say something but couldn't find my voice.

Fifth period, Callie wanted to drag me to the faculty room. But I couldn't bring myself to go.

"She's not ready," Sue said from behind her desk, looking at Callie as if I weren't there. "Just eat in Beth's office today."

Sue would have been a good journalist: accurate, terse, just the facts. If she walked into a restaurant in her tailored suit and matching pumps, you'd guess she was a reporter.

When I was pregnant with Danny, Joe and I often played "guess the profession" at the Bay View Diner. Had I seen Sue back then, I never would have guessed she was a school secretary. "Journalist," I would have said. "Newspaper. TV, maybe." Joe always smiled, despite some of my ridiculous conjectures—or perhaps because of them.

I was teaching second grade then, and school used me up. After work, I'd barely conquer the stairs of our new house. And Joe was so busy he didn't even have time to figure out what was wrong with the stove, which didn't always light. Yet despite our handyman's special, my father was proud of our move to Bay View.

"This house will be perfect for you," Dad said when we drove him by before we went to contract. "After all, Joe's a handy man. You two'll fix it up real nice. Why, I bet a year from now, no one'll recognize the place. And the best thing is, it's less than half an hour from my house."

"So you'll come for dinner often. Right, Dad?"

"Sure, honey. Once that baby's born, wild horses wouldn't keep me away."

Joe stared at the road. I had asked him not to tell my father about my emergency visit to Dr. Feinman's office the day before, after I started spotting at school. The doctor's hands were cold on the inside of my knees when he pushed them apart. "If you're determined to keep working," Dr. Feinman had said, "you go straight home after work and get off your feet. I'm sure I don't have to remind you that you've already had two miscarriages, Beth. We're not going for a third, are we?"

Now glimpses of "guess the profession," driving Dad by the house, and Dr. Feinman flitted through my mind as Sue told Callie we should eat in my office. Yes, Sue would have been a good journalist, all right. Just the facts: I wasn't ready—not for lunch with the teachers and not for troubled students. But I couldn't see that then.

Chapter Three

That first day back at Meadow Brook High School, Callie and I signed out thirty minutes after the last bell. It took a moment for my eyes to adjust to the sharp March light after a day under yellow fluorescents, but the crisp outdoor air was a quickly welcomed change from stuffy school heat. After two steps, my heel found a rut in the parking lot, battered by February's storms. I stumbled, and Callie placed a hand on my back to guide me to her white Volvo.

We cracked open the car windows as the baseball team boarded the bus for a pre-season game. Zach Stanish, the captain, called to us: "Hi, Mrs. Harris! Hey, Mrs. Maller!" I waved toward the sound, a voice like my son's. *Hey, Mom!* Danny would call as he'd bolt to his room after school, hitting every other step as if the stairway had too many risers. I had tried all day to keep the memory strings fastened. Now Zach's tug untied them.

"We don't have to talk," Callie said, popping a caramel into her mouth and offering me one, "but I'm here if you want to." I nodded and looked away, aware that if I spoke, my words would yank the scab off my still-fresh wound.

Truth be told, I felt guilty I'd been able to focus on anything in Meadow Brook other than the pictures in my office. I didn't want to let Danny go, not even for a moment. But I already knew—despite the cord that stretched from his photos to my heart and gut—that each day he would have to take up ever-so-slightly less space in my mind. Otherwise, I wouldn't be able to do my job. And then what else would I do?

Callie and I didn't speak as we headed west on the boulevard. I was grateful we could share silence without awkwardness. With anyone but Callie, I would try to fill space with sound—especially with Joe, now that our silences felt heavy.

Callie broke the stillness when a black Pathfinder swerved in front of us at the entrance to the parkway.

"Goddamn SUVs! They think they own the whole freakin' world."

"Callie Harris in road rage? I don't believe it. And your husband drives a Jeep. Remember?"

"Yeah, but Tom's not an animal like that moron."

The Pathfinder pulled to the left and roared ahead. We merged with highway traffic, then Callie glanced at me.

"There's something I have to tell you." She sounded intense, as if her outburst had been a prelude to what she was about to say. "And I know you're not gonna like it."

"What?"

Callie took her right hand off the wheel, placed it on my left. "It's about Ann. Ann Richardson." She hesitated for a second. "I have to tell you because everyone at school'll be talking about it tomorrow."

"Just tell me, Cal!"

She pulled her hand back as if I'd slapped it. I hadn't meant to sound so harsh, but Ann Richardson was one of the good guys, a gym teacher who never complained about students, even the hard core kids with attitude.

Callie cleared her throat. "Well, some of my seventh period girls have gym during sixth, and they were talking about a sign someone put on the door to the phys ed office."

"And?"

"And . . ." Callie looked in the rearview mirror, clicked her directional. "And it was really bad."

I turned to face her. "Come on, Cal. What'd it say?"

"DYKES SHOULD DIE! That's what it said. DYKES SHOULD DIE! READ THE BIBLE, MS. RICHARDSON."

A shiver worked up my spine as I watched white sunlight glint off passing cars.

"Why are the kids picking up on that now?"

"Who knows? I'm just sorry this happened—today of all days. I know you like Ann. I do too. And I know how you feel about this kind of thing."

Dammit! Why was everybody saying they knew how I felt? All day teachers had fed me a lasagna of condolence, mushy layers of sorrow and pity: "I know how you must feel . . . I can just imagine what you're going through . . . This must be so hard for you . . ."

"So I couldn't *not* tell you about that sign," Callie went on. "It'll be the talk of Meadow Brook in the morning."

"I certainly hope not."

"Me too. But I don't think the kids will drop this so fast. There's some good news, though." Callie giggled. "Wanna hear it?"

"Sure."

"Whoever wrote that sign spelled *dykes* correctly. At least that's something, isn't it?"

My keys clanked the table by the front door. Moose didn't hear me come in, didn't even awake when I climbed the creaky stairs. He had plastered himself against the closed door to Danny's room as though trapping a spirit, guarding it from slipping out through the crack between the saddle and door bottom. I lay my head on his side and breathed in the damp dirt smell of old dog. Moose batted a front paw as he slept—maybe swatting squirrels in a dream or pouncing on a tennis ball that Danny tossed. Joe had been right: Moose and

Danny had been best pals. I flashed back to the night of the accident: Moose twirling by Danny's door, turning in circles as if signaling an earthquake.

The tears I had saved all afternoon spilled onto his fur. Moose shifted and stretched his thick neck. I stroked his head and fingered the small familiar bump, perfectly centered between his ears, to ease him from sleep, and, perhaps, to ease myself too. I needed a constant—one thing that hadn't changed. The knot on Moose's head was all I could find.

Moose found a new spot in the yard as I put on a pot of coffee and tapped the red blinking button on the answering machine. My father's afternoon greeting boomed in the kitchen. The second call was from Joe, who rambled uncharacteristically. The architect had snagged his progress on a house in the Cove (something about enlarging the kitchen and adding a pass-through), so Joe had let the crew go early. All but Mike, the project manager. Joe took him to see a building site out east. They'd stopped for a beer. Joe was phoning from the pub, calling to tell me Mike had invited him for dinner. Mike's wife always cooked spaghetti and meatballs on Mondays. No problem bringing a guest. And Joe had said yes. "You're probably wiped out from work and won't want to fuss with dinner anyhow," he told the machine, then jabbed me with his last words: "I won't be home."

"Fuck you, Joe!" I said, this time aloud to the kitchen walls.

I poured my coffee and called Dad, who, I knew, would be waiting by the phone, eager to hear how I'd gotten through the day. I summarized in one sentence: "The strange thing was, Dad, the kids were easier than the adults."

"How so?"

"Well . . ." I opened the door for Moose and welcomed the clack of his nails on the kitchen tiles. "I felt as if the teachers were uncomfortable with me, like they had to make me feel better and they didn't know how."

"But you can't fault them for that."

"I know, but it made me feel . . . I don't know . . . strange. Like everyone was treating me like a child. Like the teachers were patting me on the head saying *There, there now. Everything's gonna be fine.* But everything's not gonna be fine. And the students somehow know that. So they didn't lie like the staff did, telling me they know how I must feel, that they hurt for me when they're really just glad it was my child and not theirs."

"You know why adults are like that, don't you?" I couldn't come up with anything so my father continued: "I think we're like that because we want to believe, or need to believe, that if we say everything's okay, then it really will be—as if we have some control over what happens to us." He stopped for a moment. I imagined my father dunking his tea bag, looking in his mug for a clearer explanation. "And kids know they don't."

"Don't what?"

"Kids know they don't control anything. They have no power over what happens. So they know how to act when a friend's hurting. They just act like themselves. Maybe more sympathetic, but they don't say much because . . . well, I suppose kids know their words don't count." Dad paused. "Remember when Danny sprained his ankle and you thought it was broken?"

"Sure. That time I rushed him to the emergency room and he ended up with those crutches he never used."

"Right. And what'd you tell him?"

"He'd be good as new in no time."

"But that didn't help."

"No. Guess not." I closed my eyes to see Danny standing in the kitchen, balanced against a chair and looking at the soft cast on his ankle. Crutches lean against the wall. I didn't know which hurt more then, the sprain or what the doctor told him: No sports for a month.

"You tried to talk away his sadness, Beth, but you couldn't."

"Right. And then Noah came over. And five minutes later I heard the boys laughing in Danny's room."

"See, honey. Noah helped just by being there, and adults forget how to do that. We try so hard to say the right thing, and sometimes that makes it worse. So don't be angry with the teachers who want to make you feel better. They offered sympathetic words 'cause that's all they know to do."

"You know what I think, Dad? I think the wrong one of us became a counselor."

"Oh, don't say that. You're a wonderful counselor. They're lucky to have you." Then he asked what time Joe would be home.

I wouldn't accept Dad's offer to have dinner with me. Monday was his poker night. My father would be at Saul's house, where Saul's wife, Martha, put out the best spread. Although Dad didn't tell me, I assumed Saul and Martha had invited him for dinner before the game. And I wanted him to go. He needed them the way I needed him and Callie then, to keep me upright as I stumbled through grief. There was no soft cast for my heart; it was too soon to lean my crutches by the wall. I couldn't ask Dad to let go of his either. He was grieving too. Saul and Martha kept him standing.

Yet when I hung up the phone, the stillness made me shudder. No dinner to prepare. No footsteps in the hall. And no muddy sneakers, dirty socks, wet towels on the floor. How I missed those little annoyances.

Though this wasn't the first night Joe hadn't come home to eat, it was the first I would be alone. Sitting in the silent kitchen, I thought about those times Danny and I chose Chinese food when Joe had evening meetings with clients or architects. Joe didn't eat what he couldn't recognize: vegetables diced and foreign; sauces other than tomato or Worcestershire. When we were dating, Joe's favorite restaurant was The T-Bone, named for his favorite food.

Sometimes when Joe worked late, Danny and I took Noah to China King with us. So on that day I went back to work, I called

Noah. Maybe he'd like to join me for Chinese. But I slammed the phone down before anyone answered. Though Noah had come to visit a few times since the funeral, no seventeen-year-old would want dinner with his dead friend's mother. I knew that, even then. And anyhow, I had no appetite.

Moose studied me for his cue as his tail thumped the floor. "You know what, old boy? Think we'll take a nap." I guzzled the rest of my coffee and put the mug in the sink by the one I had used that morning, the MOM mug. Moose followed me upstairs, stopping short of my room to hunker down by Danny's door.

In the king-size bed Joe and I still shared, I yanked the sheet up high. Soothed by the spring smell of fabric softener, I tucked the ivory down comforter under my chin and fingered the soft, familiar cotton. Ann Richardson's face gleamed in my mind, but it was my father's voice I heard: *Kids know they don't control anything. They have no power. They know how to act.* Wrong, Dad, I thought, while the picture changed. The sign Callie told me about came into focus: DYKES SHOULD DIE! READ THE BIBLE, MS. RICHARDSON. Some kids *do* control things, I said to myself. Some kids *do* have power. And some kids *don't* know how to act.

That afternoon I dreamed that Callie dragged me to the gym—not in Meadow Brook but in Bay View High, Danny's school. A large sign hangs on the door to the phys ed office: IT'S NOT RIGHT! IT'S NOT POPULAR! LESBIANS SHOULD DIE! "Do something, Beth," Callie says. "You're the guidance counselor." I tear the message down and pull the door open. Danny lies on the floor. Broken glass blankets his body. A huge rat sits by his head. The rat's tail whacks glass fragments on Danny's eyes.

The telephone's ring mixed with squeaky rat sounds. I welcomed Callie's voice. The dream was so fresh I shared it raw, the image unedited.

"I'm glad I called," Callie said. "So what's up with dinner?" I told her Joe was eating at Mike's. "Well, the girls want pizza, and they want to see you. So you're having dinner with us. Just tell me what you want on your pie and if Tom should come by for you on his way back from Pizza Time."

"Cal, I'm not even hungry. Maybe it'd be good for me to have a night alone."

"Not a chance. So tell me what you want or you'll be stuck with pepperoni and olives. And should Tom pick you up, or do you want to take the new car?"

I pictured the Camry, which Joe had bought the week before, in the garage where my Buick used to be. Nausea rose in my throat when I told Callie I'd drive myself.

Callie's daughters greeted me at the door. Tom came in right behind. "One pepperoni and olives, and one pepperoni and mushrooms," he announced as he whizzed by to put the pies in the kitchen. "That's what you like. Right, Beth?"

Tom's hearty voice, along with his muscles, seemed more suited to a construction worker than to an accountant. He backtracked to hug me hard. I couldn't remember the last time Joe had held me tight like that.

No one mentioned Danny while we ate, but he stayed with me as I walked to the bathroom, through Callie's house filled with girl things: a pink sock with tiny white hearts on the arm of the sofa; a bottle of perfume on top of *Teen* magazine in the bathroom. How different from my house, where tennis racquets used to hog the landing and *Sports Illustrated* decorated the bathroom vanity.

After dinner, Tom had an appointment with a couple who had started a home business and thought they could write off everything. Tom went on about how he had met with them twice already, and they still didn't understand why they couldn't deduct their entire electric bill. Tom stuffed papers into his briefcase and snapped it shut. He went over to Callie, who stood by the sink. When he grabbed her from behind and kissed her head, jealousy gnawed at my heart. "Love you, honey," Tom told her. "I won't be late."

He snatched a plate from my hands, put it on the counter, and hugged me again. "Good night, Beth. And thanks for joining us tonight."

"No, Tom. Thank *you* for having me."

He stepped back, placing his hands on my shoulders, his grip firm and strong. "Listen, you and Callie are like sisters, and that makes us family. You never need an invitation."

"I know. Thanks. I couldn't get through this without you two."

He dropped his arms and looked at me. "Tough day, huh?" I nodded. "Well, you tell that no-good husband of yours he should be taking better care of you. No more hanging out with Mike. Joe should be home. Especially now."

"It's all right. Really." I hoped I had just told my last lie—at least for the day.

At the front door, Tom called upstairs to the girls: "Good night, ladies! And don't give Mom any trouble. You hear?"

Callie loaded the dishwasher while we talked about school. "Know what I think?" she said. "You've got enough going on without getting involved in Ann Richardson's problems. I didn't tell you about that sign so you'd do something. I only told you so you'd understand the gossip."

"This isn't just about Ann. Ann's an adult. She can handle it herself. But what about the kids?"

"What kids?"

"Kids like Donna Walker. You remember her, don't you?"

"Sure. The one everyone called Donald. High school must've been hell for her."

"It was. Did I ever tell you about the time she came to see me when there was a sub in physics? The kids didn't stop picking on Donna, telling the sub to call her Donald and poking fun at her clothes. Donna showed up at my office at the end of the period. That was the only time she talked about anything other than college plans, and the only time I saw her cry."

"So what'd you do?"

"Nothing. All she wanted was for me to transfer her to another section of physics. And I didn't do it."

"Why not?"

"It was already second semester. I would have had to change her whole schedule to put her in a different class. And Steve won't let us do that—not after first quarter. You know how firm Bob and Peter are about that. But dammit, Cal. I should have tried anyway."

On the way home from Callie's, memories of Danny flooded my mind, washing away thoughts of Donna Walker and Ann Richardson. Danny, in those crinkled, shiny shorts he wore for tennis. He had them in every color. The fabric swooshed when he walked, the soft sound synchronized with his step.

March of sophomore year, the Bay View tennis team played without jackets, though I would toss Danny's in the car. A Mom thing—just in case. Just in case the breeze would make him shiver the way it did me.

Now I sought heat in the dashboard icons of my new Camry when a chill seeped through me as I turned onto Main Street. The village was deserted but well lit, a ghost town ready for visitors. I eased past Teddy's Stride Rite, where Danny got his first pair of shoes; The Village Greenery, where he bought a spring bouquet for my birthday; The Corner Deli, where he purchased Gatorade before Little League games; and Arnie's Athletics, where we acquired his rainbow of shorts. By the time I got home, the pain of missing him knifed through me.

I heard Moose howl and raced upstairs to see him circling by Danny's room. When I touched his head, Moose froze for an instant, then pawed at the door. He walked in ahead of me and moved silently on the blue carpet. I lay on Danny's bed, hugging his pillow. I didn't glance up till Moose pushed his cold, soggy nose at my shoulder. And that's when he did it: Moose raised his leg and marked the perimeter of Danny's room.

I didn't try to stop him. I thought I understood: Moose finally knew that guarding Danny's spirit behind the closed door wouldn't bring him back. It was time to sanctify this territory. And just when Moose enshrined Danny's memory in the only way he could, I saw Joe in the doorway, his face twisted with anger and incredulity.

Chapter Four

"What the hell's going on here?" Joe asked. "Don't you see what he's doing?"

I wanted to say something but didn't know what. "I'll clean it," was all I could manage.

I scrubbed Danny's carpet, then got ready for bed while Joe watched TV in the den. When I brushed my teeth, the toothpaste stung. In the mirror I saw the frayed outline of my lower lip, bitten raw like after my mother died.

Hours later, Joe roused me when his legs found mine in the rumpled sheets. As he stroked my shin with his foot, I turned away. How could he have let Danny drive that night?

For a while after, I thought it was the accident that had rent the fabric of our marriage. But now I see what tragedy did: it pulled the loose threads we used to poke back in—little things, like forgetting to say good morning. The fabric had worn thin. Our marriage wasn't strong enough to hold catastrophe. Yet I tried to keep it together. Though I had no appetite, I still cooked sometimes for Joe and me. The familiarity of our pots and pans, the dishes, and the stove we had replaced years ago gave me comfort. But my cooking changed. I threw away recipes, rarely reached for the salad spinner. And, often, we brought in: a pie from Pizza Time, chicken from The Roost, cold cuts from the deli. We'd sit in the kitchen and force conversation, chitchatting about safe subjects.

I hadn't told Joe about the problems in Meadow Brook, that at the end of my first week back, two girls asked Steve to transfer them out of Ann Richardson's class. Steve told me, in teen imitation, how they wanted a different teacher because "you know, like what if she comes into the locker room while we're changing? I mean, like she might look at us like, you know, sexual or something." Steve said no to the transfers, and the next week, when other girls brought letters from parents, he gave those notes to the principal.

"Steve, we need to do something," I said. "A sensitivity training program, maybe. We can't just keep ignoring this."

"That's not our decision. Bob wants to handle it himself. He and Peter are real concerned about what's happening. And they're determined to keep it quiet so no one gets riled up."

"So what do you mean, Bob wants to handle it? What's he doing? And shouldn't we be involved?"

"Bob's nervous, Beth. Everyone is—after Columbine. No one wants trouble now. And the superintendent told him the less we focus on this, the faster it'll go away."

"That's nonsense."

"You may be right, but there's nothing I can do. So go talk to Bob yourself if you want. Though I can't see what good it would do."

I had seen Bob earlier that day, when he'd come by to check on plans for the career fair. "Cool tie, huh kiddo?" Bob had said as he fingered the black, fake silk, a painted silver hammer in the center. His gesture obligated me to sing a bit of "Maxwell's Silver Hammer."

"It's always good to see you, Beth," Bob had said with a smile. "You have a good day now."

But later, when I raised the Ann Richardson situation, the principal's eyebrows shot up. "We're not going to talk about this. I told your chairperson I'm handling it."

"What does that mean?"

"Peter and I are taking care of it. You don't have to worry."

"But shouldn't we be doing something?"

"Beth, I'm sure you have enough on your plate right now without getting involved in Ann's problem."

My spine prickled. "This isn't Ann's problem. As far as I can see, the kids who posted that sign and the girls who want to transfer out of Ann's classes are the ones with problems." I glanced at Bob's credenza. Twin boys in orange and white soccer uniforms stared from a photo. "We've got homophobic students and homophobic parents, and you're telling us not to do anything?"

Bob nodded. "That's right. I told you, I'm handling it."

I started to leave, but a thought scratched my mind. "Sorry, Bob, but . . ."

"Yes?"

"What if one of your boys was gay?"

"That's crazy."

"But just suppose. Wouldn't you want him to be able to go to school without being afraid? Isn't school supposed to be safe for everyone?"

"Come on, Beth. You're being ridiculous."

"I don't think so. I just want Meadow Brook to be a good place for everyone, including kids like Donna Walker. You remember her, don't you?"

"Of course. But I already told you I'm handling this. Now, don't you have work to do?"

I left the main office as the fifth period bell rang and dashed to the faculty room, despite the smell of microwaved broccoli that always hung in the air there. I craved Callie's comfort and the camaraderie of our lunch group: Joanne, from social studies, and Denise, a biology teacher, whose pet white rat would snuggle on her shoulder while she ate.

As I entered the faculty room, I saw that Callie and Joanne hadn't come in yet. But Mr. Rat was there, prancing on the lunch table. Every time I saw him now, I remembered my dream—a rat's tail whacking glass on Danny's eyes.

By the time Joanne arrived, Mr. Rat slept on Denise's shoulder, his coarse tail snaking down her buxom chest. Callie came in even later. "Sorry, guys," she said when she pushed open the door ten minutes into the period. "Got a little sidetracked. But look what I have." She offered a plate of cookies from home ec.

"What's the big deal?" Joanne asked. "You know what I say: People who bake are just too lazy to go to the bakery."

That night, as Joe and I ate sandwiches from The Corner Deli, we ran out of small talk. I filled the silence by telling him about Ann Richardson.

"For Christ's sake, Beth!" Joe took his knife out of the mustard and slammed the jar on the table. "You're getting involved, aren't you? Why can't you just do your job like everyone else and not ask for more work and more problems?"

Hungry for a glimpse of the man I had married, I put down my sandwich and looked at Joe. "You know, sometimes I don't even know who you are anymore. How can you tell me not to get involved? It's my job to get involved."

"No it's not. Ann Whatever-Her-Name-Is can fight her own battles. You're not responsible for the whole world."

"But don't you think schools should teach tolerance?"

"I don't give a damn what schools should teach anymore. Why the hell should I?"

I put on the invisible armor I wore to guard myself from Joe's anger. "But remember what you told Danny when he and Noah did that AIDS fundraiser last year?"

"Jesus, Beth! This isn't about Danny!"

"Yes it is." The insight stunned me. "It's about doing what we always told Danny to do. When he signed up for the AIDS program, you said you were glad he wanted to make a difference, like his mom. That's what you said. And then Danny wrote about the murder of Matthew Shepard. Remember?"

"Yeah, well guess what?" Joe spit his words. "Danny's gone, and there's not a thing we can do about it. So what good did that stupid assignment do, anyhow?"

It's strange that I hadn't remembered Danny's words until I told Joe what was happening in Meadow Brook. I hadn't thought about Matthew Shepard, brutally beaten because he was gay. But Danny had thought about him when his social studies teacher asked students to answer this question in one page or less: What should schools do to prevent hate crimes?

Every so often, Danny wrote, *teachers and counselors should meet with students to talk about feelings. Teenagers need to share ideas with each other and with adults they trust. We should talk about issues like religious prejudice, racial injustice, and gay bashing.*

Maybe if teachers and counselors in Wyoming would have talked about these problems, the people who killed Matthew Shepard wouldn't have grown up with such hatred. Maybe if students were taught to be sensitive to differences, then Matthew Shepard might not have been beaten to death. Maybe he wouldn't have been left hanging from a fence just because he was gay.

My mother is a guidance counselor. She always asks how I feel about things, even though I sometimes wish she wouldn't. But if the people who killed Matthew Shepard had mothers like mine or guidance counselors like her, then they probably would never have committed such a horrible crime. Teachers and parents could prevent hate crimes by talking with us more.

A week after I told Joe what was happening in Meadow Brook, Callie drove me to school again. This time, I listened for the horn.

I opened the window in Callie's Volvo to welcome the soft spring air and suburban morning sounds: squirrels racing up trees; breezes sweeping evergreens. At the entrance to the parkway, a motorcycle pulled ahead of us. The biker wore a black windbreaker with red lettering on the back: IF YOU CAN READ THIS, THE BITCH FELL OFF.

"That's disgusting," Callie said.

"The jacket? Or the way he cut in front of us?"

"Both."

"Why would anyone wear that, Cal?"

"Beats me. Just no accounting for taste, I guess."

"You'd have to be an idiot to wear something like that."

Callie took her hand off the wheel and boxed my arm. "Well, maybe he's a Meadow Brook graduate."

The spring breeze didn't penetrate Meadow Brook High School. Most of the windows couldn't open. They were missing handles or glued shut with layers of paint. New windows had been installed only in the main office. But no one tried to open those: the office was air-conditioned. Yet, students and faculty sweltered, assaulted by odors which thickened the air—sweat, Lysol, and cheap aftershave.

I scanned my mail, then headed to the cafeteria for coffee. Liz Grant met me there. I noticed she had switched from orange juice to bottled water and that her jeans slid from her waist.

"Mrs. Maller, hi! I really want time with you today, okay? But I have to run now 'cause Mrs. Spinner told me to come in before homeroom if I want to go over my poetry project so I'll know if I have to change anything to get an *A*. But I really need to talk to you, so I'll come by later. I'll try to get out of gym. Ms. Richardson'll probably give me a pass."

"Sure, sweetie. Anytime." I smiled, my ease with students a pleasure I found I still enjoyed. Yet the forced lightness in Liz's voice troubled me. I went to see Debra, as Liz was one of her sophomores.

Clamping a hand over the mouthpiece of her phone, Debra motioned me into her tiny office—even smaller than mine—and pointed to the one chair angled by the corner of her desk. "Just a sec," she whispered as she pushed a catalog toward me. I looked at a bony model in a black, satin mini-dress. "Yes, that's right. Black . . . yep, size small," Debra said into the phone. "Uh-huh, same address."

She hung up and shrugged off my concerns about Liz: the urgency in her voice; her gait like a speed walker's. "Have you spoken with her lately?" I asked Debra.

"Nope. Not meeting with my tenth-graders till I've got program cards for next year."

"But maybe you could call Liz down before that. I think something's really bothering her."

Debra popped a straw into a can of Diet Coke and slowly drew the soda through her teeth. "What good would it do if I called for her? You're the only one she talks to."

At the beginning of second period, I was in Steve's office when Liz showed up with a pass from Ann Richardson.

"Listen, Beth," Steve said, having asked Liz to wait and closing his door. "Liz Grant spends way too much time with you. I don't want to see her in your office anymore. She's not your student."

"But something's troubling her. She needs to talk."

"Then send her to Debra."

"But Liz doesn't want to talk to Debra. She keeps coming to me, and she needs help."

Steve picked up a pen and turned it slowly in his hand, clicking the point in and out, in and out.

"Okay, I didn't want to tell you this, what with all you're going through now. But you leave me no choice." He put the pen down and met my eyes. "I was in the main office a few days ago when Mary Grant was running on about how much Liz likes talking to you. Peter heard her, and he said he didn't know you'd taken over the sophomores A through L. And when Mary said no, of course you're not Liz's counselor, just her friend, Peter said something like he thought we were educators, not rock stars. 'We don't need groupies,' he said. 'And if Mrs. Maller does, then she ought to find a stage and a microphone and get the hell out of Meadow Brook.' Peter's on the warpath. So I'm telling you for your own good: Send Liz to Debra." Steve played with the pen again, clicking faster. "You've been a terrific counselor, Beth. I just want you to keep up the good work and stay out of trouble. I'm sure you have enough to handle right now without looking for problems."

My back stiffened, but I didn't say anything to Steve. I pushed open the door to greet Liz. "Hi, sweetie. It's good to see you." I motioned to my office. "Go on in."

Chapter Five

At the beginning of April, Ann's second period class ran track. Liz collapsed on the third lap.

"I don't get it," Ann said as she slouched in one of my chairs, her legs stretched out as if she were at the beach. "Liz usually has so much energy. And you know what she said when she couldn't finish the run?"

I closed the door. "She wanted to do the whole thing again?"

"No. She asked if this would lower her gym grade. Said she's going for straight *A*s again this quarter, and gym counts."

"I'm not surprised she said that. You know how driven she is."

"Sure do." Ann steepled her fingers and paused as if she wanted to tell me something else but wasn't sure what.

"You know, Beth, I'm really worried about her," Ann finally said. "The girls in that gym class give Liz such a hard time. And I try my best to look out for her, but that's one tough group, that second period class." Ann shook her head. "But Liz never complains. And she's getting really thin. Have you noticed?"

Before I could answer, Steve knocked as he opened my door. "Hope I'm not interrupting anything."

"Well, actually," Ann said, "Beth and I were just talking about—"

"Nothing important." I cut her off. "What's up, Steve?"

He muttered something about next year's program cards, then turned and walked out, shutting the door behind him.

"What's going on?" Ann asked.

"Oh, nothing." I waved my hand, but the truth tumbled out, or part of it, anyhow. "It's just that Steve doesn't want me involved with Debra's students. So I didn't want him to know we were talking about Liz. In fact, I hate to say this, but you really have to speak to Debra about her."

"Yeah, right. That would be about as useful as talking to this chair." Ann patted the brown seat as she stood.

When Ann left, I went to see Mary. "I don't know why Lizzie couldn't finish on the track," she said, dusting her keyboard with a teeny brush, her red nails perfectly matched to her suit. "She never runs out of steam. Not my Lizzie. She's got more energy than ten people put together. In fact, when she got home from jazz class last night, I heard her working out in her room. She certainly wasn't tired then."

"Is she eating?"

Mary put down the brush and blew on the keyboard. "You bet. Or at least I think she is. I mean, she says she is. I'm not home every night, so I don't know exactly what she eats. She's certainly old enough to be on her own. I've been dating a bit, you know." Mary held out her left hand and smiled as if there were a diamond on her ring finger.

"Well, Mary Grant. Are you holding out on me?"

"No such luck. Not yet, anyhow. And I know Lizzie's not crazy about my going out, so I do stay home most of the time. But I must admit, she's not much dinner company lately. No time to linger at the table, she says. Too much homework, I guess. She just stresses so much over school. And all this teasing in the locker room about Ann Richardson has really gotten to her. The kids won't let it go. It has Lizzie so upset she even cried about it the other night."

"What do you mean?"

"You know, how the kids have turned on Ann. Hasn't Lizzie told you?"

"No. What's going on?"

"Well, for one thing, when they talk about her, they don't even call her Ms. Richardson anymore. They call her Mr. Richard's Son. Lizzie said the junior girls . . . well, actually it must've been Tina Roland and Jen Scotto who started it. Anyhow, they said Ann should've been a boy, somebody's son. That if her father's name was Richard, she'd be Richard's son."

Minutes later, when I went to the cafeteria for a fresh cup of coffee, Danny's words filled my head: *Teachers and parents could prevent hate crimes by talking with us more.*

Back in the counseling center, I took several "While You Were Out" slips from Sue. But I didn't look at them. Instead, I pulled Tina Roland's and Jen Scotto's program cards. This time I wouldn't have to worry about skirting Debra: the juniors M through Z were mine. I asked Sue to call for Tina and Jen.

Tina came first, in jeans like a second skin and a cropped black sweater that hugged her chest. Long bleached hair swagged across her right eye. Brown iridescent gloss colored her lips. "What's up, Mrs. M.?" Tina slunk into a chair and crossed her legs. "Why'd you call me out of Spanish? That's the one class I like. Zeitler's the only teacher who's not a total geek."

"Sorry, Tina. I won't keep you long. Just wanted to see how you're doing. I know you're in Ms. Richardson's class, and I've heard some of the girls are a little uncomfortable with the rumor that's going around."

"Okay, Mrs. M. What's up? Really." Tina leaned forward and clicked her blue enameled nails on my desk. A tiny rhinestone *T* glittered on the polish of her right index finger. "Who told you what I said about that dyke?"

I jumped in my seat. "Watch what you're saying, Tina. And nobody told me anything." My first lie in weeks. "I'm just checking with some of the girls in Ms. Richardson's classes. That's all."

"Oh, come on, Mrs. M. You think I'm that dumb? You didn't call anyone else down. I would've heard if you did." She unwrapped two pieces of gum and rolled them up. "So someone told you we joke around in the locker room. Big deal. What's the problem?" She put the wad in her mouth.

"The problem is that what you've been saying is hurtful. Ms. Richardson's a terrific teacher. And her life outside of school is nobody's business."

"You're entitled to your opinion, Mrs. M." Tina cracked her gum. "But I don't have to agree with it. In fact, my parents don't think she should even be allowed to teach. So what you're saying, I guess, is that my parents are wrong."

I swallowed hard. "This has nothing to do with your parents. Ms. Richardson's an excellent teacher. That's all that matters here."

Tina eyeballed me across my desk. "Could I go back to class now? There's only like about twenty minutes left this period." She blew a huge purple bubble.

"Lose the gum before you get back," I answered, ushering her out.

As she left the center, Tina high-fived Jen Scotto, seated at the round worktable.

"Whad'ya call me down for, Mrs. Maller?" Jen asked. "I handed in my program card, and I'm not failing anything. So I'm not in trouble, am I? 'Cause my father said he'd kill me if I get in trouble again this year." She chewed the skin around her thumbnail.

"Relax, Jen." I held open my door. "You're not in trouble. I just want to know what's happening in gym. I hear you've been talking about Ms. Richardson."

Jen sighed as she eased herself into one of my chairs. "So? You heard about that poster a while ago, right?"

"Yes I did."

"Well, after that some of us started to feel sort of creepy . . . you know . . . like it's really gross and all . . . I mean, like what if Ms. Richardson comes on to one of us?"

"Come on, Jen. You know that's not going to happen."

"But you never can tell with those lesbos. At least that's what my mother says."

"Oh? And what else does your mother say?" As soon as I got the words out, I was sorry.

"Well, here's the thing. My mother says perverts shouldn't be teachers. She says Richardson should be fired, and if she isn't, then parents should do something about it, because most parents think perverts shouldn't be allowed to teach. But what does this have to do with me? And why was Tina here?" Jen twirled a stringy strand of brown hair.

"Listen, Jen." I took a slow breath. "I'm disturbed about what's going on in the locker room. I've heard what you girls are saying, and it's hurtful and mean."

As I spoke, a fire lit in Jen. "Oh, I get it. It's that fuckin' little bitch. I'll kill her! I swear I will!"

Jen's rage forced me to my feet. "What are you talking about?"

"It's Liz Grant. That fuckin' skinny moron! She told you about Mr. Richard's Son, didn't she? If this gets me in trouble, I'll fuckin' kill her!"

I leaned against my desk and willed myself to stay calm. "Watch your language, Jen. And Liz Grant has nothing to do with this. Liz hasn't told me anything about gym. She has nothing to do with this," I repeated, motioning to the door.

I sat at my desk after Jen left and thought about what she had said. And as I did, I knew I should have listened to Joe. Because maybe he'd been right. Because now Liz might get hurt. And at that moment, I hated my don't-get-involved husband, Mr. I-Don't-Give-A-Damn-What-Schools-Should-Teach.

I shut my office door, shut my eyes, shut myself off from Meadow Brook. What had happened to Joe? To us?

Early scenes flashed in my mind—a time before Danny. Joe shirtless on a ladder. Hammer in hand, he salutes me and my college buddy, Rayanne, as we approach the house he's working on.

"Howdy, ladies!" Joe calls, lowering the hammer to his waist in a mock bow.

"He's gorgeous," Rayanne gushes. "My God! What a body!"

The next day the temperature climbs to nearly a hundred in the little upstate town where Rayanne and I spend the week after NYU graduation in her grandmother's summer cottage. We head for the lake and spot Joe at the edge of the swimming dock. His back is to us. A smaller man sits beside him.

"Oh my God, Beth! I think that's him, the guy from the ladder." Rayanne grabs my arm and pulls me toward the swimming area. "Come on," she says. "I'm not gonna blow this chance." She lets go of me to pull her red and white striped moo-moo over her head.

"What's the point? He probably has a girlfriend. And we're going home tomorrow."

"But we've got tonight." Rayanne grins. "And what muscles! We're allowed to have fun, you know, Beth. And I'm wearing my good, skinny suit. And just wait till those guys see you in that yellow two-piece. They'll fall in the lake."

In my office in Meadow Brook, I replayed that afternoon Rayanne and I spent with Joe and his friend Andy. The Dairy Freeze, where Joe claims me. "What'll it be, Red?" he asks. I can't help but smile: Joe's noticed my hair. When he hands me my cone, fingers touch. My heart somersaults.

A new scene: the warning of friends—*He's a construction worker, Beth; Yes, he's gorgeous. But come on. A construction worker?*

Dad and Rayanne rally round, swatting the doubts that buzz in my mind. "He's a good man. Hard working," Dad reminds me. "He'll be a good provider."

Rayanne's assessment: "Just think of those gorgeous kids you two'll turn out."

A year later, the wedding. Small but perfect. Then dreams about children and a house with a yard. And a dog. Joe wants a dog. A house, then kids, then a dog. My mantra: *house, kids, dog; house, kids, dog; house, kids, dog.* Say it enough, I tell myself, and it just might come true.

I'm pregnant before we even phone the real estate agent. Dad jumps out of his seat when we call him Grandpa. He hugs me hard. "You'll be a great mom, honey."

But I lose the chance to find out then. Dr. Feinman says the miscarriage in my third month isn't my fault. "Listen," he explains, "that baby just wasn't meant to be." He talks while he examines me. "This might hurt for a second. Just need to make sure everything's fine."

Dr. Feinman sees Joe and me in his office, but speaks only to Joe: "Try again after she has one regular period. No reason Beth can't have a normal pregnancy."

Two years later and another miscarriage behind us, I'm pregnant with Danny. Joe and I talk about nurseries and baby names. Joe wants a boy to shout with at football games. I dream of a girl. But when I start spotting at school, that dream fades. *Just a healthy baby, please God. Just a healthy baby.*

Nothing else matters. Not how my students will do in the school assembly. Not what Dad will think of our fixer-upper in Bay View. Not even how Joe feels about it. The only thing that counts is the child inside me, the one I can't bear to lose.

Months before Danny's birth, I became Danny's mom. Now in my Meadow Brook office—door closed, eyes shut—I thought about about Danny, about Joe. How had it all come to this?

Chapter Six

"We got a note, Beth." Bob spoke before I seated myself at the conference table in the principal's office. "It's from Tina Roland's mother." Bob swigged orange juice from a pint container. He put it down as Peter came in, carrying a white paper plate with a buttered bagel. I wished I had brought my coffee.

"As you can see," Bob went on, "I asked Peter to join us. And Steve too. But he's over at the middle school." Bob finished his juice in a loud gulp, then stood to shoot the container into the trash. "Pete and I need to talk to you about this Ann Richardson thing."

"What about it?"

Peter waved Mrs. Roland's letter in the air like a flag, then placed it in front of me. "Read."

I picked up the single sheet, ripped from a spiral notebook, and read the words in loopy bright pink script:

Dear Mr. Andrews,

Tina told me that Mrs. Maller took her out of Spanish to talk about Miss Richardson. She told Tina she has to respect that gym teacher, but that's none of Mrs. Maller's business. She gets paid to make sure Tina passes and to figure out what to do after high school, and that's all. So please don't let Mrs. Maller take Tina out of class again for no good reason. She should not talk about Miss Richardson with my daughter. My husband and I think perverts shouldn't even be allowed to teach.

Mrs. John Roland

Peter crushed his paper plate and put it in the center of the table. His thick lips glistened with butter. "Anything you want to tell us, Mrs. Maller?"

Before I answered, Bob walked to his desk and dialed the counseling center. "Sue, when Steve gets back, please remind him I need to see him right away." Bob addressed me as he sat back down. "Beth, I already told you we're handling everything that comes up about Ann. You shouldn't be discussing it."

"What do you mean?" I looked directly at Bob to avoid Peter's stare. "Tina's one of my students. I haven't done anything wrong here."

Bob stroked his mustache. "You know we don't want the whole community talking about this. There haven't been any more signs, and things have been quiet. So we just—"

"But don't you want to know why I called Tina down?"

Peter jabbed the air with his index finger. "It doesn't matter why you called her down. Bob told you to stay out of the Richardson affair. It's not your problem, and it's none of your business. What part of that don't you understand?"

Something cold and heavy settled in my chest. I fixed on Peter in eyeball-to-eyeball combat. "I don't understand any of it. When I hear that one of my students is making fun of a teacher and spreading rumors in the locker room, it's my job as her counselor to make it my problem and my business. And—"

"That's enough, Mrs. Maller," Peter said. "We've got better things to do than to listen to your locker room nonsense." He released me from his eyes and got up to leave.

"Hold on, Pete," Bob said. "Maybe we ought to hear about those rumors. What is it you were about to say, Beth?"

Peter sat down and picked up a chewed pencil. I swallowed hard, then started in. "I understand that Tina Roland and Jen Scotto have been joking about Ann and calling her names. And we can't just ignore that, because they won't stop unless we do something. So I did call Tina and Jen down. I told them that what they're saying is hurtful and mean. They need to know we won't tolerate that behavior." I paused for a moment and looked from Bob to Peter, who doodled on a notepad. I noticed the imprint in bright red letters on top of the paper: *What part of NO don't you understand?* "As I said, I didn't think we tolerated hurtful behavior in Meadow Brook."

"Don't be ridiculous," Bob said. "Of course we don't. But Peter and I have handled everything that's come up since that sign was posted on Ann's door. That's what the superintendent wants, and that's what we've done. So you don't have to worry about it anymore."

Peter struck the table with his pencil. "Just a minute. I have a question for you, Mrs. Maller. How do you know what the girls talk about in the locker room?" Without giving me a chance to speak, Peter continued. "Oh, I know. Second period. Ann's large section. Isn't Liz Grant in that class?" He kept right on, not expecting an answer. "So now I get it. The girls talk in the locker room, and little Lizzie Grant runs straight to you with the gossip." Peter pushed back from the table and turned to Bob. "Don't you see what's going on here? Mrs. Maller doesn't just do her job; she wants to do everyone else's too. You know she's not Liz Grant's counselor," Peter said, as if I were no longer in the room. "She just acts like she is. So I've got an idea. How 'bout we let Mrs. Maller run the whole goddamn school." Peter walked to the door, then turned around and hurled his last line: "Obviously she thinks she can do a better job than we do."

I wasn't surprised that Bob had let Peter go on like that, chewing me up like the pencil he'd fiddled with throughout the meeting. Peter's persistent and growing harrassment was the norm in Meadow Brook for those of us who didn't party with him and Bob. In the fall, I had even spoken with the high school union rep—one of the party-goers, unfortunately—about Peter's attitude toward me. "Oh, he's not really that bad," my colleague had said, "and there's no cause to file a grievance. Pete's basically a good guy. The stress around here gets to everyone. Just don't let him bother you."

Now I looked at Bob and hoped for an apology for Peter's behavior. But, of course, it didn't come. Bob simply waited for Peter to leave, and then said, "Beth, I'm going to remind your chairperson that you are not to get involved in anything to do with rumors in the locker room and with the sign that was posted about Ann. And remember, you're not Liz Grant's counselor. Peter's right. When Liz shows up in the counseling center, send her to Debra."

"Just for the record, it wasn't Liz who told me about the problem in the locker room."

"Well then, who did?"

I got up to leave. "What difference would that make?"

I looked at the posters by the art room while I waited for fourth period to end: ART FAIR 2000. ART IS FOR EVERYONE. THE PURPOSS OF LIFE IS ART. My God! I really should talk to Callie again about spelling, I thought.

At the bell, students flooded the hallway. Bold-colored tops bobbed on a sea of denim. I heard Tina call, "Hey, Mrs. M. What's up?"

I turned and saw the hot pink shirt that gloved her chest.

"Hi, Tina. How's it going?"

"Fine, Mrs. M. See ya!" She blew a giant purple bubble and waited for it to pop before she moved on.

Callie didn't notice me when she came to the door. In her jeans and clunky shoes, she looked ready to merge with the teens racing to Burger King. Her hand rested on the shoulder of a student I didn't know. "Great work today! Let's put that piece in the art show."

"Cal," I said when the student passed, "I need to talk to you."

"Hey. I thought we were meeting in the faculty room. Are you all right?"

"Sure. But it's just . . . just that . . ."

Callie held open the door to the art room and waved me in. Her eyes followed my gaze to her arm. A streak of yellow paint circled her wrist. "So now you know why I could never look elegant like you."

"Oh, come on. You look fine."

Callie picked crumpled newspaper off the floor. "One of the kids on the prom decorating committee's doing paper mache. Never has enough time to clean up, though."

I pulled out a stool and sat at a large worktable that looked like Jackson Pollock's ghost had paid it a visit. Around me, construction paper spilled from open cabinets. "Cal, sometimes I wish I had your job. Maybe I shouldn't be in guidance anymore."

"How can you say that? You're the best counselor we've ever had."

"I don't know what to do. Bob and Peter read me the riot act again." I picked up a clean paint brush and feathered the thin bristles. "Tina Roland's mother complained about my meeting with Tina."

"So?"

I told Callie what Bob and Peter had said. "But you know, Cal, I still can't stay out of it, because if I do, then nothing changes. And kids get hurt. And . . ." I didn't want to cry, but tears came from a place so deep I couldn't stop them. "And then Joe's right, dammit! Everything we taught Danny means nothing at all."

We got to the faculty room twenty minutes into fifth period. "Where've you guys been?" Denise asked as we opened the door. Mr. Rat wriggled on her shoulder.

"Sorry, folks," Callie said. "Beth came by my room to help with clean up."

Joanne smiled at me. "Please tell me you don't do windows."

I ignored her and opened the refrigerator to take out the yogurt I'd put in the day before. What I found didn't surprise me: an open container of cottage cheese crowned with green mold; lunch bags crammed onto shelves; an uncapped two-liter bottle of Diet Coke; and rotten bananas, pungent and brown. No yogurt.

I sat down empty handed while Callie talked. "You should see the paper mache volcano the kids are making for the junior prom. The theme's Hawaiian Luau, you know." She looked at me. "Come on, Beth. You can't live on air. Eat something."

"I know I had a yogurt in there. Guess someone's been hungrier than I."

"Well, well." Joanne stepped into the spotlight. "The backward Robin Hood strikes again, robbing the thin to feed the fat. Any guesses?"

Callie moved half her peanut butter sandwich toward me. Skippy mingled with the scent of broccoli. "Thanks, but I'm not really hungry."

"I got it!" Callie slapped down her lunch. "I know who our Robin Hood is. I'll bet it's Peter Stone. Sure looks like he eats everything. Probably hunts for food here every day."

"Hmm, you might be right." Denise tickled Mr. Rat's back as she spoke. "He certainly has plenty of time to sneak around. Doesn't seem to do much of anything around here."

"So how many administrators does it take to change a light bulb?" Joanne asked as she left the table.

Callie elbowed me. "How many, Joanne?"

"Three," Joanne called from the ladies' room door. "One to call a custodian, one to supervise him, and one to tell him he's changing it too slowly."

"Gotta go," Denise said. "Wake up, Mr. Ratsky!"

I gathered the tin foil from Callie's sandwich, scrunched it into a ball.

"You okay now?" she asked me.

I nodded as Joanne's voice boomed from the ladies' room. "Damn! No toilet paper again. I can't stand this stinkin' hell hole!"

"Rat hole, you mean," I muttered. Callie smiled and tossed me a mini Snickers bar.

Back in the center, I took my phone messages from Sue. "This must be a mistake," I said when I saw one from Mrs. Stanish, Zach's grandmother. I'd hardly seen Zach since that first day when Callie and I passed the baseball team as we pulled out of the parking lot. "Zach's not mine, Sue. He's one of Steve's."

"I know that. And believe me, Mrs. Stanish knows it too. She's called here before. But she asked me to make sure *you* got the message. She wants you to call her. Wouldn't tell me why."

I shut the door and punched in Mrs. Stanish's number. Zach's grandmother picked up the phone. I told her that if there's a problem, she should call Zach's counselor.

"No, Mrs. Maller. There's no problem. I just want to express condolences on your tragic loss. And I've waited awhile, thinking you might want a little time to get back into your work before talking with anyone."

"That's very kind of you. I appreciate it." I reached for a photo of Danny and touched his face. "But I'm quite backlogged at the moment. Thank you, though."

"Wait a second, dear. I won't keep you long." Her voice, with its hint of English accent, pulled me in. I leaned back in my chair. "I just thought we ought to talk. You know, I lost a son too. Zach's father. Eleven years ago, when Zach was six."

"Yes, I know." Everyone in Meadow Brook knew Zach's parents had died when an eighteen-wheeler plowed into their car on the highway. Zach was staying at his grandparents' house that night. He never left. "And it's so kind of you to call, Mrs. Stanish. But talking won't help right now."

"I know it feels that way. And please, call me Kate."

Something about the way she said that, the softness in her voice, I think, blanketed my sorrow. Maybe this stranger, this woman who had raised the only boy in Meadow Brook who reminded me of Danny, really did know how I felt and how I wanted to scream at everyone else who said they did. I put Danny's photo back on the bookcase.

"We don't have to talk now," Kate went on, "if you're not ready. I do understand. But please keep my number because you know, dear, people like us need each other."

"Thanks, Mrs. Stanish. Kate." I folded the "While You Were Out" slip with Kate Stanish's number and tucked it in my wallet. Then I called Gary Johnson's mother, who'd left a message about Gary's problems in math.

Home from work, I phoned my father, keeping the routine I'd established at the end of my first day back at Meadow Brook: let Moose out, make coffee, check messages, call Dad.

"You sound tired," he said after we'd chatted for a minute. "I'm worried about you, honey."

"I'm okay. Just worn out, I guess." I breathed in the comforting coffee scent. "I'm not sleeping well, and school's getting to me." I used to be good at protecting Dad from worry, but fatigue had torn down the fence around my emotional minefield. "And Joe's so busy we hardly even talk anymore, and I just . . . I just don't know what to do. And all I really want . . ." I felt the tears too late to check them. "All I want is to stand at the tennis courts and watch Danny play."

Dad let me cry, long and hard. He didn't speak until he heard me blow my nose. "I miss him too. But no one misses Danny more than you and Joe. And you've been terrific, Beth. So strong."

I blew my nose again and searched for my Mom mug. I didn't see it in the cabinet, so I picked up another, one with Not a Morning Person written in squiggly print around the middle. I'd bought that mug for Danny the year before on Valentine's Day, when he was in tenth grade and started drinking tea and sleeping past noon whenever he could.

"I'm not that strong, Dad," I finally said. And this isn't supposed to be happening to me, I thought. I'm supposed to be waiting for my son to get home from tennis practice. Dammit! Why Danny? "I'm not that strong," I said again. "And Joe . . . well, he's working so hard now, he's not home much. And sometimes after work, he hangs out with Mike. Joe's having dinner with him tonight."

"When Joe's home does he talk about Danny?"

"Not much. And he gets angry 'cause I always want to."

"Well, there's nothing wrong with that. So whaddaya say I bring dinner to you, and we can talk about Danny all night if you like. Just tell me what you want to eat."

Dad unpacked the bagels while I hung his damp windbreaker over the shower curtain rod. "You're so much like your mother," he said when I came back to the kitchen. "I look at you and I see her taking my jacket when I'd come home from work. Sometimes she'd even open the door with a hanger in hand. She took such good care of us."

I glanced at my father and saw the man my mother had married, a man with warm, green eyes and a wide smile. A man who melted worries. A rare breed: a salesman you could trust.

I set the table in silence. Dad put fruit salad in the blue ceramic bowl I'd left on the counter. He cut a sliver of cheese and held it out for Moose. "You know, your mother liked dinners like this."

"Like what?"

"Breakfast at dinner. That's what she liked all right."

I poured a cup of coffee. "I thought we had meat, potatoes, and vegetables every night."

"After you were born, your mother insisted on balanced meals. So you'd grow strong and healthy, she said. But before then . . ." Dad looked away for a moment, perhaps at a scene only he could see: maybe my mother and him newly married, sharing dinners and intimacies. "Before you were born, honey, her favorite dinner was pancakes." He smiled and reached for a bagel.

I didn't eat much that night, but I talked plenty. My father and I laughed about the time Danny was on the first grade Little League team, when he slugged the ball off the tee and raced around the bases, passing the boy who'd been on first and rounding home while the other child froze on second. We remembered one Halloween when Danny went out as Superman, got hit with shaving cream after two houses, and refused to trick or treat anymore. We talked about how proud we were when Danny won the Athletic Leadership Award as a tenth-grader. How the whole team stood and chanted: Mal-ler! Mal-ler! Mal-ler!

While my father drank his Earl Grey, he asked about work. I told him about Ann Richardson. Six weeks had passed since that sign had gone up on the door to the phys ed office. Dad grimaced when I spoke the words that had been posted.

"So, what's the school doing about that?" he asked.

"Nothing. Absolutely nothing. Dr. Sullivan, the superintendent, told the administrators not to let us do anything. We can't even talk to our students about it. We're just supposed to keep this whole thing quiet, like it never happened."

I poured another cup of coffee and let Moose take a nibble of cream cheese from my fingers. As I stroked his head, I remembered

Danny's words about Matthew Shepard. I had thought about him more in the last month than I had when Shepard's death hit the papers.

"I wanted to start a sensitivity program," I told my father, "meeting with students to talk about their attitudes. That sort of thing. But the administrators wouldn't let me."

"I guess they're scared, Beth. They don't want to open a can of worms."

"But it's not right. Not doing anything, I mean. Ann's a great teacher. She really cares about the kids, and there's never been any trouble with her. But now, all of a sudden, they look at her differently, and all the good she does doesn't count anymore. All that seems to matter is that she's a lesbian."

Dad reached for the oatmeal cookies I'd put out, dipped one into his tea. "You're right, Beth. That teacher's private life shouldn't make a difference. But you're wrong if you think it won't. Because some people feel threatened by anyone who's different."

"But how could Ann be a threat to anyone? It's not like they don't know her. She's been in Meadow Brook forever."

"Come on, honey. People are threatened by what they don't understand. They think what they've been taught is right and anything else is wrong. And when they think something's unnatural, well . . . they just want to protect their children from it. They just think it's wrong. Plain and simple. Maybe some parents think that gym teacher could influence their kids to be gay. And that's not okay with them."

Dad unknotted my thoughts the way he used to fix my mother's thin gold chain I once wore. Listening to him that night, I was a little girl again, asking Daddy to make the chain smooth.

"So you know what you have to do, Beth?"

I shook my head and waited for Dad to finish taking out the knots.

"Just keep doing your job the way you always did, because Meadow Brook's the same as it always was. That gym teacher's no different than she was the day before that sign was posted. And all those people who are scared are the same as they've always been too. That sign didn't change them one bit. And you know, honey, it didn't change you, either. So, like I said, just do your job the way you always did, because you're the same person you always were."

The moment my father said that, I knew he was wrong. I wasn't the same person at all.

Dad left just before Joe got home. I heard the crunch of gravel on the driveway a minute before Joe opened the kitchen door. "Was your father here again? I thought I passed his car at the corner."

"I needed company tonight."

"Yeah, but I can't understand why you spend so much time with him. It's not normal, you know. And he babies you, like you babied Danny."

My hands clenched, but I was too sad, too tired to fight. Tears started in anticipation of what I had to say. "Sometimes I need someone to talk to, Joe. About Danny, I mean. And about what's happening at work."

Joe slammed his thermos on the counter. "Come on, Beth. I told you to just do your job and stay out of trouble. You don't need any more problems now. And you're not the only one here who's lost a child."

Joe cradled his head in his hands at the kitchen table. I glimpsed those long fingers, which knew every inch of my body, and wondered how I'd ever let them touch me. Then I pushed my thoughts toward simple tasks: lifting coffee grounds from the pot; sponging sesame seeds off the counter; scraping cream cheese from the edge of a knife.

I didn't look at Joe until I poured detergent into the dishwasher. Slumped in his chair, he was so still I thought he might have fallen asleep. Too much beer, I assumed. But then he started jiggling his right leg, as if someone had switched on a motor.

As I swallowed cold coffee from Danny's mug, sadness lumped in my throat. "Joe?" My voice ripped the silence. "Have you seen my mug, the one I always use? The MOM one?"

Joe pulled out the chair next to his and patted the seat.

"Have you seen it, my MOM mug?" I asked again as I walked to the table.

I sat and turned to Joe. He looked old, his face darkened with shadows. "Sorry, Beth. I couldn't stand having it around here."

"So where'd you put it?"

Joe stood and moved behind me. He braced my shoulders. "I threw it away. You don't need a MOM mug. You're not a mom anymore."

Chapter Seven

I didn't come to bed that night; I dozed in Danny's room, burrowing in the comforter I'd bought him three years earlier when we replaced his blue and white children's dressers with gray Formica pieces. We kept the blue carpeting, still in good shape and soft underfoot. Danny liked it. But the children's furniture went to the basement. Joe hadn't wanted me to give it away.

Now things were different. Joe wanted to toss, and I wanted to save. Everything. Danny's clothes. His tennis racquets and trophies. Shoe boxes of photos and snips of paper and Trident chewing gum. Danny's CDs. His tiny Superman costume in a box on the top shelf in the closet.

In the middle of the night, I got up and unfurled Superman's cape. How big it had seemed when I first wrapped it around Danny's shoulders. Now I folded it again, then picked up a trophy, its metal cold against my palm. I ran my index finger over the engraved plaque on its base: CAMP CAYAHOGA INVITATIONAL. SINGLES RUNNER UP, DIVISION A. I studied a photo of Danny, his arms draped over two boys I had met on visiting day. Did they know he had died?

I held the incense his girlfriend had given him. Moist grass and honeysuckle. RAIN, the package read. I breathed in the incense as a memory unspooled. A snowy Sunday weeks before the accident. Joe yells up to Danny to turn down the Bob Marley CD, then finds me in the kitchen. "How can you let him burn that incense crap?" Joe asks. "Don't you know what's going on up there?"

"The kids are listening to music and burning incense. So what? What's wrong with that?" I stir a pot of tomato sauce. Bits of garlic stick to my fingers, gluing them to the handle of a wooden spoon. Onion and oregano invade the air.

"God, Beth, you're so naive sometimes. Don't you know why kids burn that stuff?"

The Wailers drift from Danny's room: a song about not worrying, that things would turn out fine.

"You know why they burn that stuff?" Joe asks again. He opens a beer and settles himself at the table before he gives me the answer. "It hides other smells, that's why. They close the blinds and sit in the dark with that music blasting. And the room stinks. The whole hallway stinks for that matter. It's that incense and God only knows what else. Pot, maybe. I can't even breathe up there."

Standing by the counter, I sip fresh coffee and welcome its calming aroma. "You're telling me you think Danny's smoking pot?"

"For Christ's sake!" Joe raps the beer bottle on the table. "Either nothing he does bothers you, or it bothers you but you still won't say anything. But this isn't Danny's house. This is my house, our house, and I don't want those kids burning that incense crap and doing whatever the hell they're doing and blasting me out with that music. All I want is a little peace and quiet and the sports section, which Danny must have taken."

"So go tell him he can't do whatever you think he's doing."

"No. I'm not going up there again. You tell him." Joe swigs his beer. "Oh, what's the use? He'd lie to you, and you wouldn't suspect a thing."

I turn back to the stove and stir the sauce. Funny, I think, how Joe and I actually want the same thing that day: the lull of a weekend afternoon. But for me that means music—loud as it is—and laughter, Danny's laughter with friends. And for Joe that means a house with no teen noise, no RAIN.

My silence pushes Joe from the kitchen. I stay and watch snow frost the window. Does Joe really think Danny's smoking pot? Every time we've talked about drugs, Danny's told me not to worry. *Don't worry about a thing.* The music blares from his room. I think about Joe's decision not to adopt a child when Danny was five. "If we were meant to have another child, you'd be pregnant by now," I hear Joe say. "And anyhow, one's enough for me."

"But what about me, Joe? I want another child. And you know what Dr. Feinman said. Adoption's probably our only choice."

"Well, then just forget it. I told you I don't want to adopt. Danny's already become your whole life, Beth. Between Danny and work, you never have time for me anymore."

The night Joe told me he'd trashed my MOM mug, before I tried to sleep, I lay on the floor of Danny's room. Moose hunkered down next to me. When I closed my eyes, ten-year-old Danny pillowed his head on Moose's other side. I reached over to rumple Danny's hair.

Chapter Eight

In the morning, Hilda, the Meadow Brook cafeteria aide, greeted me as she loaded bottled water into a mini-fridge. "Help yourself to coffee, Mrs. Maller. Just made a fresh pot."

I poured and saw Danny in his Superman costume. Coffee splashed on the metal tray-slider ledge. "Rough night?" Hilda asked.

"It shows, huh?" I reached for napkins.

"Don't bother. I'll clean it."

"Thank, Hil." I fumbled for quarters.

"Forget it. Catch me tomorrow." She handed me a white plastic lid. "And by the way, Mary Grant's kid was here. Asked if I'd seen you yet."

At my desk, I sipped from the Styrofoam cup as I glanced at notices and mail. Debra didn't knock. I looked up when she said, "Hey, Beth. Sorry to barge in, but I'm supposed to collect two dollars for the Sunshine Fund. I think they're out of money again."

"Sure." I fished singles from my wallet and saw the folded pink slip with Kate Stanish's number, sandwiched in the bills compartment.

"Oh, and Beth, Liz Grant's been asking for you."

"I heard." I raised my coffee. "Hilda just told me."

"Okay. Well, anyhow, she came here too, and I did offer to see her, even though the first bell hadn't rung yet. But she said no."

I handed Debra the dollar bills. "Careful," she said. "My nails are wet. Just did a top coat."

The moment Debra left, I reached for my coffee and swallowed quickly. Too fast. Too hot. Tears came easily. Or maybe it was fatigue that made me cry. Or the photo on the bookcase: Joe and me at the Clam Shack in Maine. *Charlie's Clam Shack. Fresh Seafood Since 1950. Eat Clams!* I unfolded Kate's number and dialed.

The machine clicked on. "You have reached the Stanishes. Please leave a message after—"

"Hello?" Kate answered before the beep. "Hello?"

"Mrs. Stanish?" I reached for a tissue.

"Yes. This is Mrs. Stanish. Who's calling?"

"Kate?" My voice cracked.

"Yes. This is Kate Stanish. Who is this, please?"

"Mrs. Maller. It's Beth Maller from the high school." I squeezed the words out.

"Beth. What a pleasant surprise! Now, can you hold for a moment, dear? I was just getting out of the shower when I heard the phone."

"Sorry. I didn't mean to bother you. I'll call some other time."

"Don't be silly. You just stay put. I'll be with you in a moment."

Embarrassment crept in. Why had I called?

"Now then, you sound upset. Do you want to talk about it?"

"No, I really don't." I didn't mean to sound rude.

"Well, that's all right. I'm glad you rang all the same. And I want you to keep my number. You will, won't you?"

Something in her voice made me feel as if I were in a rocking chair. Rocking slowly. Very slowly. *Hush, little baby. Don't say a word.* I took a long, deep breath. "Thanks, Mrs. Stanish."

"Kate."

"Yes. Thank you, Kate. This is crazy. I don't know why I called."

"Maybe you remembered what I said: People like us need each other. So I want you to know you can call anytime."

"Thanks. You don't know how much I appreciate that."

"Well, maybe I do. And when you're ready to talk, I could refer you to someone who might help."

"What do you mean?"

"His name is Dr. Goldstein. Elliot Goldstein. He helped me when Zach's parents died, and then again three years ago, when I lost my husband."

"But I don't think anyone can help. I just go through the motions." I reached for the photo of Danny in his backward baseball cap. "Sometimes, Kate, I don't even want to be here anymore."

"Beth, listen to me now. I'm going to give you Dr. Goldstein's number."

Though my voice wouldn't come, I was sure Kate knew I heard her. I wrote Dr. Goldstein's number under hers on the pink slip of paper.

Two hours later Liz Grant ran into my office. She slammed the door, tucked herself into a chair, knees to chest, and cried. "Don't tell my mother. Please, Mrs. Maller, don't tell my mother." Liz looked up when I squatted in front of her. I pushed a strand of hair from her face and handed her a tissue. She scrunched it in her fist.

"What happened, sweetie? What's wrong?"

Liz leaned forward, placing hands on top of her head. "Promise you won't tell my mother. They'll kill me if anyone finds out I told. They'll kill me if they see I'm talking to you, but I didn't know where else to go."

I lowered her arms, then lifted her chin. "I'm always here for you, Liz. You know that, don't you?" She nodded.

I sat in the other brown chair and faced her. "Now, tell me what happened."

"I thought they were . . . they were . . . I thought they were gonna rape me. They emptied my locker. And they made me take my gym clothes off. I was so scared, and I didn't know what to do. And they said if I called for help, they'd . . . they'd—"

"Okay, sweetie. Back up a minute. I need to know who's *they*." I placed my hands on hers.

She pulled back. "I'm sorry. I can't tell you. I never should have come here, and I have to go to English now. I've probably missed half the class already. So just forget it, okay? Forget it."

I stood her up and hugged her. Liz folded into my arms. "I can't forget it, 'cause you're a terrific kid, and I care about you. This is serious, Liz, and I want to make sure no one will hurt you. So, this is what we're going to do. You're going to tell me exactly what happened, and then we'll figure out what to do." I felt her whole body sigh. "But first, how 'bout we go wash up?"

Liz backed away and sat. "I can't. What if they see me in the hall or the girls' room?"

"I'll go with you. No one'll bother us."

"No." She lowered her head, spoke softly into her lap. "They said they'd kill me if I told anyone."

"Okay, Liz. You stay right here then. I'll be gone for just a minute. No one will see you in my office."

I closed the door behind me and headed to the cafeteria for a bottle of water and a paper cup. Then I stopped in the girls' room for paper towels. Peter and I nearly crashed into each other in the hall outside the counseling center. He looked at the towels and grinned. "Cleaning day, Mrs. Maller?"

"No. I just need to take care of something."

"Well, I hope it's nothing pressing, 'cause I have to talk to you about Gary Johnson. Bob and I just went over third quarter grades with Steve. I assume you know Gary failed math again."

"Yes. But I've got a student in my office now. I'll get back to you about Gary."

"Why don't I wait? Take a load off my feet." Peter opened the door to the center and followed me in.

"I may be awhile. I'll buzz you when I'm finished."

"I said I'll wait. How long could you be? Oh, and I see Debra's not with anyone. So I'll just keep her company while you finish with . . . who did you say you're with?"

"I told you I'm with a student. I'll see you in a few minutes, okay?"

A smirk tugged at Peter's mouth. "No. Not okay." He opened the door to my office. "What the hell's going on here?" Peter asked as he looked from Liz to me.

I kept my voice low and even. "She's got a problem. I'll find you as soon as we're finished."

"You're finished right now." Peter walked in and hovered over Liz. "Okay, missy. This isn't kindergarten." Liz hugged her knees.

"Please, Peter," I said.

He marched from my office, motioning for me to follow. "Mrs. Maller—"

"I'll fill you in later. Right now we've got a problem, and I'd like to do my job and handle it."

"Your job? Is that what this is about, doing your job?"

I put the water and paper towels on the round worktable and closed the door to my office, hoping to save Liz from Peter's rage.

"If you want to do your job, Mrs. Maller, then I suggest you stay the hell out of everyone else's business. Liz Grant is not your student. Bob told you not to meet with her, to send her to Debra. Why can't you understand that?"

In a way, Peter was right, I suppose. I wasn't handling Liz correctly. But, of course, I couldn't see that then. All I saw was a fragile child who ran to me for help, and a menacing adult who smashed us with his power.

"Listen, Peter." I tried to lessen the blow. "Liz has a problem, and she came to me. I couldn't just turn her away."

Peter's knuckles whitened as he gripped the back of a chair. "No, you listen, Mrs. Maller. And you listen good. I've had just about enough of your nonsense. You send Liz to Debra right now or I will."

I caught sight of the door and prayed Liz hadn't heard us. "Peter, I—"

"Forget it. I'll do it myself."

Liz looked up when Peter barged in. "Okay, Liz. I don't know what's going on here, but—"

"Mrs. Maller?" Liz called in a five-year-old voice.

"It's okay, sweetie. I'm right here."

Peter turned to glare at me, then faced Liz again. "No, it's not okay." He moved closer to her. "This isn't kindergarten. I'm trying to run a high school here. So if you have a problem, you see your counselor. And that's not Mrs. Maller."

"Please, Peter, just give me a minute with her."

"No. I'm talking to Liz now. And this is none of your business."

I leaned against the round table and squeezed its edge. From where I stood, I saw Debra on her feet by the door to her office, Peter towering over Liz in mine.

"As I was saying, missy, this is high school. You have a problem, you go to your assigned counselor. So, you have two choices. You can see Ms. Greene right now—I know she's in her office—or you can go back to class. Which will it be?"

Liz didn't answer.

"I'm talking to you, Liz. And when I talk to you, I expect an answer." Peter waited a moment. "Do you hear me?" His voice grew louder. "I said I'm talking to you, and I expect an answer."

"Peter, please!" I bolted for my office. "She's not feeling well."

"Then send her to the nurse. Or better yet, I'll have Mary take her home."

That did it for Liz. "Please, Mr. Stone," she begged. "Please don't tell my mother."

Peter looked at me as a red blotch sprouted on his neck. "Jesus Christ! I don't believe this. I'm running a preschool now." He stormed out to the secretary's desk, brushing past me at the door. "Sue, when Steve comes in, tell him to see me right away."

Despite Peter's warning that Liz's problems were none of my business, her words stayed with me—temporarily overriding thoughts about Danny. Did Liz really think she was going to be raped? Clearly something had happened in that second period gym class—something that surely involved Tina Roland and Jen Scotto.

I needed to talk to Ann, but I knew she'd be outside with a class. And Steve wasn't in his office. So, I saw Debra. I had to convince her to change Liz's gym period without saying much. Liz wouldn't survive if word got out that she'd told what had happened, and I couldn't trust Debra not to talk about it. So I simply said Liz was upset because the kids in Ann's second period class had bullied her.

"Well, it's no wonder, Beth. They probably tease her when she changes. Why, I bet she doesn't even weigh ninety pounds. And the fact that she's nonstop mouth can't help. That's for sure."

"Look, we don't know exactly what's going on." Fatigue pushed me into Debra's visitor's chair. "But it's really important that we get her out of that gym class."

"You mean change her schedule? Now? You've gotta be joking."

"But if she stays in that class, things could get worse. There are tough kids in that group. If we don't make a change, Liz could get hurt."

"Oh, come on. It's fourth quarter already. You know we can't change schedules." Debra wrapped a curl around her finger. She saw me watching and unwound her hair. Then she popped open a can of Diet Coke with a nail file. "Look, I'm sorry. I'd like to help. Really I would. But rules are rules. Liz'll just have to deal."

Steve entered with a plate of brownies. "Just came from home ec. Want some?" Debra picked up a burnt chocolate square and took a tiny bite.

"No thanks," I said when Steve turned to me. "But I really need to talk to you."

"I'll get to you later. I hear Peter's been looking for me. I have to see him first."

"No. It's important." I stood and faced Steve. "It can't wait."

"Whoa. What's eating you?"

"There's a problem, and I need to tell you about it before Peter does."

"With a student?"

I nodded. Steve looked from me to Debra, who grinned like a child with a secret. "Let me guess. Liz Grant?"

"Bingo!" Debra said.

"Come on, Beth. Haven't we been through this already? If Liz has a problem, Debra'll handle it."

"No, she won't."

"Okay, ladies. That's it. Into my office, both of you."

Scattered program cards surrounded *Newsday*'s sports pages, centered on Steve's desk. He pulled up two chairs. "You first, Beth. Tell me why you're involved with Liz Grant when Debra's available."

"It's not like I wouldn't see her or anything," Debra said before I could answer. "I was in my office, but Liz went to Beth."

Steve hooked me with his eyes. "Let me get this straight. Liz came to see you again, Debra was available, and you took Liz in anyhow?"

"No. It wasn't like that. It wasn't just *I have a little problem. I need to see a counselor.*"

"Gimme a break, Beth. You had an obligation to send her to Debra."

"Obligation? I thought my obligation was to help kids. Liz was in a crisis."

"Then you should've called for Debra."

"You don't get it, Steve. Could I talk to you alone? Please?"

"Look," Debra said, "if Beth wants to talk to you in private, I don't mind. I'm ready for lunch, anyhow. And she already told me about Liz. Beth wants me to change Liz's schedule to get her out of Ann Richardson's second period class. But I know we can't do that, it being fourth quarter and all. So there's nothing I can do, right? Liz will just have to deal."

Debra left, and I told Steve there'd been an incident in the locker room.

"What kind of incident?" he asked.

I should have told Steve, should have known I couldn't protect Liz. I see that now. But all I said then was, "Some kids gave Liz a hard time. And she was really upset. She wouldn't talk to Debra. And when Peter saw her in my office, he freaked out. That's why he wants to see you."

"Beth," Steve's voice softened, "we've been through this before. Seeing Liz was a mistake. I told you: the big guys are on the warpath, and they're not pleased with your performance lately. I need to know I can count on you to do your job properly, and that means listening to Bob and Peter. And me. So, I'll tell you again for the last time: You are not, under any circumstances, to meet with Liz Grant. Do you understand?"

"I hear you. But please, trust me on this. You've got to get Liz out of that second period class."

"Jeez!" Steve stood and spread his hands on his desk. "Maybe Peter's right. Maybe it's not a good idea for you to be working with teenagers now."

Steve's words smacked me hard. Working with teenagers was what I did. It was all I had.

Back in my office, I fingered Danny's photo, seeking clues as to what to say to Mary. I didn't want to betray Liz's confidence, but I had no choice now: I had to tell Mary that her daughter was in trouble. I needed to convince her to push Bob to get Liz out of gym. And Bob might do it, I thought, because he wouldn't want Mary announcing that he didn't go to bat for his kids. Why, just a month earlier, the *Meadow Brook News* had praised Bob's leadership following a visit from the Middle States Accreditation Committee. Their report cited Bob as "a principal who has created an academic oasis in which all students learn in a safe and nurturing environment."

The superintendent got good mileage from that. Dr. Sullivan lauded our safety record: no violent incidents; only two bomb threats in the previous year; and just one student suspended for bringing a weapon into the building. At a recent Board of Education meeting, Bob had been commended for the Middle States write-up. Mary told me she had even heard rumors about Bob sliding into the superintendency whenever Dr. Sullivan retired. So Bob definitely wasn't looking for any problems.

If Mary urged him to get Liz out of gym, Bob might listen. After all, she was not only his secretary, but also a Meadow Brook parent. And wasn't her child entitled to four years in the *academic oasis*? I would talk to Mary and then catch Ann between classes, I decided. Liz counted on me. I had to take care of her.

But Peter got to Mary first. "I already heard," she whispered as I neared her desk. "Lizzie does tend to get hysterical at times. Thanks for listening to her."

I spoke in a normal voice. "I never mind listening to Liz. She's a great kid."

Mary put her index finger to her lips. "If Bob or Peter hears us talking, they'll go ballistic."

"But I'm so worried about—"

"Look, Peter already filled me in. So don't worry about it. It's just Lizzie being Lizzie. Any little thing sets her off lately, and she blows everything out of proportion."

"But—"

"Beth, listen to me. I heard Peter ranting in Bob's office, even with the door closed. He's really after you. So I don't think he should see you here. Lizzie will be fine."

"But," I whispered, "Liz has had—"

"Don't worry. She'll be fine." Mary stood and leaned in close. "And nothing real bad could have happened. 'Cause if it did, Liz would have come right to me. I know my own daughter."

At the end of fourth period, I found Ann stacking softball bats against the back wall of the walk-in equipment closet in the rear of the gym. A stench of sweat radiated from the sleeveless smocks used to differentiate teams.

"Hey, Beth!" Ann lay a bat on the floor and brushed the dust from her hands. "What brings you to the wonderful world of fizzle ed.?"

I backed away from the closet and allowed myself to breathe. "I need to talk to you about Liz Grant."

"Sure. Just a sec." Ann shut off the light and locked the door. "Let's talk in the gym office. I've got a few minutes till my fifth period kids get suited up, and you look like you need to sit. Been some crazy morning, huh?"

"What do you mean?" I asked as we crossed the empty gym toward the small glassed-in office near the entrance.

"Well, first that long fire drill. Some of the kids said it was bogus, that someone pulled the alarm. They think it was Fred Morris. You know, the one who follows Tina Roland everywhere. And then I get this weird call from a man who says he's Linda Marshall's father, and he wants to know every detail about his daughter's accident in softball, when Tina blocked first base, causing Linda to fall. Anyhow, he asked what I planned to do so his daughter won't fall again. Crazy, huh? And he wouldn't let me off the phone." Ann shook her head and wiped her hands on her jeans. She opened the door to the gym office.

I sat on one of the hard chairs in the corner of the tiny room. Ann turned another one around so its back faced me, then slung her leg over the seat. "So, you said you wanted to talk about Liz."

I told her some girls had emptied Liz's gym locker and forced her to strip. Probably Tina and Jen, though Liz hadn't admitted that.

"Shit! That's when I was busy with that stupid phone call. I told you I've been watching those girls. I have been for a long time. So I'll bet that call was planned to keep me out of the locker room. Dammit! I should have known better."

"It's not your fault, Ann. But I just don't know what to do now. I tried to get Liz's schedule changed, to get her away from Tina and Jen. But no one's willing to listen to me."

Ann got up and gripped her chair. "Look, you've been doing everything you can to help that child. Liz won't get hurt again. At least not in gym. I promise."

Chapter Nine

I pieced together what Ann had said—and what she had already shared with me earlier in the year—with what I had heard from Mary and Liz. The rest of the saga I imagined, which wasn't hard to do. After more than ten years in the high school, I knew what went on and how kids like Tina and Jen behaved. Their poison permeated the air, making it hard for students like Liz to breathe. And their mean-girl voices echoed through my haze of grief.

Looking back, I hear them as if they're standing next to me. Picturing it now, I see them as if I'm right there in the locker room. Liz's story still plays in my mind.

It starts in the fall. Tina and Jen go after Liz, and it doesn't matter that her mother works in the school. Liz won't rat on them; Tina and Jen are certain of that. The only sophomore girl in gym class, Liz is a perfect target—so easy to keep her threatened and quiet.

Liz asks her counselor, Ms. Greene, if she can take gym some other time. She's willing to change her lunch period, to skip lunch altogether. Liz knows she won't survive gym without a female classmate. But Debra says, "No way. Mr. Stone won't let anyone change gym sections." Debra won't even ask him.

So Liz asks him herself. "Please, Mr. Stone. I'll do anything to have a different gym period. I don't want to be the only tenth-grade girl in that class." But Peter doesn't budge. No changing schedules once programs are printed. No time for that nonsense. No sir. No way.

Liz toys with asking her mother to speak with the principal. He's a nice man, Mr. Andrews, Liz thinks. He'll probably help—especially if Mom asks him. But Liz decides not to have her mother do battle for her after all. It's bad enough her mom works in the school and knows everyone and everything that goes on. Better to just accept things than to have Mary intercede.

Liz tells me what happened in October. Tina takes Liz's watch, the one her father sent last year for her birthday, the only decent gift he ever gave her. Tina steals it from Liz's open gym locker when Liz races to the toilet after the mile run. But Liz suggests it wasn't such a big deal, actually, and she did get her watch back. "So promise you won't say anything, Mrs. Maller," Liz says. "I never should have told you, 'cause if my mother finds out, she'll say it was my fault."

But I can't get this image out of my head: Tina sitting on the bench in the locker room, sticking out her arm to show off Liz's watch. "Better hurry, Liz," Tina says. "Wouldn't want you to be late for your next class."

"Give it back. Please," Liz begs.

"Hey, Jen!" Tina calls to her sidekick. She takes off Liz's watch and dangles it from her fingers.

"Give it back, Tina. Please," Liz says again. "It's a good watch. I need it."

"Of course it's a good watch. I wouldn't have taken it if it wasn't a good one. I'm not stupid, you know. So, you want it back? Well, if you catch it, you can have it. Now what do you say we make time fly? Jen, look alive. Catch!"

Tina and Jen toss Liz's watch like a ball. Girls cheer as it sails over them. Or they leave. Or they pretend not to notice. They can't get involved, can't tell Tina to stop. If they do, their lockers will be next.

Ann Richardson walks in on the action. "Hustle, ladies," she calls. "Let's go! Don't want to be late for third period, do you?"

Tina pockets the watch. "Of course not, Ms. R. Jen and I are just helping Liz look for her watch. Aren't we, Liz?"

Liz keeps her head down. She doesn't speak.

"Liz, I'd like to see you," Ann says when the bell rings. "Meet me in my office. And Tina, you and Jen go on to class now."

"Maybe you should give it back to her," Jen says when the teacher leaves. "It's an ugly watch anyhow."

"I think you're right," Tina answers. "It is an ugly watch." Tina sidles next to Liz. "Listen, loser. Here's your fuckin' watch. And if you tell anyone about this, you're dead. You hear?"

Liz doesn't tell when Ann asks if everything's okay. "You can always come to me if there's a problem, Liz. Those girls can be tough."

"Thanks, Ms. Richardson." Liz studies the floor. "But everything's all right. I just need a pass to English, that's all."

Liz doesn't wear her watch anymore. She keeps her locker open only while she's changing, and she never leaves her lock on the bench.

A few weeks later, Ann tells me, they get her during volleyball. Liz starts by playing front right. After four rotations, she's next to Tina, who's center at the net. Jen's on the other side and knows the plan: Hit to Liz and watch Tina slide into her. Volleyball's tough. Sometimes you've just got to knock into the player on your left, especially if that player is Liz Grant, who must have told about the watch 'cause Richardson's been keeping guard ever since—even supervises in the locker room, though no teacher's done that since second grade.

Liz will have to be warned again, Tina must think. Adults can't know what goes on in our school. It's our world. We make the rules.

Rule number one: *If you snitch, you get hurt.*

I picture Liz on the floor near the volleyball net, her breath sucked out by Tina's impact. Ann rushes to check Liz's knee.

"I'm okay," Liz says. She doesn't look at Ann. She doesn't look at anyone. She struggles not to cry. If eyes meet, she might. Ann helps Liz to the bleachers, packs her knee in ice. Then Ann calls for Tina.

"No. I'm okay. Really, Ms. Richardson," Liz says again. "It was just an accident. I'm sure Tina didn't mean to bump into me." She speaks loudly so Tina can hear—as loudly as she can without breaking into tears.

Ann tells me about the rest of that game. She brings in a substitute for Liz. Tina and Jen hit without force, as if it's a beach ball they're pushing around now. They're just passing time, waiting for the kill, Liz must think.

But it doesn't come then because Ann stays in the locker room. "Get a life!" Jen says under her breath when she sees the teacher spying on them.

"Maybe this *is* her life," Tina answers. "Everyone knows she's a fuckin' homo." Tina turns toward the door, where Ann stands guard. "Might as well give her something to dream about," Tina says as she adjusts her bra, wiggling her breasts.

"You sure you're okay?" Ann asks Liz when the class leaves.

"Fine. Thanks, Ms. Richardson. See you Thursday."

Liz tries not to limp. She can't risk anyone asking what happened. Telling would make her feel the hurt, and then she might cry. Liz knows the rules.

Rule number two: *If you cry, you get laughed at.*

Liz doesn't tell anyone the truth about what happened. Not her mother. Not Ann. Not even me. When I see Liz in the hall, she shrugs off her slow walk.

"Just a banged knee," she says. "No big deal."

Tina and Jen wait for Liz after fourth period. They corner her in the corridor between the science labs and Liz's locker.

"We're not morons, you know," Tina says. She blows an enormous purple bubble, then picks the stringy remnants from her lips. "Jen, you want to tell her why volleyball was so rough?"

"Oh, yeah. Sure. You told Richardson about that stupid watch. We know you did. She's had her eye on us ever since."

"That's right." Tina blows another bubble. "And next time it'll be worse. You snitch, you die. Got it?"

Liz nods.

"So, we have an understanding now. Right, Liz?"

Liz doesn't answer.

"I'm talking to you, Liz Grant. We have an understanding now, don't we?"

"I didn't say anything about the watch. Honest." Liz stabs at the truth.

"Yeah, like I really believe that. Who do you think I am, an idiot?" Tina takes a package of Big Chew from her bag, unwraps a piece, drops the paper on the floor. "But today you did good. I liked what you said after the . . . after the volleyball accident. Shows you're not completely brain-dead." She kneads the gum between her fingers and offers it to Liz.

"No thanks."

"Take it, loser. It's the only time I'll ever give you anything."

Liz takes the gum. Tina watches until she puts it in her mouth.

Ann tells me she separates Liz from Tina and Jen in basketball. Ann knows what's up. She's known all along. But she can't force Liz to squeal. Ann has rules too.

Richardson's rule number one: *Be discreet. Or the kids won't trust you. And they'll make your life miserable.*

Ann doesn't tell anyone trouble's brewing in the locker room. Not the teachers. Not the counselors. Not the administrators. That would only make it worse. Bob and Peter would call Tina to the office. They would listen to her story, then be nowhere to be found when she attacks Liz.

But Ann stays visible. She lingers by the locker room, listening to sex talk, to put-downs, to laughter. She protects Liz now, stands inside the door to stem the abuse from Tina and Jen.

Richardson's rule number two: *When you smell trouble, stay close to the garbage.* Or they'll hurt Liz even more, which is what they'll do if they get the slightest chance. They'll hurt Liz if she talks. And they'll hurt her if Ann says anything to anyone. Because somehow they'll find out. And they'll say that Liz snitched.

I picture Liz in the locker room, trying to be invisible. She speaks only when spoken to, and always answers when Tina asks, "How's it goin'?" Liz doesn't wear jewelry on gym days. She doesn't talk when kids make fun of Ms. Richardson, who's one of Liz's favorite teachers, who actually seems to care. Liz doesn't comment even when they say, "Ms. Richardson's a dyke." Even when they announce, "Homos shouldn't be allowed to teach."

And they joke about Ann's name. It starts when Ann comes into the locker room after softball.

"Let's get a move on, ladies," she says. "Wouldn't want to be late for your next class."

Liz thinks Ms. Richardson's checking on Linda Marshall, who fell at first base when Tina stretched to catch the ball, blocking the bag with her arm.

"God, that teacher's so annoying," Tina says. "She's really starting to creep me out." Tina looks straight at Ann and tugs at her panties. Ann turns away.

"Didya see what Richardson just did?" Tina asks Jen. "She wouldn't look. Well, fuck her! Like I'm not good enough, not her type maybe. Or maybe I turn her on. Whaddaya think, Jen?"

"If she's into women," Jen says, "she's gotta be turned on by you, Tina. You got it where it counts."

"Yeah, well whatever. I just can't stand Miss Girlie-Eyes watching us dress. I mean, fuck it! We're entitled to some privacy."

"You're right, Tina. This sucks."

"Yeah, big time. And I was just thinking: I wonder if Richardson's parents know about her being a homo and all. I mean, I wonder if they even think of her as a girl, or if she's more like a son. You know, with all her sports and stuff."

"Yeah. And you know what would be so funny? What if Richardson's father's first name is Richard? Then she'd be, like, Richard's son."

"That's great. Richard's son. Mr. Richard's Son."

I hear about the laughter. They laugh in the locker room all the time. "Poor Richard," Tina chuckles when Ann's around. "Always wanted a son, and look what he got. A fucking dyke. Mr. Richard's Son."

Everyone calls her that now. In the locker room, they all say *Mr. Richard's Son this* and *Mr. Richard's Son that.* Everyone thinks it's funny. Or they pretend to. Or they pretend not to hear.

Then one night at dinner when Mary doesn't have a date and Liz doesn't run to her room, Mary asks about school. The way I picture it, Liz stares at her spinach and cries.

"What's wrong, Lizzie?" her mother asks. Liz can't tell her about the watch or the volleyball game or the meeting in the hall. She can't talk about the hurt or the threats or the fear. She can't tell her mother. She can't tell anyone, really. Tina will kill her if she does.

But when tears come, Liz has to say something. So she spills the one thing she thinks can't get her in trouble because it's not about anything Tina's done to her. She tells Mary about Mr. Richard's Son, and how that makes her sad because Ms. Richardson's such a nice teacher.

"I bet it's Tina Roland who started this, isn't it?" Mary asks.

"Oh, Mom. It's just everyone." Liz warns herself to be careful, not to say much—just enough to explain the tears. "It's no big deal. It's just that they're all so mean to Ms. Richardson."

"But it's Tina who started it, right? Tina and that one who follows her around. Jen Scotto. Am I right? Those two are just mean. Been that way ever since I've known them. So you stay away from those girls. If you ignore them, they won't bother you."

Liz clears the table and goes to her room. She thinks she's safe now. She didn't really snitch, so why should they get her?

But Mary tells me about Mr. Richard's Son when I see her after Liz collapses on the track. She tells me Liz is stressed about school and anxious about what's happening in gym.

I meet with Tina and Jen separately. Jen freaks out. "That fuckin' skinny moron!" she cries. "If this gets me in trouble, I swear I'll kill her!"

I speak with Ann, who says she's on to them. Has been for a long time.

"Why didn't you tell me everything's that's been going on?" I ask. "Maybe I could've helped. Liz talks to me all the time, but she never said anything about this."

"She can't, Beth. It's her private war. The minute Liz makes it public, she loses. She's a smart one. She knows silence is her only defense. And I respect that. I understand it."

But Liz's defense isn't working. She knows they're after her again, even though she hasn't said anything to anyone—except that one night at dinner when she told her mother about Mr. Richard's Son. But why would her mother say anything about that? Her mother doesn't blab much, except maybe to Callie and me. Liz hopes I don't know, and that if I do, I haven't said anything to Tina and Jen. She looks for me in the cafeteria.

Ann tells me about guarding the locker room. But Tina knows that Ann can't stand there forever. Tina has a plan. She asks Liz, "How's it goin'? And how's poor Mrs. Maller doin'? What a pity her son died. And just how old was he, anyhow?" And while Liz answers— because she knows she has to—Jen snatches Liz's lock from the inside corner of her locker, where she puts it while she changes. Tina's sure Liz won't say anything. And the whole period while they're out at softball, Liz knows her locker's open. But there's nothing worth stealing. No jewelry, at least.

What Liz doesn't know is that Tina told Fred Morris to pull the fire alarm at exactly 9:22, when the gym class always comes in. Fred will do anything for Tina. Anything for that blow job she's promised him. And everyone will listen to Ann when she hurries the class back outside. Everyone but Tina, who'll dally just long enough to take the clothing from Liz's locker.

Fred knows to call the gym office as soon as the "all clear" sounds. And when it does, Ann shepherds the girls in and hears the phone. So she doesn't stay in the locker room. Instead, she sits in the gym office and talks with a man who says he's Linda Marshall's father, and he wants to know how his daughter got hurt in a softball game and what Ms. Richardson's going to do to prevent future accidents.

And while Ann's on the phone, Liz pulls off her sneakers and T-shirt, looks in her locker, and finds only her backpack. No clothes. Tina and Jen corner her. Tina swipes Liz's T-shirt off the bench. "Want your clothes back, Liz?"

If she answers, she'll cry. So Liz simply nods as other girls grab what they need from their lockers and move away.

"Okay then," Tina says. "We'll trade you. Take off your sweatpants, and we'll give you your clothes."

"And don't even think of calling for help," Jen adds. "'Cause if you do, we'll strip you butt naked. Bet Mr. Richard's Son would love to see your skinny little ass."

"But don't you worry," Tina says, "'cause we always play fair. All you have to do is give up your smelly sweatpants and you get all your stuff back."

"Sounds fair to me," Jen says.

"Please give me my clothes," Liz pleads.

"Sure thing," Tina says. "Just take off your sweatpants and they're yours." Liz doesn't move.

"Hey, come on!" Jen says. "We haven't got all day here. Just listen to Tina, and you'll get your things back. Tina doesn't lie."

"Maybe she needs help," Tina says. "How 'bout we give her a hand, Jen?"

"Yeah. Put our hands there. Get it? See how it is for Mr. Richard's Son."

"Wanna see how it feels, Liz? Feel what it's like for a fuckin' dyke? Or you wanna take your pants off yourself?"

Liz pulls off her sweats.

"Okay, give." Tina grabs the pants from Liz's hands. "Now just be patient, Liz. As soon as Jen and I are dressed, you'll get your clothes back."

I picture Liz sitting, knees to chest, on the bench. The locker room's silent. Everyone's already gone to third period.

"Oh no you don't," Tina says. "No sitting. You stand right where you were and let us have a good look while we finish getting dressed. See if we can feel what it's like to be a homo. Come on now. Hands at your sides. That's good. Stand still. Give us a view." Tina looks at Jen. "Hey, I don't feel anything. Do you?"

"Nope. Don't know how Mr. Richard's Son gets off on that."

"Well, maybe we need to see more. Whaddaya say, Liz? Maybe butt naked's the way to go, after all." Tina unhooks Liz's bra and flicks it off her shoulders. It falls to the floor. "Now can you get out of your panties yourself, or do you need help with that too?"

The door opens. The next class straggles in. Tina and Jen rush out. Liz darts to the toilet and vomits. She hears Ann in the locker room. "Let's go, girls. Hustle! Quick change and out for softball."

Liz is silent in the stall. I imagine her running her hands over the goose bumps on her arms, deciding what she'll do. She'll wait for the locker room to empty. If she can't find her clothes while the third period class is out on the field, she'll call for help when they come back in.

Her bra's on the floor, where Tina dropped it. The way I picture it, Liz shivers when she touches the straps. She looks under the bench, scans the aisle. No clothes. She searches by the toilets, under the sinks, around the radiators. Then she lifts the top of the black metal garbage can. The glint of a belt buckle catches her eye. She pushes the can on its side and pulls out her jeans and cotton sweater.

Liz throws on her clothes and runs from the locker room. She races to my office.

Chapter Ten

I drove home with the radio blasting that day, trying to get locker room images out of my mind and hoping to drown out what Peter had said, the words Steve shared with me in his office. They played over and over in my head: *Maybe it's not a good idea for you to be working with teenagers now.*

Hunger pulled me to an empty parking spot in front of Kregel's Ice Cream Shoppe on Main Street. I hadn't eaten lunch that day. When Callie found me in my office after I'd seen Ann, I was more eager to tell Callie about Liz than to join the lunch group in the faculty room.

"I don't need Denise and her rat now, Cal. This school's crawling with rodents."

"But you still have to eat. How 'bout I see if Hilda can make you a sandwich?" She put a hand on my shoulder.

"No. But you want to be a really great friend? I'll take more coffee." I tossed my empty cup in the trash. "Just coffee. And please don't give me a hard time about that."

Callie came back with her paper bag lunch and a half-filled, unlidded cup for me. "Sorry. Spilled a little. You know what a klutz I am."

"No problem." I took a slow sip. "What would I ever do without you?"

Callie pushed a chair in front of my desk and settled in to face me. "Regards from the lunch group, by the way. I told them you're having a hard day. And you know what Joanne said?"

I shook my head.

Callie unwrapped a squashed bologna sandwich with heavy fingerprints. "Mollie made lunch today," she explained as she pushed half the sandwich toward me.

"No thanks. And what did Joanne say?"

"Oh, right. She said something about a hard day being tolerable if it follows a night of something hard."

I must have smiled.

"Come on, Beth. It's not even funny."

Now Kregel's mocha chip dripped down my cone as I read the sign in the window of Arnie's Athletics: YOU DON'T NEED THE MALL— WE'VE GOT IT ALL! A memory pulled me into the past: the first time Danny and I shopped at Arnie's. Fall of first grade. Cleats and shin guards for his soccer league.

"We'll take Moose to the games, right Mommy?" I hear Danny's six-year-old voice. "'Cause he'll like the big field."

"I don't know, honey. We'd have to keep him on a leash. Maybe he'd be happier at home."

"No, Mommy. That's silly."

"What's silly?"

"Moose won't be happier at home. *We* won't be there."

The first pair of cleats is too big. "Hmm . . . his feet are really small," Arnie tells me. He smiles at Danny. "Let's see if I have something that'll fit you better, champ. Be back in a jiff."

Danny studies his feet, which dangle from the red leather chair. "Mommy, remember you said Moose will be big 'cause he has big feet?"

"Uh-huh. Big paws. I think he'll be huge."

"Mommy?" Danny pumps his legs as if on a swing.

"Yes, honey?"

"Will I be little 'cause I have little feet?"

"Oh no, Danny. You'll grow up to be big and strong."

Arnie comes back with two boxes. He squats on a stool in front of Danny. "Okay, sport. Let's try these." He pulls out a pair of cleats, threads the laces with hands that look too big for the task. Then he holds Danny's ankles and slips his feet in.

"Mommy, they're gr-r-reat!"

Arnie smiles at Danny's Tony the Tiger imitation. "On your feet, champ. Let's see if they feel as good as they look." Arnie presses the toecaps. "Hold on, sport. Stand still for a minute so I can see if they fit."

"They fit. They fit great. Please, Mommy. Let's buy these."

"How 'bout taking a little walk to make sure," Arnie says.

The cleats leave Cheerio imprints on the carpeted area of the shoe section. "They're gr-r-reat!" Danny announces again as he hops back into his seat.

As the memory played out, I tossed my drippy ice cream into the trash can in front of Arnie's and started for home. But at the light on the corner of Main Street and Bay Avenue, Danny's voice came again. "Mommy, I forgot. When's the game?"

"Saturday, honey."

"I want Moose to come."

"We'll see."

"Mommy, Billy Kramer's dog died."

"That's sad."

"And Billy said Moose will die before I grow up 'cause dogs don't live long like people."

"That's right, honey. But some dogs live a long time—fourteen or fifteen years, even. So don't worry about Moose. I think he'll be around for a very long time."

"That's good, Mommy. 'Cause I'll be very, very, very sad when Moose dies."

Without stopping at the blinking answering machine, I headed upstairs. Moose lay still in Danny's room.

"Hey, old boy. Let's go out." He lifted his head, but his body didn't budge. I curled up beside him. "Hey, Moose-Moose." I stroked the underside of his chin. He craned his neck for more. "I know, Moosey. You miss him too."

The old yellow Lab struggled to get up, his legs unfolding like rusty hinges. He labored down the steps and stopped for water from his bowl in the kitchen. Once outside in the sun, though, his joints seemed to loosen. I watched Moose loop around the basketball post till he found his spot. When he finished spraying the azaleas by the driveway, he looked almost majestic, so unlike the shrunken spirit on Danny's carpet just minutes before.

A squirrel froze by the giant oak in the yard. Moose barked and took off for the tree. I flashed back to Moose as a puppy, sprinting out the front door, coming back with a dead squirrel. Joe put on gardening gloves before he yanked it from Moose's mouth. Danny laughed at their tug of war. "Pull, Moosey! Pull!"

"It's not funny, Danny," Joe said. "He could get sick from this."

Danny stood next to me while I called the vet. "Just watch him today, Mrs. Maller. He probably didn't kill it, just picked up the carcass from someone's lawn, I'd guess. Call back if he doesn't seem right. And Mrs. Maller, try not to let him run out again."

"Is Moose gonna die, Mommy?"

"No, honey. We just have to watch to make sure he doesn't get sick."

"Mommy? Do you think Billy Kramer's dog caught a squirrel?"

I clicked on the answering machine while Moose trotted around outside. Dad checking in. Then Joe announcing he'd be home early and "how 'bout we go out for dinner? Something light. The diner, maybe." And then my college buddy, Rayanne, telling me Andy's deal had come through. She and Andy and the boys would be in London for a year. Wouldn't dream of trying to sublet their apartment, and wouldn't I love a place in the city?

I returned Dad's call.

"Hi, honey. How was your day?"

"Fine." The truth was too hard. "And what did you do today, Dad?"

"Oh, not much. This afternoon, Saul and I went to Home Depot. Martha's been after him to fix the deck before summer, so I thought I'd give him a hand."

"You're a good friend, Dad." I gazed at Moose as he pawed a patch of grass. "Saul's lucky to have you."

"Beth, you don't sound right. Something happen at school?"

"You're too smart. Remember when I told you that *you* should have been the counselor?"

"Sure, but you were wrong. I could never do what you do. I wouldn't want to work with teenagers every day. Especially now."

"Actually, it's not the kids who make it hard. It's the administrators." I let Moose in and watched him stamp muddy prints on the kitchen floor. "I don't know . . . it's like . . . like doing the right thing is suddenly wrong."

"Listen, Beth. I don't know what happened today, and I guess you don't want to tell me. But I'll tell *you* something: Doing the right thing is never wrong. And I know you believe that because that's what you always told Danny." My father waited for me to speak, but I didn't know what to say. "I'm here if you need me, honey," Dad finally continued. "If you feel like talking, just call back."

I cleaned up Moose's prints as little boy Danny played in my mind again. I pictured us in Maine, the summer before first grade, before soccer. Even now, I can close my eyes and still see us there. Danny wants to build in the sand. He whines for help. Yet I don't want to pull myself away from *To Kill A Mockingbird*, though

I'd already read it in high school and had seen the movie twice. So Joe goes with Danny. They're gone a long time.

"Mommy!" Danny's voice brings me back from Maycomb. "Come see what we built. It's gr-r-reat!" I brush sand off the back of my legs as I stand.

"Lead the way, buddy!"

In the distance, Joe guards a section of the beach. "Where's the castle, Danny?"

"You'll see." He giggles.

"I don't see any building over there."

Joe blocks my view. "Come on, Joe," I say as we approach. "Let me see."

Joe doesn't move. "We had fun. Didn't we, Danny?"

"Yep."

Joe winks. "Ready to show Mommy our castle?"

Danny looks up at me. "Well, it's not really a castle. It's much, much better than a castle." He turns to Joe. "Okay, Daddy."

"Ta-da!" Joe steps to the side.

"Ta-da! Isn't it great, Mommy?"

I stare at the face of a dog, in sandy bas-relief on the beach. Joe's perfect block lettering forms an inscription: DANNY'S DOG.

"Whaddaya think, Mommy? Isn't it great? Daddy said we can get one. Right, Daddy? When we get home."

I carried that memory upstairs and found Moose in Danny's room again. "Think I'll go rest too, old boy."

In my bed, I curled under the down comforter, which should have already been stored for next winter. I pictured Rayanne's apartment in the city and welcomed sleep.

I dreamed we were back in Maine, back on the beach. Danny and Joe are off somewhere. I'm with Rayanne. We lie side by side, our sun reflectors like starched silver collars. The beach is deserted.

"Let's go for a swim," I say.

"Nah. I just wannna soak up the sun."

I tug Rayanne's arm. "Come on. Let's go in."

"No way. There aren't even any waves. What fun is that?"

I look at the water. "Okay then. I'm gonna find Danny and Joe."

My feet sizzle when I hit the sand. I jump back on the towel. "It's burning, Ray. Where are our shoes?"

"Beats me, Beth. I don't need them 'cause I'm not going anywhere. And you shouldn't either. No one's calling. No one needs you."

"But I just wanna see what they're up to." I stand on the towel, scanning the beach for Danny and Joe. "Come on, Ray. I need my shoes. I don't see the guys."

"I told you. I don't know where your shoes are." Rayanne sits up, still collared in cardboard and foil. "But Peter Stone probably does."

Peter appears, his belly hanging over bathing trunks. He holds my flip-flops like an offering. "Want your shoes, Mrs. Maller?"

"Please, Peter. Yes."

"Well . . . let's see. You catch them, you can have them. Now what do you say we see how high these babies can fly? Rayanne, look alive."

Peter tosses my shoes, like Frisbees, in Rayanne's direction. They spin upward. I spring for the catch.

When I come down, I'm alone. The heat is gone. I shiver in my bathing suit and walk toward the sound of Danny's voice. "Mommy! Come see what we built. It's gr-r-reat!"

"Danny, where are you?"

"Mommy! Look what we built!"

"Mrs. Maller!" I hear Liz Grant call as the sun starts to sink in the ocean. "Come see."

"Danny! Liz! Joe! Where are you?"

"Come see, Mommy. It's not a castle. Come see." Danny's voice grows louder. "Where are you, Mommy? Where are you? I need you!"

"Mrs. Maller, I need you."

I fling off my flip-flops and run to the children.

Joe stands next to them. He pushes me back when I reach for Danny.

"Daddy, show her."

"Show her," Liz echoes.

Joe steps aside. "Ta-da!"

"It's my dog, Mommy. Daddy said I can get one."

"I don't know, Danny. Who's gonna take care of a dog?"

"He will, Mrs. Maller," Liz says. "Won't you, Danny?"

"Yes. Can I go swimming now?"

"No way, honey. It's getting cold. It'll be dark. It's not safe."

"Go ahead, Danny." Joe picks up a stick and scrapes the sand. "Go on and swim if you want. You too, Liz."

"Okay, Mommy?"

"Okay, Mrs. Maller?"

"No, kids. It's not safe."

"But Daddy said I could. He said I could get a dog, and he said I could swim." Danny takes off his shirt. Liz steps out of her cover-up. In the dimming light, I make out hip bones that cap her bikini.

"Come on, Beth. You've got to let him grow up already. He's not a baby."

"But he's only six."

"Look. The water's still calm. If it wasn't safe, do you think I'd let him swim?"

"Please, Mommy." Danny drops his T-shirt on the dog's face. "I'll be careful. Promise."

Liz takes Danny's hand. They run to the water, laughing as the ocean nips their feet.

"Yikes! It's freezing!" Danny shouts.

"Be careful, Danny!" I call.

Joe tosses Danny's shirt with the stick, then letters DANNY'S DOG in the sand. "Let him be, Beth. He's got to grow up."

"Joe, listen. You hear that?" The ocean churns. "It's dangerous. Go get them!"

"Relax, baby. How 'bout a little time, just us." Joe pulls me down. "How 'bout it, baby? We've never done it on a beach."

I push him away. "Listen. The waves. Get Danny! Hurry!"

"Mommy, help! Help!" Danny calls before the ocean swallows him.

"Mrs. Maller, help me!" Liz screams.

Joe rolls down my bathing suit straps.

"Stop it! Get Danny! Get Danny!" I yell.

Joe grabs my shoulders.

In bed in our house in Bay View, I opened my eyes and cringed at Joe's touch.

"Beth, you were calling out in your sleep. Are you okay?"

"Yeah, sure."

Sometimes, I still think, it's better to lie.

Chapter Eleven

Joe and I went to the diner, where I tried to erase the dream. But Danny and Liz stayed with me. Through my scrim of grief, the diner glowed with loneliness, highlighted by torn seats and the smell of burnt grease. Although the place hadn't changed, its garishness glared, as if I were seeing it for the first time. Artificial light bounced off mirrored walls. Painted flowers on the windows, like elementary school decorations, blocked the outside world.

Our waitress, Penny, hadn't seen us since the accident, and there is no anonymity in Bay View. I accepted her condolences with the coffee she pushed in front of me. "We don't need that," Joe said when Penny brought a creamer to the table. "She takes it black."

I used to find comfort in Joe's familiarity with my habits. Immersed in each other's nuances for so long, we often communicated needs without speech. But that night Joe's intimacy irked me. I separated a stack of pancakes and heard Danny's and Liz's cries for help from my dream. As I sipped my coffee, Liz huddled next to Danny in my mind.

"You've got to stop thinking of him every minute," Joe said, taking a bite of his hamburger. He dipped a fry into ketchup and held it out to me.

I shook my head no. "I wasn't thinking about Danny," I said. "I was thinking about something at school." The lie rolled off my tongue. I focused on scooping butter to the side of my plate, then drank my coffee and swallowed anger with the tepid liquid. So what if I were to admit I was thinking of Danny? Why should I have to apologize? And to Joe, of all people.

He flagged Penny to refill my cup. "Do you want something instead?" she asked when she saw I hadn't eaten. "It's no trouble, really. Let me bring you something else. Some eggs, maybe? A toasted bagel?"

"No, thank you. I'm fine. Just not very hungry."

Joe ordered apple pie. "So I heard the message from Rayanne," he said. "What did you tell her about the apartment?"

"Nothing. I haven't called back yet."

"You know, I don't understand why you still talk to her. All that bragging about how well Andy's doing. And their big apartment in Manhattan. And private school for the boys. Doesn't that bother you? Aren't you just a little sick and tired of hearing how wonderful her life is?"

"I know she's annoying, but Rayanne's been a good friend since college. I can't just forget that." As I spoke, I looked at Joe, as if watching him on a screen. My celluloid husband, the projection of a man I'd believed I would love forever. It was then I saw the truth: Danny had glued us together, even when we argued about him. And now we were peeling apart.

Joe jabbed his pie. "So, what's happening at school these days?"

I should have lied again. It would have been simple to say everything was fine. But without pause, I reported on Liz. I didn't get far, though.

"You did *what?*" Joe said when I told him I hadn't sent Liz to Debra even when Peter ordered me to. "What's wrong with you, Beth? You're gonna end up losing your job. And for what? She's not even your student, for Christ's sake." Joe glanced at the check. "And this all started in gym. So I'll bet it has something to do with that gym teacher, Ann Whatever-Her-Name-Is. Didn't I tell you to stay out of that?" The coffee soured my stomach. How dare Joe tell me what to do at work.

He didn't ease up on the ride home either. "Explain something to me," he said as we turned onto Main Street. "Why are you doing this?"

I nestled by the window, as far from Joe as I could get. "Doing what?"

"Come on. You know damn well what I mean. You've had such a good career. So why are you intentionally ruining it?"

"I'm not intentionally doing anything. Certainly not ruining my career." I studied the streetlights and longed for Callie or Dad, who didn't demand explanations and justifications whenever I spoke.

"That's it? You don't think you're screwing up? End of story?"

I didn't answer, just looked out the window and thought about the tennis team. Noah hadn't called in a while. Who was his doubles partner now? The dream I'd had three weeks after the accident came back to me.

Hey, Noah! Where's Dan?

Don't know. Can't help you.

Joe stopped for me to get out before he pulled into the garage, a routine we'd established when we moved into the house. I went in through the kitchen door and saw the blink of the answering machine. Joe walked in as Dad's voice boomed, "Hi, honey. I was worried about you this afternoon. You sounded so down. And even though that's to be expected, well . . . anyhow, I'm just calling to tell you I'm here if you want to talk. But I guess you and Joe are out for the evening. So I hope you're okay. Love to you both. I'll talk to you tomorrow."

I picked up the phone. "Jesus, Beth! You're calling him back?" Joe asked. "Once a day isn't enough?"

I slammed the phone down before it rang on my father's end. "Why do I have to explain everything I do? Wouldn't you want to talk to *your* father if he were alive?"

"*My* father? Nobody talked to *my* father about *anything*. And what difference does that make? You're a grown woman. You shouldn't have to talk to your father every day. There's something wrong with that—how often you see him, how much you talk to him."

I rinsed the NOT A MORNING PERSON mug I'd left on the counter. "You know what, Joe? What's wrong has nothing to do with my father. What's wrong is being married to a man who makes me explain everything I do."

I threw the sponge in the sink and went upstairs, where I snuggled next to Moose, asleep in Danny's room. I craved the dog's stillness, the rhythm of his breathing. "Hey, Moose-Moose," I whispered. "I love you, old boy."

Tears flowed with the image of a picture Danny had made when he was in first grade. It still hung on the basement wall, stuck with yellowed masking tape. A fat smiley face with green-and-orange-striped legs sits on a red brick wall. And at the top of the paper, in labored, little boy print:

Humpty Dumpty sat on a wall.
Humpty Dumpty had a great fall.
And all the king's horses and all the king's men
Couldn't put Humpty together again.

Chapter Twelve

In the morning, I pulled Bob's message from my school mail-box—one line written under the notepaper imprint WHAT PART OF NO DON'T YOU UNDERSTAND?—*Beth, please see me ASAP.*

I stopped by the cafeteria on my way to his office. Hilda poured the coffee when she saw me coming. "Mary Grant's kid's been around again. Asking everyone if they saw you yet."

As I headed toward the counseling center, Meadow Brook unfolded like a movie set, a replica of a place I used to love. Lockers banged. A hat flew by my nose. Backpacks skidded, like shuffleboard disks, across the floor. And teen voices rankled me: *Outta my way, loser. Anyone goin' to Taco Bell later? I'll pay five bucks for the bio. lab. Fuck you!* Almost eleven years at the high school, and I had never before been bothered by this blast of teen anger and the pumped up volume as the weather warmed, as if students rehearsed for noisy summer days.

I welcomed the silence of the center, where Sue picked at a muffin in the Dunkin' Donuts box by her computer. "Beth, thank goodness you're here."

"What's going on?"

Sue lowered her voice. "She's waiting in your office."

"Liz?"

Sue nodded. "She insisted on waiting for you, and I didn't know what to do because of what happened with Mr. Stone yesterday.

So I figured I'd let her wait in there before anyone saw her hanging around."

"Thanks. That's fine."

Sue gave me a thin smile and held out the box of muffins. "Look, Beth. No one saw her. Just thought you should know. Steve's over at the middle school. He won't be here till about ten. And Debra's not in yet." Sue looked at the clock. "But she'll probably be around any second."

Liz didn't turn when I entered my office. She sat as if a steel rod were stapled to her back, so different from her curled posture the day before. "I'm sorry, Mrs. Maller." Sadness clung to her measured words. "I shouldn't have come to you yesterday. I should have worked it out myself."

"Don't be silly, sweetie. Why would you say that?"

She avoided my eyes. "My mother said I really shouldn't talk to you 'cause it gets you in trouble. So, I'm sorry."

"You have nothing to be sorry about. You can come to the counseling center anytime." I moved behind her and tried to ease her shoulders. Protruding bones interfered.

Liz shifted in the chair. "But I told you not to tell my mother. And I know you talked to her."

I sat at my desk. "I'll be honest with you, Liz. I wanted to get your gym class changed without telling anyone what happened. And I couldn't. So I did see your mom, though I wasn't going to tell her the whole story. I just wanted her to ask Mr. Andrews to make the change for you. But we didn't even have a chance to talk. Your mother said Mr. Stone had already told her you were having a rough day." I paused for a reaction, which didn't come. "So what did *you* tell your mother?"

Liz spoke into her lap. "I said some kids were stealing stuff from lockers. That they took my clothes, but I got them back. No big deal."

"Didn't she ask who did it?"

Liz poked at a snag in her jeans and shook her head. "No. She just said trouble finds you if you go looking for it, and that I must have bothered those kids or they wouldn't have picked on me."

"But you didn't do anything wrong, Liz. None of this is your fault."

Liz pulled her backpack from the floor and stood. "And then my mother told me about getting you in trouble. So, I can't talk to you anymore." She turned to the door. "But I just wanted to say thanks, Mrs. Maller. Thanks for trying to help."

I brought what was left of my coffee into Bob's office, where he sat alone. Peter's absence made me smile. "Good morning, Bob. Is this a good time?"

He put his orange juice on the conference table and motioned to a chair. "Have a seat."

I noticed his tie: a girl with huge eyes, fractured in kaleidoscopic image, floats on sparkling clouds. Before I could say "Lucy in the Sky With Diamonds," Bob spoke. "Listen, Beth. Peter will be coming by in a minute, and I just want—"

I let out a long breath, then cleared my throat.

"Are you all right?" Bob's gentle voice tricked me into thinking we were on the same team.

"Sure. Fine."

"Good. Then as you know, we've all been pleased with your work in the past. You've done a great job with the kids, always going above and beyond. And I don't think you've missed a performance or an evening event since you started in Meadow Brook. I believe I've indicated that in your year-end evaluations. Haven't I?"

"Yes. I've appreciated that."

"So, do you know that Peter reads the evaluations of every faculty member? We work on them together in fact. I write a draft, then Peter looks it over and tells me if he thinks anything should be changed before Mary puts it into the computer. And not once, not even once, has Peter asked me to change anything I wrote about you. He's a good guy, Beth. Does a good job for this school."

I prickled at Bob's words. How could he praise the man who tormented Liz, the man who tormented me?

"Yet it's no secret," Bob went on, "that you and Peter have been at odds since day one. But even so, I have never, ever heard him say a bad word about your work until you got involved in this mess with Ann Richardson. So, I think you should know this isn't personal. Peter's just trying to do his job. And you're getting in his way. First, getting Mrs. Roland riled up, then not doing what you're told. You're making Peter's life difficult when all he wants is order and safety in Meadow Brook. And isn't that what we all want?" Bob didn't wait for my answer. "So we're really all on the same page, aren't we?"

I glanced at Bob's credenza and saw he had replaced the photo of his twins in their soccer uniforms with a family shot. As I looked at the picture of Bob and his wife, their boys in the middle, Peter walked in, bagel in hand. He shut the door and nodded at me. "Mrs. Maller," he announced, as if labeling an item in a stamp collection.

Bob spoke first. "I told Steve we'd be meeting this morning, but he's tied up with the middle school counselors. And this afternoon, Peter and I'll be in a staffing meeting with Dr. Sullivan. So, because we're all anxious to get this resolved, Steve said to go ahead without him."

Peter put down his breakfast. "Mrs. Maller, let's cut to the chase. Didn't I remind you that Liz Grant is not your student and that you are not to see her under any circumstance?"

I waited for Bob to jump in, but he simply focused on shooting his juice container into the wastebasket.

"Mrs. Maller, I asked you a question, and I'd like an answer." Peter's words dripped with arrogance. "Didn't I tell you not to see Liz Grant?"

As I glanced again at Bob's family photo, anger couldn't cut through my sadness. "Yes, you did," I answered.

"That's it? That's all you're gonna say?" Peter looked at Bob.

"What is it you want me to say?" I asked.

"Well, for starters," Peter said, "how 'bout explaining your behavior? I'd like to hear why you chose to blatantly disregard what I told you." He balled a napkin in his fist. "Is it that you think you're so much better than everyone else around here that you can just do whatever you want?"

Bob pulled at his mustache. "I think you should answer Peter's question, Beth. I want to know why you assumed it was okay to ignore what he said."

"Bob, if this is an interrogation, then maybe I ought to ask my union rep to be here."

"Jesus Christ!" Peter stood up and leaned against the table, bracing himself with beefy fingers. His eyes bulged. "I can't believe you said that! You're gonna bring the union into this? Well, you go right ahead, and we'll just see what Dr. Sullivan has to say when he hears you're turning our little problem into a union issue. First you want some stupid sensitivity program to get all the kids talking about our lesbian gym teacher, and now you're threatening to bring the union in. I don't believe what's going on here. We're nice enough to meet with you when we could just bring you up on charges of insubordination and get this over with. And now you're threatening to call the union in. Ha! Dr. Sullivan will sure love that all right."

I wanted to scream, but I couldn't. It took all my energy to fight the tears that flooded my eyes. Bob must have seen them. "Okay, that's enough, Pete. Sit down now. We're gonna work this out. And Beth, you don't need a union rep. Nobody's bringing anyone up on charges. We're not gonna make this bigger than it already is. So let's just calm down and talk about what's going on here."

"Right," I said. "Then I have a question for Peter."

Peter drummed the table. "Go ahead," Bob said. "As long as we're all civil, I'm sure Peter will be happy to answer."

"Okay, what would you do, Peter, if a student had a serious problem and came to you saying she couldn't talk to anyone else? Would you turn her away?"

"Oh, don't be stupid, Mrs. Maller. Of course I wouldn't. But that's not the point. The point is Liz Grant shouldn't have been in your office in the first place. How many times do you have to be told not to encourage a relationship with her? Did it ever occur to you that maybe she doesn't go to her own counselor because you've never given her a chance to work with Debra?"

"Maybe the reason she comes to me is I know what I'm doing."

"Now you hold on there." Peter raised his voice. "You're saying Debra Greene doesn't know what she's doing?"

Bob's hands flew from his mustache. "Enough! Both of you, just listen now. I'm pulling rank here, Pete, and I'm not gonna let either of you drag anyone else into this. Why can't you just talk to each other like colleagues, for God's sake?"

"See, that's the problem," Peter said. "We *are* colleagues, but that doesn't mean we're equals. There's a pecking order here that Mrs. Maller forgets. She thinks she can make whatever rules she wants. But you know what, Mrs. Maller? You don't run Meadow Brook. Bob and I do. And we're telling you not to see Liz Grant. You want to help her? Then let her get comfortable with Ms. Greene so Liz *does* have someone to talk to.

"And stop trying to take over, because you're just making things harder for Liz and harder for me. Because Bob and I run a damn good school where kids learn and get the support they need. And you undermine us when you let Liz stay out of class, because all she learns from you is that she can avoid anything she wants by crying in your office.

"So I'm warning you, for the last time: Stay away from the Grant kid. And if you're not busy enough with the students assigned to you, then Bob and I can find plenty of other things for you to do. Can't we, Bob?"

"Look, Beth," Bob answered. "We all know you've got enough to do. Especially now, with what you've been through and with all that must be on your mind. So I want to make sure we understand each other. You'll just go back to doing your job the way you used to. Listen to what Peter tells you from now on, okay? And we'll forget we ever had this meeting."

I heard Joe's voice, the words he had fired at me the night before: *You've had such a good career. Why are you intentionally ruining it?* Anger rolled through me.

"No, Bob. That's not okay." I forced myself to breathe. "Aren't you at all concerned about Liz? We're accomplishing nothing here when we should be talking about how we can help her. For instance, how about changing her gym section? She's traumatized in that second period class, and isn't helping students what we're about?"

"Of course that's what we're about," Bob answered, his voice slow with exasperation. "But you know, Peter and I run a tight ship. It's the rules that keep us afloat. We've established a good safety record here, and Dr. Sullivan expects that to continue—especially now, with Columbine still cropping up in the news from time to time. So even if you don't understand why we do things a certain way, and even if you don't always agree with our rules, it's still your job to follow them."

I couldn't let Liz down. I hadn't stood up to Joe; I hadn't saved Danny. Now, I'd fight to save Liz. "What if we just exempt her from gym for the rest of the year? No big deal, right? You could do that for her, Bob."

"You're right, I could. But I won't. It's fourth quarter. No one gets a schedule change or permission to drop a class this late in the year. If I change Liz's class, it will set a bad precedent. I'm not willing to do that."

"And you know, Mrs. Maller," Peter chimed in, "if Ms. Richardson can't control what goes on in her classes, I'd say she's got a really big problem. Wouldn't you?"

"Oh, come on," I answered. "Ann has great control of her classes, and you know it. She does everything she can to keep all the kids safe. She and I have talked about that many times."

Peter tilted his chair back. "Oh, I'm sure you have."

"What is it with you two?" Bob asked again. "Why can't you just be civil to each other?"

"I don't know. It seems as if Peter's been angry with me since my first day in Meadow Brook."

"Then let's clear the air, once and for all," Bob said. "What's going on?"

Peter planted his chair on the ground and sat taller. Hands folded on the table, he looked directly at me. "Well, here's the thing. I know you like stories, Mrs. Maller, because you sure as hell listen to Liz Grant tell them all the time when she hangs out in your office. So here's a good one for you."

I pulled in closer and challenged Peter with a cold stare. "You remember," he said, "years ago when you came for an interview and I asked why you'd become a guidance counselor? You said you wanted to make a difference for kids and you could do that as a counselor in ways that other faculty members can't. And then I believe you said something like, 'Counselors have one of the most important positions in a school.' And as soon as you left, I told Bob you'd be nothing but trouble. Because you know, Mrs. Maller, counselors aren't the most important people on a faculty." Peter wiped his lips with the back of his hand. "You know who's more important? We are. Bob and I make this building run. And we do a damn good job of it.

"So I told Bob we shouldn't hire you because you wouldn't know your place. I've always been a pretty good judge of character. But Bob wanted to give you a try. And it took a long time for your attitude to get in the way of your work. But I knew someday it would. And now I'm sure even Bob's sorry he didn't listen to me in the first place. Because lately, Mrs. Maller, your attitude's getting in the way of everything around here, and I'm sick and tired of it."

Peter shot out of his seat and stormed off. Bob stood and put a hand on my shoulder. "Sorry, Beth, but it was finally time you two got things out in the open. We can't work well together when we hold grudges. So, now you know. I went to bat for you . . . how long ago? When was that interview?"

I turned in my chair to escape Bob's touch. "Almost eleven years ago."

Bob moved to his desk. "Right. And I probably should have had you two air your feelings right at the start. But you know, Beth, hiring you was a good thing. You've done a great job. So why not just go back to being the old Beth Maller and stop sticking your nose where it doesn't belong." Bob shuffled papers on his desk, then looked up. "By the way, you haven't said anything about my new tie. Ready to sing?"

"No." I looked hard at the man who made the rules and steered the ship. "We're not playing games here anymore."

Chapter Thirteen

Callie huddled with three girls and Fred Morris in the back of the art room. "Yo, Mrs. Maller!" Fred called as I walked in. "How goes it?"

When Callie looked up, I gestured toward the door. "Okay, photo bugs," she said, her voice rising above student conversations and a rap artist blasting from an old boom box on the window ledge. "Listen up! Bell's gonna ring in two seconds. Stay in the room till it does. And remember, outdoor shots tomorrow. So ladies, bring your sweaters."

In the hall, Callie saw the anger and sadness that must have tangled in my eyes. She placed a hand on my back. "What happened?" Her gentle touch loosened the knot that tightened around my chest, but the bell rang before I could say anything. Students flooded the corridor. Fred bumped into me on his way out of the art room, then blended into the flow. At the end of the hall, he looked back and shouted, "Hey, Mrs. M., d'ya know where Tina is second period today?"

Kenny Roberts, a toothpick junior, cornered Callie. "Mrs. Harris, I have to talk to you about the art show."

Callie's hand dropped to her side. "What do you have this period, Kenny?"

"It's okay, Cal," I said. "We'll talk later." I tried to smile, to convince us both I was all right. Then pushing myself into the swirl of Meadow Brook, I greeted students hurrying past. In the cafeteria, Hilda told me to help myself to coffee. "You can pay me tomorrow," she called out from the kitchen.

Back in the center, I took four "While You Were Out" slips from Sue. Two students had been looking for me, and a parent had called to make an appointment. I held the fourth pink sheet while I sipped my coffee. *Kate Stanish*, it read. A check mark filled the box next to *Please call*. I studied the message as if Kate's name were a code.

She picked up on the second ring. "Beth, I'm so glad you called back."

"But this isn't a good time for me to talk."

"I understand. I just want you to know I've been thinking about you, and I wanted to make sure you're all right." I wondered why this woman I didn't even know seemed to care so much about me. Was it only because we had both lost our sons?

"Actually, I'm not. I got off to a bad start this morning. It's already one god-awful day for me." I struggled not to cry.

"Well, I know how hard it must be for you, especially doing the kind of work you do." She paused, clearing space for me in the conversation. But I stayed silent, knowing I wouldn't be able to rake the tears from my words.

"Beth, would you like to have lunch someday? I'd love to get to know you better. You could come to my house, get away from school for a spell. How does that sound?"

"That's very kind of you."

"You see, dear, I know what you're going through."

I couldn't find anything to say.

"Beth, are you there?"

"I'm sorry." I labored to get the words out. "I can't talk now. It's just . . . just that I'm having some trouble at work."

"I see. But I do want to connect with you. You sound like you need a good friend and a good cry. I know how that feels. I've been there. And I do so admire you—the way you went right back to work. The way you get up and go to Meadow Brook every day. I could barely do anything for a year after Zach's father died. But you're a fighter, Beth. I know that about you already. Because if you weren't, you'd be home in bed right now, crying under the covers."

Kate's understanding kept me on the phone. I thought about the luxury of bed, that sanctuary from grief. How I wished I had stayed there this morning.

"So, will you come for lunch? We could talk about your problems at work, or we could talk about Danny. You need to talk about him."

I swallowed lukewarm coffee and thought about Joe in the diner the night before. His voice pounded in my head like the music in the art room: *You've got to stop thinking of him every minute.*

"I'd like that, Kate. I will come for lunch someday. Just not now. I hope you understand."

"Of course. We'll get together whenever you're ready. And please remember, anytime you want to talk, just pick up the phone and call. Will you do that?"

"Yes. And thank you," I whispered.

"And you know you can always call Dr. Goldstein. Do you still have that number I gave you?"

I lifted my purse from the bottom desk drawer and took out my wallet. There, behind a dog-eared photo of Danny and Dad, was the pink paper with Dr. Goldstein's number under Kate's. "Yes, it's right here."

"Good. Now one last thing, and then I'll let you get back to work. It's something Dr. Goldstein told me three years ago when Carl, my husband, died and I had to decide whether or not to sell the house. Dr. Goldstein said that grief spills over onto everything. It stains our judgment. And right now your grief must be spilling onto Meadow Brook. But things will get better with time. Trust me."

I didn't question then why I trusted her from the very beginning, why I embraced Kate's words like a kind of religion. I simply said goodbye and called Valerie Gordon's mother to set up a meeting. But when I hung up, I couldn't remember which class she said Valerie had been complaining about. Then I checked the program cards to track down the two students who had come to see me. "Beth? You need something?" Sue asked when she noticed I stood frozen by the file cabinets.

"No. I'm fine," I lied. "Just thinking about something a parent said."

"Anything I can help you with?"

"Sure. Could you buzz the music room? I want to see Alison Thompson, unless they're in the middle of something she can't miss."

I knew why Alison had been looking for me: she wanted a call slip for seventh period. She had used me twice to get out of chemistry, where her lab partner, Mark Bolton, squeezed his pimples and gave off an odor like sour milk. I should never have given in to Alison. I knew the rule about pulling students from major subjects. But Alison was a solid kid with a better-than-decent academic record. And she said she needed to talk about colleges. Her mother was already giving her a hard time about going away to school the year after next. I suggested we meet during gym or music, or better yet, during lunch. That's when she hinted at problems with Mark.

"I just need a day off from my lab partner. Please, Mrs. Maller. And we can talk about colleges some more."

I broke the rule then. I'd broken it twice. Now I knew she would want me to do it again.

It didn't take Alison long to get from the music room to my office. When I looked up as she walked in, I noticed the poster by my door; a corner had peeled from the wall. "Come on in, Ali," I said as I stood to tack it back.

Alison turned to read the message: WHAT'S POPULAR IS NOT ALWAYS RIGHT; WHAT'S RIGHT IS NOT ALWAYS POPULAR. MAKE A DIF-FERENCE! DO THE RIGHT THING.

"You believe that, Mrs. Maller?"

"Believe what?" I scooted around her, back to my desk.

"You know," Alison said as she pulled up a seat and settled in, "that bottom part: Make a difference! Do the right thing."

"Sure. Don't you?" As I spoke, though, I wondered how I could expect my students to do the right thing when I couldn't even find the strength to protect Danny and Liz. I hadn't told Danny he couldn't drive that snowy night, and I hadn't made Meadow Brook safer for Liz. So, Danny was dead, and Liz still faced Tina. The truth was, I hadn't made a difference at all.

Alison seemed to consider my question. "Do the right thing," she repeated. Finally, she answered, "I don't know, Mrs. Maller. I mean, it's really hard to do the right thing. Like with Mark Bolton. You know how the kids pick on him 'cause he's kinda gross? But he's not really a bad guy. I mean, like he does smell and his face is disgusting sometimes, but he probably can't help that. I sorta feel bad for him."

I smiled. "You're a good kid, Ali."

"But even so, I really, really don't want to work with him today. And that's the truth. I don't want to lie and tell you I need to see you about colleges. Not that our discussions aren't helpful or anything. But please, please could I have a call slip for seventh period today? This'll be the last time, I swear."

I wrote the pass and made a deal. From then on, Alison prom-ised, she would do the right thing: be kinder to Mark and tell her friends he's not so bad.

Alison left, and I thought again about the meeting with Bob and Peter. Why couldn't *they* do the right thing? How could it be more important to follow protocol than to help Liz? I'd have to make sure Ann would keep up her guard during second period.

"Bob and Peter are a pair of eight-hundred-pound gorillas," Callie said at lunchtime when I told her what had happened in Bob's office. "They get to do whatever they want. And they're at war with you now. I know it's unfair. But come on, they have all the power. Who do you think's gonna win?"

"But I don't get it. Why now? Bob even said I've done a good job in Meadow Brook."

"Listen. That doesn't matter. It's like what Tom always tells the girls: If you do something wrong, fix it right away. Because the only thing people remember about you is the very last thing you did."

"Hold on a sec. Are you saying that I did something wrong? I have something to fix?" I sat at my desk.

"Uh-uh. Don't get comfortable. We'll talk on the way to the faculty room. I'm starving." Callie pulled a carrot stick from her lunch bag. "And I promised Denise we'd be there today. So let's go."

"Hang on, Cal. You think I did something wrong, don't you?"

She pulled up a chair and unwrapped a peanut butter sandwich. "Well, just think about this: Didn't they tell you to forget about Ann Richardson? And didn't they tell you not to see Liz Grant? Didn't Peter tell you to send Liz to Debra?"

"But none of that makes sense, and you know it. I can't just ignore how the kids treat Ann. And I can't ignore Liz. And I certainly can't send her to Debra. What good would that do?"

Callie put down her sandwich. "You want to know what good that would do? It would save your job, that's what. Because what doesn't make sense is how you're acting like you don't care whether or not the big guys make your life miserable. And believe me, they will. You're acting like you have choices around here. You think they tell you something and you get to decide whether or not to listen. But you don't have a vote, Beth. They make the freakin' rules, and we follow them. And if we don't like it, well that's just too bad."

Callie stood and threw her sandwich in the garbage can by my desk. "This sucks! It's the last time I'll put Mollie in charge of making lunch."

"No, Cal. What sucks isn't your lunch. What sucks is what's happening in Meadow Brook."

"You wanna know the truth?" Callie sat back down and waited till my eyes found hers. "I'm scared because you're doing some pretty stupid things lately. And because you're getting yourself in a big mess. And because . . ." She looked down and lowered her voice. "Because I don't want to lose you. I can't imagine being here without you, and everyone knows Peter's out to get you. They'll bring you up on charges if you keep ignoring what they say, or they'll transfer you to the middle school, or they'll make you so miserable you'll leave." Callie looked up then, tears glazing her eyes. "And it scares me you don't see what's happening. I mean, wanna try wiping out homophobia? Fine, be my guest. But while you're at it, you decide to help Liz Grant and to fight Bob and Peter all at the same time. So, how can you not see you're gonna lose? 'Cause you will. And when you do, I'll be here all alone. And that, my friend, is what sucks."

Alison showed up five minutes into seventh period. As she was telling me about a fight with her mother, Peter pushed open the door to my office. He addressed Alison as if he didn't see me. "Where are you supposed to be now, young lady?"

"Here. See?" Alison twisted in her chair and flashed the call slip. "I have a pass."

"Did Mrs. Maller give that to you?"

"Uh-huh."

"And what do you have this period, Alison?"

"Chem lab. But see?" She waved the call slip again. "We're doing college planning."

"But there's not going to be any college if you don't pass chemistry. Will there?"

"But I got an *A* last quarter and a 91 on the last quiz."

"And you want to keep those grades high, don't you?"

"Yeah. I will."

"Not if you miss a lab you won't. And we're not even fifteen minutes into the period, so I suggest you hightail it back to class this instant."

"But that's not—"

"No *but*, young lady. Back to class. Let's go."

Alison looked at me. "Sorry, Ali," I said. "We'll talk some other time." She stood, clutching her backpack.

"And have the time stamped on that call slip, Alison," Peter said.

He stepped out to let her pass. At the door, Alison turned toward me. I shrugged.

"You win, Peter," I said when she left.

He started to go, then looked back. "Now that's the first smart thing I've heard you say, Mrs. Maller."

Chapter Fourteen

April slipped into May. Students taped posters all over the school. Art Fair—Be There or Be Square! First Show of the Millennium. Come One, Come All to the Greatest Show on Erth! No *A* in *Earth*, but *millennium* spelled correctly. Why not have the *millennium* speller proofread all notices? I suggested that to Callie when I pointed out the poster.

"I can't believe you let them put that up. How are these kids ever gonna learn to spell if they get away with that?"

"Spell check. They don't have to know how to spell."

"That's nuts. Doesn't it bother you that a high school student leaves out the *A* in *Earth*?"

"No. What bothers me is that you're so uptight about it. Nobody else around here will even notice. It's a new world. Computers. Spell check." She threw a playful punch at my shoulder. "Get with the program."

A few days later, I stayed after school to help Callie finish hanging the art show in the cafeteria. The building was quiet, the only sound an occasional yell from the gym, where cheerleaders must have been working on new routines for the fall.

"You know," Callie said as I hung a black-and-white draw-ing of a clown, "Meadow Brook's the one steady thing in your life now, and there're only six weeks till vacation. So if you keep your nose clean, as the big guys would say, we're home free. All they'll remember is how peaceful things were at the end of the semester. Dr. Sullivan'll pat them on the back for another good year, and that's all they're after. They're climbing the ladder. Everyone knows that. Bob wants to be superintendent. That's why he doesn't want anyone making waves. And Peter? Well, you know how he can't stand being second-in-command, how he always has to be big man on campus. I mean, it's no coinci-dence he divorced his wife when she became principal over at Hilldale. So now if everything stays quiet till Dr. Sullivan retires, then when Bob moves up, Peter'll take over the high school. He's just biding time till then."

I listened to the voice of reason from my best friend—the woman who knew that spelling didn't count anymore. The rules at Meadow Brook were clearly changing. Not rocking the boat was all that seemed to matter now.

"You're right, Cal. Right as usual." I stood back and looked at the clown drawing. "This is such a sad picture. But really good. Who did it?"

"I don't remember. But if it's not signed on the front, the name's on the back." She tossed me a peppermint and left to get a staple gun.

I pulled the tacks from the drawing and flipped it over to find the artist. Zach Stanish had printed his name in thin, penciled let-ters. I held the black-and-white drawing and thought about Zach, a teenager with no parents. How much sorrow does it take to strip the color from a clown?

Joe never saw Zach's drawing. He didn't even come to the art fair.

"Whaddaya mean Joe's not coming?" Callie said when she called me at home to find out what time we'd be there and if we wanted to grab dinner first.

Tom, home early from work, got on the phone. "Hey, Beth, are you and Joe all right?"

I forced an upbeat in my voice. "Sure. I'll see you later. And by the way, the show looks great. Your wife did an amazing job."

"Always does. But what's this about Joe not coming to the show? He always comes." Tom stopped for a moment, then said, "Remember last year when we went to Friendly's after we put the easels back in Callie's room? And Joe and I each had that Super Sundae thing with four flavors? And you and Cal were betting on which one of us would get sick first?"

Last year. A lifetime ago. Before the accident. "Sure I remember. But . . ."

"What is it?" Tom asked.

"You know what? Let me see if I can find Joe. Just give me a few minutes. I'll call you back."

I reached Joe at a project site in High Hollow. "I can't talk now," Joe said when he heard my voice. "We're on a tight schedule."

"I know, but I just talked to Callie and Tom, and they really want both of us at the show tonight."

"And you thought that was important enough to bother me at work? Jesus, where's your head these days?"

My stomach tightened, but my voice came strong. "You know, sometimes I think my head's on straighter than yours." I had never countered Joe like that, donning boxing gloves as I spoke.

"I can't have this conversation now, Beth. I'm in the middle of something important here."

"But this is important too. It's important to me. You've always gone to the art fair. Callie and Tom are counting on it. They want to see you. They're our best friends, remember?"

"What I remember is that if my crew doesn't get the sheetrock finished today, this project won't be done on time."

"Please. I told you, this is important to me."

"So you go. I'll hang out with Mike."

"But why can't we do just one thing the way we used to?"

"Jesus! We're not the same people anymore. The last place I want to be tonight is at your school looking at art by other people's children."

I called Callie to tell her to go without us, that Joe wasn't coming, that I'd see her there. "Then we'll pick you up," Callie said. "Can you be ready by five-fifteen? We can go to the diner and make it to Meadow Brook by seven, easy. And Mollie might even come. She'll be so disappointed if you don't join us."

I inhaled the coffee that steamed from my mug. "Cal, why don't I meet you at school? I really could use a nap and a shower."

"You've got to eat, though. We can stretch it to five-thirty and still make it on time. How's that?"

"Thanks, but I'll go myself. And Callie? You know how you said Meadow Brook's the one steady thing in my life now? Well, you were wrong. *You're* the one steady thing in my life." I sipped my coffee. "So . . . I just want to say thanks."

"Come on. No more thanks. You never have to thank me for being your friend. Just go do what you have to so you can get to the show."

When I called my father, I didn't tell him Joe wasn't going with me. I didn't want to make excuses for his behavior. So I steered the conversation toward Dad, who told me Saul and Martha had gotten a new car, an Oldsmobile, a big boat-of-a-thing. Dad went to see it in the morning, and Martha insisted he stay for pancakes. When he got home, he planted a flat of impatiens by the front walk.

My father asked if Joe had done our planting yet. Dad knew our landscaping routine, how Danny and Joe always put in annuals around Mother's Day. What my father didn't know, though, was that

I had lied about Mother's Day, telling Dad that Joe and I wanted quiet time at home and not to bring over bagels. I never told him that Joe went for a run, then spent the afternoon with the Sunday paper. I slept through as much of Mother's Day as I could. Joe and I had an early dinner at Boey Louie's just outside Bay View, where the food was mediocre and the service poor. Neither of us had wanted to bump into anyone we knew, and no one we knew would eat there.

Now, on the day of the art fair, I let Moose out and poured another cup of coffee while Joe's words boomed in my mind: *The last place I want to be is at your school looking at art by other people's children.* Moose hobbled around the basketball post, then lay down under the basket. "Let's go, Moose," I called. "Come in, boy." He didn't move. "Come on, Moose-Moose," I called louder. He raised his head and looked at the door, as if waiting for Danny to push it open, to dribble toward the hoop. "And he scores!" Danny would shout, making a hook shot, then a lay-up. I went out and pulled Moose to the side of the basket, where he sat while both of us watched Danny's ghost practice foul shots.

Then I phoned Rayanne and apologized for not having returned her last call. "That's okay," she said, though irritation filled her voice. "I know things must be really hard right now. But what do you think about the apartment? If all goes well, we'll be away for a year. And Andy and I know how much you love the city. So?"

Joe's voice came again: *We're not the same people anymore.* "Thanks, Ray. Let me think about it."

"What's to think about? A big apartment on the Upper East Side. Three bedrooms, two baths. A terrace with a view of the river. What's to think about?"

"I appreciate it. Really, I do. But I need to talk to Joe. He hates the city, and he works out here. We both do. You know that."

"But you've got the summer off. And once school starts, you can use the apartment whenever you want—weekends, vacations. Why not? It'd be good for you. Some time away from home."

"Thanks. That's really generous. I'll let you know."

"Well, it's yours if you want it, with or without Joe. We wouldn't think of letting anyone else use it."

I washed the coffee pot and crawled into bed, welcoming solitude. I pulled the comforter to my chin as images flooded my mind. First Rayanne's apartment—not the marble baths or the doorman who'd grab my parcels and ring for the elevator—but the anonymity of the city, where no one would notice my grief. And then Joe coming into our room the night before, only to find me scrunched on my side of the bed, pretending to sleep.

Joe's right, I admitted to myself. We're both different now— separate, unconnected. Yes, it was Danny who had kept us together. But as I tried to nap, I knew it was Danny who had actually torn us apart. Not his death, but the closeness between Danny and me, a bond Joe couldn't share. I'd known Danny longer than Joe had, since the first time his kick woke me at night. *I'm in charge now*, those tiny feet announced.

Nothing was the same after Danny was born. Being a mom changed everything for me. I shaded my marriage in motherhood and ignored the cloud over Joe. Maybe I didn't have enough love for a husband and a child. Or maybe I didn't know how to divide it.

I found the last spot in the Meadow Brook lot. THE GREATEST SHOW ON ERTH had pulled them in. Callie had been right: the missing *A* hadn't mattered at all.

Parents and students crammed the building, where the linoleum glowed as if it were the first day of school. The smell of seven hundred students had been Lysoled away. As I entered the cafeteria, my eyes caught the polished kick plate, which had worn a thick coat of black scuff just that afternoon. But what I noticed most was the hum of quiet speech. Even the students spoke in hushed tones.

I spotted Callie by the refreshment table. Bob and Dr. Sullivan stood next to her, Dr. Sullivan pumping Callie's hand. At the end of the table, Peter piled cookies on a paper plate. I headed for Callie as Peter moved away. Then Liz appeared out of nowhere, elbowing toward me. She looked like a ten-year-old in her purple tank top and denim miniskirt. Her matchstick arms waved, knocking a cookie from the hand of a ninth-grade boy. "Watch it, loser!" he said, his voice sounding louder than it probably was.

Liz picked the cookie off the floor and held it while we spoke. "Hi, sweetie," I greeted her. "It's good to see you."

"This is okay, right?"

"What do you mean?"

"Talking to you here. I mean, like this won't get you in trouble or anything, right? Because I know I'm not supposed to talk to you, but this doesn't count because it's not like we're in your office or anything, right?"

"Of course you can talk to me, Liz. I miss seeing you. And you never did anything wrong. So please don't worry about getting me in trouble."

Liz tossed the cookie in the trash and raced back to me. She bounced from foot to foot as we talked. "Anyhow, Liz, you and I are friends, but we both need to remember I'm not your counselor." While I spoke, I noticed Fred Morris walking toward us. "So when you come to the counseling center, you really should see Ms. Greene. Okay?"

"Gotta go." Liz turned to the door and disappeared just before Fred reached me. He wore a black shirt, unbuttoned nearly to the waist. Chunky gold chains dangled from his neck. "Yo, Mrs. Maller. How goes it? And what's up with skinny Lizzie?"

"Nothing. Why?"

"Oh, just looking out for—"

Peter's voice blasted from a speaker over the door. "May I have your attention, please. This is Mr. Stone. I want to welcome everyone to our tenth annual art fair. We hope you're enjoying the show. And you're in for a special treat this evening because in a few minutes, the concert band will perform by the north entrance to the cafeteria. Concert band members, please report to the music room immediately."

"Now, what were you saying, Fred?"

"Just looking out for my girls, that's all."

"I don't understand."

"Well, Tina and Jen have more important things to do than come to the art fair. So I'm just scouting around for them, making sure everyone's behaving. Know what I mean?"

"No, Fred. I don't know what you mean."

"Oh, nothing for you to worry about, Mrs. Maller." He scanned the room. "Just keeping tabs on skinny Lizzie. I know she's been talking to you."

"What Liz and I talk about is not your business, Fred."

"Well, I just want to make sure she's not telling lies about my girls."

"Really, Fred, I don't know what you're talking about," I said as I turned to make my way toward Callie. She had left the refreshment area and stood now with Tom and Mollie. They studied photographs on a hinged bulletin board, unfolded like an accordion. Tom grabbed me in a bear hug.

"Missed you at dinner. And where's that no-good husband of yours? He's supposed to be here."

Callie put her arm on my shoulder and answered for me. "I told you, Tom, Joe's working late."

"So, he'll meet us at Friendly's?" Tom asked.

"I don't think so. You might have to do all the eating yourself this year," I said.

"But you're coming with us, Beth, aren't you?"

"Let's see how I'm doing later."

"You know what, guys?" Callie turned to Tom and Mollie. "You two look around a bit. I want a little time with Beth." She steered me toward the refreshments. "How 'bout a cup of coffee?"

As we stood by the table, I told Callie the truth. Joe wouldn't come to the art fair, and it didn't matter that I wanted him to. We'd hardly spoken about it. We hardly spoke about anything these days. I sipped my coffee, then confessed out loud, "It feels like we're not even married anymore." Tears worked up to my eyes. *Don't cry*, I told myself. *Not here. Not now.*

"You want to go somewhere to talk? I can make myself scarce for a while. How 'bout your office?"

Two parents tried to trap me in conversation as Callie and I headed out of the cafeteria. "I'd love to stay and chat," I told them, "but I've got to take care of something. I'll be back in a minute."

"Wow. You're good," Callie said as she pulled me through the crowd. "I could never shelve my emotions like that."

In the hall, a student bumped me with his clarinet. "Sorry, Mrs. Maller. Aren't you gonna listen to us play?"

"We'll be right back," Callie answered for both of us.

I didn't cry till we entered the counseling center, where I fumbled with my keys. Callie grabbed them and opened the door to my office just as Peter came by. "Mrs. Maller. Mrs. Harris." He nodded at us. "Thought I heard someone in here. But the center's closed for the night. And Mrs. Harris, you're supposed to be at the art fair for the entire evening. Isn't that so?"

"Absolutely," Callie said. "But I need masking tape, and Beth said she has a roll I can use."

"Well, get it quickly then. I'll expect you both in the cafeteria in a minute."

"Of course, Peter," Callie said. "And I hope you're enjoying the show. The kids worked really hard this year."

We laughed, Callie louder than I, when Peter left. "And you think *I'm* good, Cal? You're a pro."

"You okay to go back now?"

"I guess we have no choice. Gorilla's orders. But I can't tell you enough how much it helps to know you're here."

Callie socked my arm. "Enough with the thanks already. I told you, you never have to thank me for being your friend."

A large group gathered around the concert band. Callie went back into the cafeteria. I stayed by the entrance waiting for a medley from *The Phantom of the Opera*. A tap on my arm startled me. "Hey, Mrs. Maller," Zach whispered.

"Zach, it's good to see you. And I'm really moved by your drawing. Did your grandmother see it?"

"She did, and we've been looking for you. My grandma wants to meet you."

"I'd like that. I'll wait over by the photo display while you track her down."

I would have known Kate Stanish even if Zach hadn't escorted her. Perhaps it was the quickness with which she approached, or her smile that grew wider the closer she got. Without a word, she reached out and placed her hands on my shoulders. Her eyes found mine in a flash of recognition. We stood still for a moment, long enough for me to smell the spring flowers in her perfume. Then her arms were around me, and I felt—all at once—my mother and Callie and the second grade teacher who had hugged me every day after my mother died.

Peter walked by and looked at us. And I didn't care.

Chapter Fifteen

"Whaddaya mean you're not coming?" Tom said when I told him I wasn't going to Friendly's after the art fair. "I know you're gonna stay to help take down the show, so why aren't you coming with us?"

Callie smiled at me. "Who needs her, Tom? I've got great student helpers this year plus you and Mollie. We can do it in no time. And the faster we do, the sooner the hot fudge."

By the time Kate and I got to the Athena Family Restaurant, all the booths were taken. It seemed as if half of Meadow Brook was there. The hostess offered us a table in the side room.

"Do you mind waiting, dear?" Kate asked me. "I'd rather have a booth. Unless you're pressed for time. Is your husband expecting you home soon?"

"No rush," I said. "I'm on my own tonight." What I didn't tell her was that I wasn't eager to get home. Lately, whenever Joe and I were in the same room, I itched to escape. He irritated me like a scratchy sweater. I needed a layer between us—I needed Danny.

Kate and I waited on a black bench, a remnant of the diner the new owners had tried to disguise. Now tapestries in pink and purple covered banquettes, Formica tables mimicked wood, and the Mozart Clarinet Quintet replaced hits from the '60s and '70s. But the fluorescent lighting and mirrored walls reminded me of the Bay View Diner, where Joe had warned me about my job.

At the Athena that night, students seemed to compensate for their hushed voices at the art show, as if they had been carrying around sacks of volume that finally burst. Yet Kate spoke softly, her velvet voice filling the space between us. "Tell me about Danny," she said while we waited. I let memories tumble through time: tennis and Little League and day camp; sleep-away and sleep-overs and school.

"Table'll be ready in just a few minutes," the hostess said.

"And he made me laugh, Kate. More than anything, Danny made me laugh."

"Yo, Mrs. Maller." Fred held the door open for Tina and Jen. "What's happening, Mrs. M.?"

I stood as if Fred had issued a command. "Not a thing. And how are you, ladies? Didn't see you at the art fair. Fred said you had other things to do."

"Yeah. Other things," Tina answered. "We've got a life. Don't we, Jen?"

"Right," Jen said to the floor.

Tina pulled two cigarettes from a pack and handed one to her sidekick. "Fred tells me you've been meeting with the snitchin' bitch again, Mrs. M."

"What are you talking about, Tina?"

Tina rolled her eyes, her lashes heavy with mascara. "Clue her in, Jen."

"Oh, yeah." Jen kept her head down and twirled the cigarette in her hand. "Umm, we hear you were at that art thingamajig with Liz Grant."

I held Tina with my eyes. "Now, listen to me, both of you. I don't know what your problem is with Liz, but my conversations with her have nothing to do with you. Do you understand?"

"Yeah, sure," Tina said. "We understand."

Jen flicked bits of tobacco with her thumb. "Yeah, we hear you, Mrs. Maller. But if she says anything that gets us in trouble, well . . . she'll be sorry."

"The only way you'll get in trouble, Jen, is if you *do* anything that gets you in trouble. So, have you done anything? Anything you want to tell me?"

Now Kate got up from the bench and wandered toward the hostess. I guessed she was eager to find out when our table would be ready, when we'd be able to pull ourselves away from these obnoxious, rude students.

Tina dangled the unlit cigarette from her lips, smeared in purply-brown. She planted hands on her hips. "Of course she hasn't, Mrs. M. We're not troublemakers. So, don't you think it's time you called off the guard?"

"Yeah," Jen said. She looked at me then, her eyes cold and narrow. "Ms. Richardson still stays in the locker room. So, either the skinny bitch is talking about us or that lesbo gets her kicks watching us change."

Fred smiled. "Lucky Richardson."

"Enough! All of you! If you want to talk to me, then make an appointment at school. And if you talk to me this way there, you *will* be in trouble." I walked over to Kate, standing by the cash register. The hostess told us our table was ready.

"Enjoy, Mrs. M.," Fred called. I felt Tina's eyes burn into my back as Kate and I walked toward a booth in the rear.

"Hey, how come you didn't introduce us to your friend?" she called.

"Oh dear," Kate said when we settled in. "Those girls are awful! Are they always like that?"

I folded my arms on the table. "Those two are tough," I said softly. Kate reached over and put a hand on mine. I welcomed her touch, like Callie's pat on my back, a reminder I wasn't alone. At the same time, I hoped no one was watching. "Meadow Brook's changing." I pulled my hand away, then was sorry I had.

"It seems all schools are, Beth."

"There's just so much hostility in these kids."

A waitress slapped down two heavy menus. "Coffee, ladies?"

"Decaf for me," Kate answered.

"It's like there's an explosion building up." I tugged at the thread of a thought as I looked at Kate. Her eyes smiled with encouragement. "And we need to defuse it before it goes off, but they won't let me get close enough to try. Thank God, there's no trench coat gang in Meadow Brook. Not like Columbine. Not yet, anyhow. But still, we need to do something about the anger in these kids before it's too late."

The waitress brought coffee. I took a sip, welcoming the bitter taste.

"I think it's wonderful, Beth, how committed you are to helping kids. Especially now." Kate picked up her cup—beige with a faded green rim. I noticed the braided gold band on her right hand and wondered if that had been her wedding ring, moved now to the lonely hand of widowhood.

"I actually worry about those girls, Tina and Jen. I don't think they have anyone to talk to." I forced myself to stop.

"Go ahead, dear."

"No. This isn't very professional. I shouldn't be telling you this."

Kate reached for my hand again. "You know, I think we're going to be friends—very good friends—so you don't have to worry about what you tell me. Now, what is it you were saying about those girls?"

This time, I let her hand rest on mine. "They're so filled with rage. It's like they're about to plant a bomb, and nobody's gonna stop them."

We took a break to order: a muffin for Kate; a bagel for me. Then I picked up my thought. "Zach's getting out just in time. He's a terrific kid, Kate. You've done a great job with him."

"Thank you. And I'm sure you did—"

Laughter from the senior cheerleaders at a table near ours chopped her sentence. "Hey, what's the joke?" a boy called from across the room, where he sat with a group of sophomores.

"Get a life!" the girls shouted.

The boys shot straws, like arrows, toward them. Two landed on our table. I tucked them behind the ketchup.

"Perhaps you're right, dear. Maybe it *is* a good thing Zach's about to graduate. Though the thought of being all alone next year isn't very appealing. I've never lived in an empty house."

I ate slowly, enjoying Kate's company, enjoying a conversation in which I didn't have to weigh my words. Kate talked about her husband, about Zach, about relatives who still lived in Australia and wanted her to visit. "I haven't gone back there since we moved to the States a lifetime ago, when I was ten."

"That must have been so hard for you, moving to a new place so far away."

"No. Actually, it was exciting. My mother's older brother was already here, settled with his family in New Jersey. And my mother was so excited about seeing him again and about all those things we'd do together: Sunday dinners and holiday gatherings. And I would have cousins here—her brother's two girls, not much older than I. I couldn't wait to meet them." Kate's eyes got hazy, as if she were reliving that first meeting, watching family outings on the screen of her mind.

"So, it all worked out?"

"Not exactly." Kate paused for a moment, sipping her coffee. "My mother got sick shortly after we arrived, and her brother wanted her hospitalized in Jersey, so he could see her, he said. He told my father he could arrange for the best care in a small hospital not far from his house. But my father said no. He wanted my mother in the city, where we could be with her. There was a big argument. And later, after my mother died—cancer, it was—I found out her brother never liked my father to begin with. And my cousins? Well, I saw them only a handful of times after the funeral." Kate sighed. "Families. They're hard to figure out sometimes. So . . . tell me about yours."

I met her eyes. "We really do have a lot in common. I was seven when my mother died."

"Cancer?"

I nodded.

Kate laced her fingers with mine as the waitress approached, a coffee pot in each hand. She nearly crashed into Tina, heading for the rest room with a cigarette. I pulled my hand away from Kate's.

"Ladies' night out, Mrs. M.?" Tina asked as she paused at our table. "And who's your friend?"

"I'm Mrs. Stanish," Kate answered, sparing me the introduction, "and you must be Tina."

"Yeah, whatever." Tina moved on, then stopped and turned back. "Stanish . . . wait . . . as in Zach Stanish?"

"Yes, young lady. I'm Zach's grandmother."

Tina stuck the cigarette in her mouth. She looked puzzled, as if she wanted to say something but couldn't remember what. When she moved away, Kate shook her head. "Let's talk about something else. Tell me about Joe."

Chapter Sixteen

On my way home, I thought about what I had told Kate: that Joe always did what had to be done, but that he wasn't often accessible. I'd told her that Joe paid the bills on time and never forgot to let Moose out. He always returned phone calls, picked Danny up at Noah's when he said he would, and never missed Little League if he'd promised to be there. But shortly after Danny was born, Joe's heart had seemed to harden toward me. Perhaps he sensed that being a mom was more important to me than being a wife. And though Joe softened on vacations and at the garden supply shop before Mother's Day, he often squelched my laughter and taught me to measure my words. In the months after Danny died, Joe's heart had turned even harder.

Maybe mine had too—with Joe, anyway. We couldn't break the wall between us, and we couldn't move around it. Separate from each other, we tossed blame like a ball. Yet we lingered in our relationship. How could we not? We had a history together. We were Danny's parents.

Joe didn't ask about the art fair when I greeted him from the doorway to the den. "How was your evening?" I asked.

"Fine. I ate with Mike."

Moose stood by the ottoman. He stretched his solid neck and looked at me. Then he plopped down, resting his head between front paws, inviting me to join him and Joe.

Joe just stared at the TV. *And at four-thirty this morning*, a newscaster reported, *fire swept through a two-story house in Woodside.* The camera zoomed in on the charred building, then pulled back to the sidewalk, where blackened firefighters gathered by a hook and ladder. *Two boys, six and nine, were trapped in an upstairs bedroom.* Neighbors, jackets over sleepwear, surrounded a sobbing woman in a yellow nightgown. *A smoke alarm was found in the upstairs hallway, the fire chief said later, but batteries had not been installed.* Two photos filled the screen: round-faced boys with large, dark eyes and curly hair.

"No fuckin' batteries," Joe said under his breath. He didn't face me. "Stupid parents."

"I'm going upstairs, Joe. Come on, Moose."

The camera panned a slick news center as theme music grew louder. *Sports and weather up next. Stay tuned.*

Moose stood slowly. "Let's go, Moose-Moose. Time for bed." He followed me to the stairwell, pausing for a moment at the bottom before starting up the steps. I went after him, poised to catch his rump if his legs gave out. In this slow-motion climb, the weight of the day pushed hard on my shoulders.

Upstairs, Moose moved faster as he headed for Danny's room, where he stretched out on the blue carpet. "Good night, old boy," I said softly, kneeling to stroke his head. I ran my hand down his back, then rubbed his front paws. *Mommy, remember you said Moose will be a big dog 'cause he has big feet?* Moose rolled on his side. I lay down, pillowing my head on his soft belly, and breathed in a fresh, herbal scent.

Joe must have bathed him, I thought as I caressed Moose's smooth, thick coat. But when had he found time? My arm looped under Moose's chin to pet his fleshy jaw. For a while, I stayed that way, listening to the silence, trying to conjure the sound of Danny's laugh. When I took a deep breath, the air pressed on my heart.

I stood to look for Danny's tennis racquets, which I had propped against his bookcase. Gone. Then I pulled open the second drawer of his dresser, where tennis and camp clothes enfolded memories. Only one shirt remained—a worn white T with deep blue lettering: BAY VIEW TENNIS.

Joe and I hadn't talked about Danny's belongings. I just accepted their gradual disappearance as a needed step in my walk through grief. As always, Joe simply did what had to be done. He would bid on a project, take out the garbage, bathe Moose, and pack up Danny's life.

I studied the few trophies that Joe had left on Danny's bookcase. An open carton in the corner of the room held special prizes: Danny's Scholar-Athlete plaque, an All Conference commemorative plate, and a Coach's Award trophy, which I lifted from the box. I fingered the engraving at the base of the statue: BAY VIEW HIGH SCHOOL COACH'S AWARD. 1999. DANIEL MALLER.

I carried the trophy down the hall and placed it on my nightstand. The silver figure of a tennis player rested against a tall blue column. I ran my hand from player to base. COACH'S AWARD. DANIEL MALLER. Danny and Meadow Brook and Kate tossed with Rayanne's message as I fell asleep. *An apartment on the Upper East Side. Three bedrooms, two baths. What's to think about?*

In the morning, the trophy was gone.

Chapter Seventeen

"So, where was Mr. Maller last night?" Tina asked, cracking her gum, when she stopped me in the corridor by the art room the next morning. Her raccoon eyes stared, daring me to look away.

"Tina, that's none of your business."

"Oh, isn't it?" Her hands flew to her hips, drawing attention to her midriff, visible below a blue, baby-doll top.

"No, it's not."

"You're so wrong, Mrs. M. You see, Jen and I were talking last night, you know, when we saw you at the Athena? And everything makes sense now."

"What are you saying?"

"Well, now we know why you went off on us about what a good teacher Richardson is." Tina blew a slow, perfect bubble and waited for it to pop. "My parents still say that dyke shouldn't be allowed to work here, especially since she's been eyeing us in the locker room. And we all know who put her up to that, don't we?"

Students quickened their pace in the hall. A backpack banged my side. "I don't know what you're talking about, Tina, and I'm not going to have this discussion here. If you want to talk about the locker room, then make an appointment in the counseling center. We'll talk about it in my office." I spoke slowly yet forcefully, hoping to quash the anger that rose in my throat.

"You really don't get it, Mrs. M.? We're on to you now." She leaned against a locker, shoulders back, chest forward.

The bell rang. Students ran. A wake of debris trailed them to their classrooms: chewing gum and candy wrappers and crumpled papers. I stooped to pick up an empty Tootsie Roll box. Tootsie Rolls, the biggest seller in the Key Club's fund-raising drive. Then I stood and faced Tina again. Just the two of us, alone in the hall. A tingle worked down my arms. I crossed them and breathed slowly.

Later, I'd remember this run-in with Tina as a recognition of one of my father's lies: that kids don't have power. Or that, if they do, it's linked to good grades and good values. It was a complete lie, because Tina had neither, yet she grabbed all the power. And though my colleagues nodded in agreement when I shared the problems I had with Tina, they knew, as I did, that speaking with the administrators would not help at all.

"Really, Mrs. M., it's simple," Tina went on, ignoring my request that she make an appointment if she wanted to speak with me. "See, the way I figure, maybe Richardson spies on us to report to you. Know what I'm sayin' here?"

"I certainly don't. And this discussion is over!"

"Well . . . I guess you're even denser than I thought." Tina turned and walked away. I bit my lip and opened Callie's door, wondering why I had let Tina corner me like that, harassing me with innuendoes. Of course, I couldn't yet see how grief obscured my judgment.

Paintings and drawings from the fair filled half the art room; junior prom decorations cluttered the rest. A giant paper mache volcano sat in the middle of the floor, separating art fair pieces from prom ornaments. The volcano reached toward the light fixtures, from which paper birds hung on lengths of colored yarn. As students moved from cabinets to worktables, the birds darted overhead, as if flying.

Three junior girls slopped orange and brown paint around the volcano's base. One of them looked up and caught me hugging the wall just inside the door. "Hi, Mrs. Maller!" she called over the sound of a female vocalist on the boom box. "Whaddaya think? Pretty good, huh? Wanna give us a hand?"

I stuck to the wall like a small child at an ice rink, scared to move in from the rail. "Looks like you're doing just fine on your own," I answered.

Callie stood up from a group cutting paper pineapples in the back of the room. Her smile steadied me. I moved to the table where girls worked in assembly line fashion.

"Grab scissors," Callie told me. "We need all the help we can get. Prom's in two weeks, you know."

Susanna Smith, a junior with the raspy voice of an old smoker, pulled out the empty chair to her right. "I don't know how we'll ever get these done this period," she said, "though it does go faster without the boys."

Callie stayed focused on cutting spiky, green leaves, which the after-school decorating committee would later glue on the paper pineapples. "After all these years, Mrs. Maller, I've finally learned how to do this," she said as she feathered the leaf tips. "The boys get passes to the computer room, the girls choose the music, and bingo! We pick up the pace."

I didn't sit at first, but rested my hands on the back of Susanna's chair. "I can't wait till the prom," Susanna said to no one in particular. "My boyfriend's wearing the most outrageous tux."

An image came into focus: Danny in the rented tuxedo he'd worn to Noah's stepbrother's wedding two years earlier. For a moment, I couldn't breathe.

Callie walked around the worktable and placed a hand on my shoulder. "You okay?"

"I . . . I don't know." I ran my tongue over my bottom lip. "We'll talk later."

Callie inched out the chair Susanna had readied for me. "Come on. Sit for a minute. We really could use your help."

I pulled scissors from the coffee can in the middle of the table. Susanna handed me a sheet of brown construction paper and pointed to the pineapple stencil. Callie went back to her seat, where she chatted easily with the girls, like friends at a coffee klatch.

"How many more, Mrs. Harris?" a student asked. "My fingers are cramping from all this cutting."

"We're almost there, girls." Callie thumbed the stack of pineapples like a deck of cards.

I finished the piece in my hand, careful not to clip off the prickly points, and placed the scissors in the can. "Sorry, ladies, but I've got to get back to the counseling center." My voice sounded fake to me, as if I were reading from a script that called for a happy tone. I pushed out my chair. "Fifth period, Mrs. Harris. I'll see you then. And by the way, the art fair was terrific. Great job."

Callie winked. "Well, Friendly's wasn't the same without you, though Mollie managed to down a sundae in your honor."

As I entered the center, Sue held out a message. I looked at Kate's name on the slip of paper.

"She wants you to call whenever you get a chance," Sue said. "Oh, and I think you should know Mr. Stone came by just a little while ago and asked where you were." She lowered her voice, causing me to stand closer to her desk. "I told him you just stepped out for a minute. And when I asked if I should give you a message, he said no, he was just making the rounds. But I thought you'd want to know."

I thanked Sue and went into my office, where I closed the door and picked up the phone. Kate answered on the first ring. "I'm so glad you called back. I didn't know what your schedule would be today." Her voice flowed over me like a warm bath. I slumped a bit in my chair. "Now I don't want to disturb you if you're busy, Beth. Tell me if this isn't a good time."

"Actually, it's not. But it's good to hear your voice."

Danny in a tuxedo. That vision again. I closed my eyes and felt tears heat the back of my eyelids.

Then another image: Tina in the hall. I told Kate about that—which I knew, even then, was totally unprofessional. Kate allowed me to speak fully. No interruptions. No judgments. How different from my conversations with Joe. And when I finished, Kate explained and excused my behavior: "You're not yourself, dear, and you can't expect to be. It's still too soon. You remember what I told you about the spillover of grief?"

"Yes, but I've got a job to do. And I can't do it when I don't think clearly." Tears, which had started slowly, now ran unchecked down my cheeks.

Kate seemed to know I needed a minute. "Just put down the phone, dear. No need to hang up. I'm not going anywhere. I want to hear how things were with Joe when you got home last night."

I followed Kate's suggestion, laying the phone on a stack of college catalogs, and reached for a tissue. I looked up when the door opened and Peter walked into my office. He put fisted hands on my desk. "Is that a parent on the line, Mrs. Maller?" He spoke in a loud voice, as if addressing a student assembly.

My breath caught in my chest. If I said yes, I was talking with a parent, Peter would ask which one. And Peter knew I wasn't Zach's counselor. But if I said no, then Peter would nail me for using school time for personal business. I hung up the phone.

Callie was right: An eight-hundred-pound gorilla does whatever he wants. And Peter wanted to crush me like a cigarette. He rapped my desk. "When I ask you a question, Mrs. Maller, I expect an answer."

"It was a personal call. Sorry."

He closed the door, closeting us together, and pulled up a chair. "Now you listen to me, Beth. I don't know what's going on around here, but I do know that we pay you to do a full-time job. And that means keeping your personal business out of Meadow Brook. That phone is not for personal calls. And if you have a cell phone, don't let me catch you on that, either. Not during school hours. Do I make myself clear?"

I met his gaze. "Perfectly."

"And another thing while we're at it. We don't pay you to wander around this building. So, when you're out of the office, you need to let Sue know where you are. Understood?" Peter got up and opened the door, then faced me one last time. "So, would you mind telling me where you were a little while ago?"

"I was in the art room. Some of my students asked me to come by to check out the prom decorations."

"So, you went to see Mrs. Harris."

"I told you, Peter. I stopped by the art room."

"Well, that's something else we don't pay you to do, to hang out in the art room, especially when there's supposed to be a class going on in there. I guess you think you decide when you and your gal pal get time off. But you know what? You don't. And that art room's not your private playground."

Sue brushed against Peter as he marched from my office. "Beth," she said, "Mrs. Stanish has been trying to reach you again. She wants you to call her right back."

Chapter Eighteen

I apologized to Kate for hanging up and promised to call her from home. The rest of that morning, I busied myself with interim reports and scholarship applications. When Callie came by during fifth period, I told her about my separate clashes with Tina and Peter. "So, let's eat here, Cal. Two rats in one day are enough."

"Sorry, but my lunch is in the fridge. So we've got to go to the faculty room. I can't just pick up my sandwich and come back here. Last time I did that, Joanne made mince meat out of me. I guess she's jealous of our friendship." Callie tugged my arm, steering me away from my desk. "And you know what they do with mince meat, don't you?"

"No, what?" I stepped back to grab my purse.

"Hah, hah, hah," she said in comic vampire tone. "They feed it to rats. Because rats eat anything."

"Well, they certainly took a bite out of me."

Callie smiled and ushered me to the door. We stopped at Sue's desk. "I'll be at lunch, just in case anyone asks," I reported as I glanced at the clock. "And if Mr. Stone comes by, please tell him I went to the faculty room at eleven-o-six."

"Yeah," Callie said. "And you can tell him I'm there too, since we don't have a private playground."

"Just tell him I'm at lunch," I said, my voice dry and cold.

But Callie wouldn't quit. "And if Mr. Stone has a problem with that, tell him it sure looks like *he's* been taking plenty of meal breaks lately."

I elbowed Callie on the way out of the center. "Watch it. Aren't you the one who told me to stay out of trouble so those bastards don't get me?"

"Yeah, well, they finally got you. And you know what? I'm not gonna let them get away with it."

"You've got to stay out of this, Cal. It's enough they're gunning for me. I don't want them coming after you too."

"Hey, this is Callie Harris you're talking about here." She resumed her vampire speech, which made me smile. "Nobody messes with the woman who gave them that fabulous art show. Nobody!" She linked her arm in mine and gentled her voice. "And nobody messes with her best friend either."

We entered the faculty room. Callie tilted her head and sniffed like a dog. "The vegetarian's out sick today," Joanne said, explaining the absence of odor. "See what happens when you eat all that broccoli and healthy stuff? You get sick."

"Well then, I guess the opposite's true too," Callie said. "Explains why I'm so healthy." She pulled her lunch bag from the refrigerator. "It's all this poison I consume. Garbage, my friends." Callie tossed her brown paper sack onto the table. "Pure unadulterated garbage. My very own health food."

I took the chair across from Joanne, whose fingers explored a school salad. "Checking for worms?" Callie asked, settling into the seat next to mine.

"No. Bugs," Joanne answered. "I hear the cafeteria's crawling with them—cockroaches the size of Mr. Rat. So, I thought I'd better take a look." She flipped a slice of tomato, rearranged carrot sticks. "It's funny, isn't it?"

"What?" I asked.

"Give her a moment to crank up the wit machine," Callie muttered.

Joanne grinned. "Well, in the real world, people look before they leap, but in Meadow Brook, we look before we eat."

Callie shook her head as she unwrapped a bologna sandwich. "Cool it, Joanne. We're not in the mood."

"What's the matter?" Denise asked, cradling Mr. Rat in her lap. She stroked him with her right hand, ate Fritos with her left. "Are they giving you a hard time again, Beth?"

I nodded. Callie spoke for me. "And not just the big guys. Now a student too."

"That's impossible," Denise said. "No student would ever give Beth a hard time." She looked at me. "The kids love you."

"Thanks," I said, "but we've got a few rats around here."

Denise lowered her eyes.

"I'm sorry, Denise. I'm not talking about *your* rat. I'm talking about the ones who ruin this place."

Denise crumpled the empty Fritos bag and lifted Mr. Rat to her shoulder. "I know. There are all kinds of rats. White rats, like Mr. Rat here, they're the good guys." Mr. Rat's tail swished over Denise's chest. "Scientists use them to study behavior, disease, and all kinds of things." Denise bent her head, nuzzling her chin on Mr. Rat's tiny head. "You're a trailblazer, Mr. Ratsky."

"Oh, let's not get carried away," Joanne said. "The only trailblazers around here are the Key Clubbers, marking the halls with candy wrappers. I take it you've all noticed the litter. It's amazing they're allowed to sell that junk in school."

"What's amazing about that?" Callie asked. "Lana's the adviser. The Key Club gets to do whatever Lana wants." Callie jabbed my shoulder. "Hey, maybe she's a small gorilla in disguise."

"I don't get it," Joanne said.

"You don't have to," Callie answered.

Joanne pushed her chair back and headed for the ladies' room. "Bell's about to ring," Denise announced. Mr. Rat squealed as Denise stood and walked around the table. "He's really very sweet, Beth. Feel how soft he is."

I shook my head.

"I won't let his tail hit you. I promise." Denise squatted and took my hand. "Don't think of him as a rat. Think of him as my pet, like a dog."

I thought of Moose and scratched Mr. Rat's head with my index finger. His fur calmed me, like the rabbit's foot I had carried in elementary school. Denise smiled. "I really hope things get better for you, Beth."

Callie and I dashed into the ladies' room. "Oh my God!" Callie whispered. "I can't believe you touched the rat."

I pulled the lever on the soap dispenser. It spit only air. "Dammit! Why isn't there ever any soap in here?"

The bell rang. Joanne called from one of the stalls, "Wait! Could you please find me some toilet paper? No toilet paper. No soap. What do they think we are? Animals?"

"That's right," Callie said, as I slipped paper under the door to Joanne. "Welcome to Meadow Brook, home of the roaches, rats, and gorillas."

"Again with the gorillas. What's with that?" Joanne asked as the toilet flushed.

"Sorry, can't hear you," Callie said. She laughed and pulled me from the bathroom.

Joe went for a run after work that day. When he came in, I told him Dad had offered to bring dinner. "Guess I can't say no," Joe said, his words muffled by the towel mopping sweat from his face. "But I sure don't want him here again." Joe ripped off his T-shirt and balled it in his hands. "All this pretending. I hate it."

"Pretending? What pretending?"

"When your father's here, we have to pretend we're the same as before."

"No, we don't. We don't have to pretend anything."

"Of course we do. We always pretend when he's around. We pretend we're still a family."

"Then you know what, Joe? Don't. Don't pretend. Don't talk to us. Don't even come to the table."

Joe ran upstairs. I heard the bathroom door slam, then water whooshing through the pipes. The house hissed like a snake.

Dad called again to ask what we wanted for dinner. I told him neither Joe nor I was hungry. Joe had mountains of paper work, I said. He'd probably pass on dinner. But an hour later, my father barreled through the door with his familiar greeting, suddenly sandpaper on my brain: *Hey, honey. How's my girl?* The smell of meat and peanut sauce filled the kitchen.

"I brought you a surprise," he said as he unpacked a brown paper bag. Egg rolls and spare ribs, moo shu shrimp, chicken with mushrooms, rice, and packets of condiments. Cellophaned fortune cookies tumbled onto the counter.

I set the table. Two places. I was certain Joe would hide. And as I reached for serving bowls, I realized that I hoped he would. I'd had enough confrontation for one day.

"You're awfully quiet tonight," my father said as he plated the moo shu pancakes.

"Just tired, Dad." The lie came so easily. "And let's not put everything out. There's way too much food. It's only the two of us. Joe'll probably work through dinner."

"What's keeping him so busy?"

I poured water and brought the glasses to the table. "Just catching up on bills, I think."

"Well, shouldn't we call him? I know he's not a big fan of Chinese food, but I bought the chicken with mushrooms for him.

Figured he'd be okay with that, seeing as nothing's chopped too much and he'll know what he's eating. And maybe he'll even try a spare rib. Wouldn't hurt him, you know."

"He'll come down if he's hungry."

"Well, he could come down just to say hello. I haven't seen him lately."

"Dad, please. He knows you're here. Maybe he needs time to himself tonight."

I scooped a thimbleful of rice onto my plate and looked at Danny's empty seat. He and Noah would have loved this feast, I thought—especially the moo shu shrimp, which they always wanted instead of moo shu chicken. And though the egg rolls wouldn't have been a big hit—Danny hated the egg rolls from China King—the spare ribs would have gone over well. I picked one up and turned it in my hand. In my mind, Danny and Noah staged a spare rib duel, bones clunking like swords.

Dad intruded on my fantasy. "You're supposed to eat the spare ribs, honey, not study them."

"Oh, I was just thinking how Danny loved Chinese food, how I used to take him and Noah to China King when Joe worked late." Longing mixed with the anger I had carried home from Meadow Brook and with the bile in my throat from the scuffle with Joe. I put down the spare rib and wiped my hands. "Sorry, Dad. I just have a lot going on right now."

My father halved an egg roll and passed me a piece. "Wanna talk about it?"

I shook my head.

"Okay. Well then, how 'bout I talk? You just relax and try to eat a little." Dad touched my hand. I pictured the Meadow Brook staff lining up to pat me on the head. A chorus of teachers: *There, there now, Beth. Everything's going to be fine.*

I tuned in when my father said something about Saul refusing to take his car back to the dealer. "So, don't you think Martha's right, honey?"

"I'm sorry. What were you saying?" I picked at the egg roll.

"Oh, nothing important. Just blabbing about Saul and Martha again."

"You're lucky you have them." I spooned moo shu onto a pancake. "I don't know where I'd be without Callie and Tom."

"And without Joe. That's your most important relationship. Don't you forget that now."

"Actually, Joe and I are having problems." I bit into the pancake and willed my tears to stay back. "He hates it when I talk about Danny." My voice broke on Danny's name. Dad got up and pulled me from my chair. For the very first time, I resisted his hug. "You can't make it all better, Dad."

He pulled back and took his hands off my shoulders. I stood still, listening to Joe's footsteps on the stairs. My father sat down. I ran my hands over my eyes and moved to the counter, where I pushed around cartons of food.

"Hey, Al," Joe said as he pulled a beer from the refrigerator. I inched away from him and took out a plate and silverware.

"I know this isn't your favorite, but Beth told me you probably wouldn't be joining us. So I thought I'd give her a treat. Though it seems she's not hungry."

Joe fell into his chair and turned over an egg roll.

"You probably won't like that," I said matter-of-factly. "But there's some plain chicken with mushrooms. I can heat it for you."

Joe gulped his beer. "Don't bother. I'll try it the way it is. Probably won't eat it anyhow."

I emptied the container of chicken into a bowl and avoided Joe's eyes when I put it on the table and took my seat.

Dad started the conversation. "So, I take it you've been pretty busy, Joe."

"Uh-huh." Joe segregated the mushrooms, then scooped chicken onto his plate.

"What's going on at work?"

"Nothing much. The usual, I guess."

My father turned to me. "And you, young lady? What's happening at work with you?"

"Oh, the usual, I guess." In copying Joe, I knew I had spoken the truth: confrontation had become the norm in Meadow Brook.

"Well I'll be." Dad slapped the table. "This is a first for this family. We haven't got anything to share."

Joe put down his beer. "Maybe a first for you, Al, but not for us."

"I don't understand."

"It's simple. Beth and I haven't had anything to share since the accident." Joe stood up. "And don't call us a family. We're not anymore." Joe grabbed his beer and left the kitchen.

"What's going on?" My father reached for my hand. I drew away and began clearing dishes. "Whatever's happening between you and Joe can be fixed, honey. And please, don't pull away from me too."

I put a plate on the counter and watched an egg roll slip off. "What makes you think I'm the one who's pulling away from Joe?"

"I didn't mean it like that. I'm not blaming you. I just want things to be good between you two. You need each other."

"How do you know what I need, Dad? You always think you know what I need and how I feel. But . . . but you don't."

I bit my lip as I filled the coffee pot and put the kettle on for Dad's tea. "You can't possibly know what I need," I went on. "Sometimes I don't even know."

"Then let me help you, honey. We'll figure it out together."

"No, Dad. You can't always help me."

"Sure I can. I always have, haven't I?"

"No," I said softly. "You haven't always helped me. I know you've always tried, but you haven't always helped."

"How can you say that? When haven't I been there to help you?"

"I didn't say you haven't always *tried* to help. What I said was you haven't always helped."

"I don't understand, Beth."

"So much of what you tell me is wrong, Dad. And you know what? I don't want to hear it anymore." I turned on the water to muffle my sobs.

My father came over and placed a hand on my back. "Please, honey, come sit and tell me what you mean. Are you calling me a liar? I've never lied to you. Never." He guided me to the table. "You sit right here now." Dad placed me in my chair. "I'll get the coffee and tea, and we'll talk about this."

I thought of Tina, puffed up with power in the hall by the art room. And Peter, his fisted hands on my desk. Then, through my tears, I pictured Joe leaning into the doorframe of the bathroom. *You've got to let Danny grow up already. You have to stop babying him. If it wasn't safe, do you think I'd let him go?*

Dad put a cup of coffee in front of me. He set down his tea. I watched steam curl up the spoon sitting in his mug. "Now what's all this about, Beth?"

I tried to pin my rage on something Dad had said, anything to explain my anger and the reason I chose to aim it at him. In the connect-the-dots drawings I had done as a girl, a picture always emerged. I searched for an image now, trying to connect the dots from Tina to Peter to Joe. The allegations. The put-downs. The reprimands. Their faces formed an ugly border around my thoughts. I connected the dots, and in the center, my father stood alone.

Hot coffee trickled down my throat, fueling the fury that threatened to explode. I put down my cup and looked at Dad, older now than an hour ago. His eyes glazed. Yet, I couldn't stop the volcano that was bubbling inside me. "You are a liar, Dad." My words spewed like lava.

He jumped in his chair. "Please, Beth. You have to tell me what you're talking about. I don't understand what's happening. I've never, ever lied to you."

"You do it all the time. And the sad thing is, I've always believed you."

"Honey, please. Tell me what you mean."

"You lie when you say you're always there for me, because nobody, not even you, Dad, can always be there for me."

"But when haven't I been?"

"At school this morning. You weren't there when a student laced into me. And you weren't there when the assistant principal barged into my office."

"But you could've called me, and we would've figured out what to do, how to make things better."

"No! You can't always make everything better. No one can do that."

"But I could help."

"No, you can't. You wouldn't know how. You haven't done anything since you retired—except watch TV, hang out with Saul, and play poker. God, it makes me so angry. You never date. You probably can't even remember the last movie you saw. And when was the last time you read a book? Come on, Dad. You don't even have a life. So, how can you help me with mine?"

"*You've* been my life, Beth. That's been enough for me. And I always thought you appreciated that."

"But I can't be your whole life. I'm all grown up."

"But you'll always be my little girl."

I trembled as anger rushed through me. I had never stood up to my father, and I had never before wanted to shout *I'm not your little girl anymore!* "I have to be strong, Dad. I have to face problems by myself now."

"I'm sorry, honey. Maybe you're right. Maybe I do too much for you. But it's just that I love you so much, and after your mother died, well . . . I just wanted to protect you, to take care of you."

"But don't you see? You never gave me a chance to learn to take care of myself." I softened my voice again. "You told me to be generous, to work hard, to respect others. You said people value integrity and honesty. And I believed you, Dad. I believed you. But now, I see it's all a big lie. Because now I'm up against people who don't give a damn about those things, and I don't even know how to deal with them."

I moved to the sink and began rinsing dishes. The clatter of cleanup pushed my voice louder. "You made me believe that if I did the right thing, then everything would turn out fine. But life isn't a fairy tale. The good guys don't always win. And we all don't get to live happily ever after, do we?"

I looked at my father, who stared at the table. "I'm sorry, Beth. I've done the best I could. And if that wasn't good enough, then all I can say is, I'm sorry." He swirled the spoon in his tea. "You know, there are plenty of people who wish they had the relationship you and I've always had. Remember how Rayanne used to love staying at our house, how she always said she wished her father cared for her the way I care for you?"

"Well, you know what? Turns out Rayanne's a helluva lot luckier than I am." I pictured Rayanne with her boys. "Because she learned to take care of herself, and her kids aren't dead."

Joe walked in, the empty beer bottle dangling from his hand. "Jesus! What's goin' on in here?"

"I was just leaving," Dad said. He carried his mug, still full, to the sink. "Beth's had a long day. I'm going home."

Joe looked at me. "What's going on?"

"I don't want to talk to you now. I don't need another liar."

"What are you talking about?"

My father answered. "Beth thinks everything I've taught her is a lie."

"I don't understand," Joe said.

My anger boiled. "Well, you should, 'cause you know all about lies."

"What are you saying?"

"You told the biggest lie of all, Joe. You said it was safe for Danny to drive to Noah's."

Chapter Nineteen

I stayed in Danny's room again that night. The sound of Moose breathing finally lulled me to sleep. In the morning, Danny and Dad mixed in my thoughts. My explosion had lifted a weight, like Danny's barbells, from my chest. Yet the guilt that replaced it pumped acid into my gut.

I remembered Joe's building rule: Build it right the first time so you won't have to tear it down and start again. As I dressed for work, I worried about having to build a new relationship with my father.

I called him as soon as I got to my office—not even thinking about Peter's ban on personal calls, not stopping to go through the mail or to check my appointment book. Dad answered on the first ring. "Beth, are you all right?"

I'd expected anger. "I'm not sure, Dad. I'm . . . I'm just so sorry about last night. I never meant to take everything out on you."

"It's okay, honey. I'm glad you called."

I tried to find words to explain my behavior, but none came. After a moment, my father asked if I was calling from work.

"I do better when I keep busy," I told him. "Too many memories in the house. They make me crazy sometimes, like last night. But I never should have exploded at you. I feel so bad about what I said. And you're not a liar, Dad. I don't know where all that anger came from."

"Do you want me to tell you?" My father chuckled, assuring me I hadn't destroyed our relationship. "Or will you accuse me of pretending to know how you feel?"

"No. I won't accuse you of anything. Don't you think I did enough of that?"

"What you did last night was probably healthy."

"You know, you're the only person who could take such a beating and then tell me he's glad I hit so hard."

"That's because I'm your parent. I root for you even when I'm the opponent."

A lump rose in my throat. I sipped my coffee, hoping to forestall tears. "I just wish I weren't so angry."

"It's no wonder you're angry. You miss Danny. And you're angry about what's happening between you and Joe. I'm an easy target, honey. You know I'll always love you, no matter what you say."

I pictured my father in his kitchen and wanted to be there with him—fixing his breakfast, pouring his tea.

"And Beth, I don't want you to be hard on yourself for last night. What's surprising is not that you got angry but that you've held yourself together for so long. You've been holding your feelings in ever since the accident. It's good you finally let some out."

"I don't know, Dad. It's scary to explode like that."

"I wish I knew someone you could talk to. Saul and Martha's daughter and son-in-law in Cleveland went to some counselor or therapist. Saved their marriage, Saul says. Maybe you and Joe need to see someone."

"I don't think Joe'll go."

"But you need help, honey. There's no harm in suggesting it."

I was comforted by the recognition that my father hadn't dropped the reins of parenthood. Yet I knew he'd begin to loosen his grip.

Sue buzzed me as I pulled Dr. Goldstein's number from my wallet. "The student support team's waiting for you. Mr. Stone just called." I stuck the pink paper in my desk and raced to the conference room.

"Mrs. Maller," Peter said as I walked in, "glad you finally decided to join us." I sandwiched myself between the school psychologist and Nevil Clark, a math teacher sporting a tan warm-up suit and stubble from a too-quick shave. Without looking at Peter, I addressed the group. "Sorry. I got held up."

"Well, now that Mrs. Maller's graced us with her presence, we can finally begin," Peter said. "And thank you all for your patience. I know how busy you are."

Folders opened in unison, spilling Gary Johnson's math tests and interim reports. Peter tapped the table. "Mrs. Maller, we'll start with you. I assume you have report cards and standardized tests to help us understand Gary's trouble in math." Peter fixed on the empty space in front of me.

"Well, I can talk about Gary without my folder, or I could run back to my office for it."

"You know, Mrs. Maller," Peter said, his voice brimming with condescension, "why don't you do just that? Go back to your office. But do us all a favor. Don't bother coming back."

Without a word, I walked to the door. "Sorry to have wasted your time, folks," I heard Peter tell the group. "Now that Mrs. Maller's left, we can start. Mr. Clark, let's begin with you."

Back in my office, I held the pink sheet with Kate's and Dr. Goldstein's numbers. I called Kate first. "What's the matter, dear?" she said. "You sound upset."

I told her about dinner with Dad. "And where was Joe while this was going on?" she asked. "Didn't he have dinner with you?"

"No. Most of the time he stayed upstairs."

"Oh my. You two are in trouble, aren't you?" Kate paused, expecting an answer, then went on. "Beth, I do wish you'd call Dr. Goldstein."

"I was just about to do that."

"Good. He won't be surprised to hear from you. I told him you might be calling." When had Kate spoken with him? And why had she talked about me? She had told me that she was in therapy with Dr. Goldstein three years ago. Was she still seeing him?

"Well, then," I said to her, "let me call Dr. Goldstein now so I can get to work here." Embarrassed by the situation with the student support team, I chose not to say anything about Meadow Brook. Never before had I forgotten a meeting. And never had I been so unprepared. I didn't need Kate to remind me of the spillover of grief. My behavior reminded me of it constantly.

"Oh, and one more thing, dear. How about lunch today? You sound as if you could use a friend. Why not come to my house?"

"I don't know, Kate. I always have lunch with Mrs. Harris, the art teacher."

"But it's such a beautiful day. We could eat outside. The fresh air will do you a world of good. And anyhow, Mrs. Harris gets to see you every day at school. Surely she can share you this once."

Kate's voice steadied my breathing. "You're right. I'd love to see you. What's a good time?"

Before I phoned Dr. Goldstein, I looked at the student support team agenda: three students to discuss after Gary Johnson. Two were Debra's; one was Steve's. Peter couldn't intrude for at least another hour.

Dr. Goldstein surprised me by picking up his phone. I had expected a secretary or an answering machine. "Kate Stanish said you might call."

"Dr. Goldstein, I need help." I sounded weepy.

"Kate told me about your loss. A son, wasn't it?"

"Yes. Danny. And I thought I was handling it, but last night I exploded. It scared me. And the awful thing was, I raged at the person I least wanted to hurt."

"And who was that?"

"My father."

Dr. Goldstein was silent for a moment. I pictured a man who looked like Tom, seated in a huge leather chair, balancing an oversized mug and an appointment book. "You're married, aren't you?"

"Yes. Though we're having problems."

"I'd like to see you and your husband together, at least for one session, if you think that would be possible."

I scheduled an appointment for the following week—an evening appointment, in case Joe said yes to attending. Then, walking the long way around the building to avoid the conference room, I went to see Callie. Her second period boys were in the computer room again, engrossed in battles of Air Warrior and Silent Death. The girls, serving as the ad hoc prom committee, sang to a CD. The paper mache volcano had been pushed to the rear of the room. Callie sat on the floor, helping Susanna Smith outline a lopsided palm tree. Both were shoeless, their sandals clustered, like coconuts, under fan-like fronds.

"Ah, our wandering helper has returned," Callie called when she saw me. "Welcome to the luau production line. Kick off your shoes and color some leaves."

"Sorry, Mrs. Harris. I can't stay today. Just need to see you for a minute."

"Excuse me, ladies." Callie unfolded her body and reached for her sandals. "I'll be right outside. Susanna could use some help with this tree. Oh, and a few of you might want to count the leis in those boxes by the window."

Callie and I stood in the empty corridor, the building still, the eye of a hurricane. Callie pulled two Tootsie Rolls from the pocket of her jeans. She handed me one. "What's up?"

"Peter finally did it."

"Whaddaya mean?" Callie unwrapped her candy and stuck it in her mouth. I told her how Peter had spoken to me in the meeting. "What a freakin' zoo this is," Callie said, shaking her head.

"He humiliated me, Cal. And I let him, dammit!"

She rested her hands on my shoulders and smiled a weak grin. "How 'bout lunch in your office today? Just us. No rat. No wit. And we'll close the door so the gorilla doesn't see us. I'll grab my stuff from the fridge next period."

"That's the other thing I came to tell you. Kate Stanish just invited me to her house for lunch. I'm sorry."

"You mean you said yes?" Callie dropped her hands.

"I like her. She's easy to talk to."

"And I'm not?" Callie pushed open the door to the art room.

"Come on, Cal. I thought you'd understand. It's a gorgeous day, and she talked about eating outside. I guess she tempted me."

"Yeah, well, the serpent tempted Eve too." Callie slipped into the art room and shut the door. Was she simply jealous that I was having lunch with Kate instead of with her, or did she sense something about Kate that I couldn't see then? In the silent hallway, I gasped for breath, loneliness heavy on my chest.

Three hours later, I turned onto Pebble Lane and saw the cherry tree that canopied Kate's lawn. She used it as a landmark, the only thing that differentiated her dormered Cape Cod from other houses on the block.

Kate hugged me as if I were a youngster returning from summer camp. I breathed in her perfume as a gentle breeze poked through my cotton sweater. "What a glorious day, isn't it?" She loosened her grip. "I'm so glad you decided to share it with me." Kate took my hand and led me through the front door, into a living room dipped in sunshine. Even the sofa and wing chair shimmered in pale yellow, accented by sky blue pillows.

"Your house is beautiful," I said as we walked to the kitchen. A large wicker tray on the table held two luncheon plates with sliced turkey, cheese, and perfect, tiny tomatoes. Condiments and olives filled miniature dishes. A pitcher of iced coffee and crystal glasses completed the arrangement. As Kate lifted the tray, I picked up a basket of dark bread in one hand, and in the other, silverware bundled in green cloth napkins. For a moment, I thought of Callie in the faculty room, rummaging in the refrigerator for her brown paper bag amid containers of moldy cottage cheese and an open carton of milk.

But Meadow Brook disappeared as soon as Kate and I moved to her brick patio, bordered by tidy impatiens. Kate placed the tray on a wrought iron table and pulled out a chair with a floral seat cushion. "Please, dear. Make yourself comfortable."

"Danny used to help Joe plant impatiens on Mother's Day," I blurted out. Kate came up behind me and squeezed my shoulders. She asked about Joe's relationship with Danny. And she listened, not like Joe did, even when I thought our marriage was good—glancing up from the sports section or racing out the door—but as if what I had to say was more important than anything else.

Yet, what I remember most about my first visit to Kate's house that late May afternoon isn't the conversation but the ease of being with her, that sense of absolute acceptance I hadn't felt since Rayanne and I had gathered with friends at the student union decades earlier. When I spoke, a smile rose from Kate's lips to her deep blue eyes. And when I cried, Kate swept her hand to my face, tracing tears with her index finger. No friend, not even Rayanne, had ever done that.

As I finally pulled myself away to go back to work, Meadow Brook didn't seem to matter so much anymore.

Chapter Twenty

I heard the phone before I walked into the house. "Hey, Beth," Callie said, when I picked up. "I was just about to hang up. Glad you're home. So, tell me about lunch with Mrs. Stanish."

"Cal, I'm sorry."

"It's okay. I shouldn't have been so snippy. It's just that it's not the same without you. But anyhow, how was it?"

I told Callie about lunch with Kate: that I wished Callie could have seen the wicker tray and the luncheon plates and the sunlight in Kate's yard. But I didn't tell her how I had thought about Kate as I drove home, and how, when I raced for the phone, it was Kate's voice I was hoping to hear. "I really wish you could have been there, Cal. You'd love Kate. Now I know why Zach's such a great kid."

"Well, I've always said there're advantages to being a counselor. You don't have to jump when the bell rings. I couldn't have come with you even if you'd asked. Forty-two minutes isn't time to go anywhere."

"We just jump to different sounds. You listen for the bell. I listen for the gorilla."

"I know. And bells are easier. They can't hurt you."

"So, how was lunch with Joanne and Denise?"

"Same as always. Denise asked for you. And Joanne . . . well, when I said Zach's grandmother had invited you for lunch outdoors, you know what Joanne said?"

"I couldn't begin to guess."

"She said your leaving us on a sunny day puts a new spin on the expression *fair weather friend.*"

"Cal—"

"You know, I've been thinking. I'm glad you met Mrs. Stanish. I mean, I guess she knows what you're going through in a way that I can't. But just don't abandon me at school, 'cause I couldn't stand that hell hole without you."

"Rat hole, you mean, don't you?"

We laughed. But even as we did, I knew I'd continue to choose Kate's patio over the faculty room. After that first lunch, I began calling her every day during homeroom, when Peter broadcast announcements on the PA system and then headed to the cafeteria for his bagel. Kate always invited me to lunch outdoors when the forecast called for sun. And on dark days, she'd ask if I could meet her at the Athena.

Those phone calls became as much a part of my daily routine as my afternoon check-ins with Dad. I'd anticipate my chat with Kate as I drove to work, sometimes even turning off the radio to replay our previous conversation in my head. At traffic lights, which I had developed the strange habit of counting, I'd let Kate's words wash over me, cleansing the pain of the night before, when Joe and I barely spoke, when he stayed late at Mike's, or when he found me in Danny's room, cuddling with Moose.

Callie started coming by my office every day during third period for my lunch decision: Kate or Callie, sunlight or faculty room. Kate's house was a magnet on bright days, pulling me to the wrought iron table where we'd eat and to the chaises where we'd unwind for a few minutes before I'd race back to school. In our quiet time on the lounge chairs, I'd listen to the birds and to the breeze sweeping the bushes by Kate's back fence. And I would smile at the easy silence between us.

Silence at home with Joe had grown heavier yet, pushing us down in a sea of grief. We had whittled our conversations: *How you doin'? Fine; Everything okay at work? Uh-huh.* We protected ourselves with lies as if they were life jackets.

Still, I had to ask Joe about Dr. Goldstein. I waited until two days before the appointment. Joe was working late, taking advantage of the longer spring days. I had gone to the mall after work with Callie and Mollie. Callie encouraged me to buy black nubuck sandals at the shoe store as Mollie begged for a new pair of Nikes. Mollie and I swung our purchases as we strolled from the shop, her free arm linked in mine.

As we approached the food court, Mollie pulled me in step to her off-key rendition of *The Wizard of Oz*. Callie winked when I looked back at her.

I asked Mollie where we were heading. "Just follow the yellow brick road."

"Where to?"

"To the Land of Oz and thirty-one flavors."

We slowed to a walk. "And your mom knows this?"

"Sure. I asked her while you were buying those geeky sandals, and she said it was fine."

I boxed Mollie's arm as Callie caught up with us. "This is really okay with you, Cal? Ice cream before dinner?"

"Sure. What's the big deal? We're having pizza tonight. It's not like we won't eat if we have ice cream now. And you said Joe won't be home till much later. So you're joining us."

"Oh, is that so? I don't even have my car. You drove here, remember?"

"So what? We'll get you home. I just want more time with you. We hardly talk at school anymore, if you haven't noticed. But I'm looking forward to tomorrow."

"And why is that?"

"It's supposed to rain. Kate's patio'll be closed. So you'll be stuck with us peons in the faculty room."

Mollie sidled next to Callie and studied the tubs of ice cream at the Baskin Robbins counter. "You know what you're having?" Callie asked her.

"Either jamoca almond fudge or chocolate marshmallow. And Mom, what's a peon?"

"Just another word for loser, honey. So, what'll it be? We're next." Callie draped her arm around my shoulder. "You, too, Beth. Choose your poison. My treat."

Joe got home before I did. Buoyed by my time with Callie and Mollie, I started right in as soon as I returned.

"I've got to talk to you about something, Joe."

"Shoot." Joe folded the sports section, clearing the kitchen table.

"I made an appointment to speak with someone. A therapist. And he wants to see you too."

"You did what?" Joe's eyes narrowed.

"I have an appointment to meet with a therapist this Thursday at six. Maybe he can help us."

Joe walked to the sink. "And you just decided to do this on your own without talking to me first? Don't you think you should've at least asked before you made an appointment that includes me?"

I didn't turn to look at him. "But I knew you'd say no."

"And what the hell do you think I'll say now?" I heard the cabinet open, a glass bang on the counter.

"I'm hoping you'll say you'll go with me."

"Well think again, 'cause there's no way I'm gonna go talk to a stranger. Jesus! We can't even talk to each other anymore. What makes you think we'll be able to talk to someone we don't even know?"

"But I spoke with him on the phone. He has years of experience in bereavement counseling. Dr. Goldstein's helped lots of people who've suffered losses."

"Oh, so that's what they call it nowadays, huh? Our son dies, and they call it suffering a loss. And tell me this, Beth: How many of his own children has this therapist guy buried? Because I don't need to talk to someone who can't possibly know what it feels like. Someone who's gonna throw mumbo jumbo words around. Because it won't make a difference. Danny's dead. And there's nothing anyone can do about that."

Joe's anger caused a quake in my chest. I recognized this feeling: the shakiness I felt around Peter. I breathed slowly, willing myself to stay calm. "But *I'm* not dead, Joe. And neither are you. And I'll do anything that might help me feel even a little better."

"Then go. You go and talk to the shrink. Why not? You talk to everyone else. Everyone on the planet probably knows our business. But see, I don't believe what's going on with us is anyone's business but ours. I don't broadcast our problems to the world."

"But you talk to Mike."

"Sure. We talk. We talk about the Mets and the Yankees and the Knicks. I talk to forget my problems, not to think about them. So, if you want to talk to Dr. Whatever-His-Name-Is, you go right ahead. But leave me out of it."

"Please," I said as he came back to the table. "Maybe if we see Dr. Goldstein together, we'll learn how to help each other. We've got a history here. We've had a life together. We can't just throw that away like garbage."

"Why not? Seems to me you already have. You threw it away the moment you blamed me for the accident. But it was an accident, God dammit! It wasn't my fault!"

"But you told him he could go."

"Jesus, Beth! Accidents happen. Nobody *causes* them."

That's a lie, I screamed in my head as I stormed from the kitchen. *You caused it when you said he could drive.* I headed upstairs. *When it was supposed to snow again. When another storm was coming. You caused it, Joe. You caused it.* I crawled into bed, pulled a pillow to my face to muffle sobs. *And so did I. So did I when I didn't say no. Dammit! Why didn't I just say no?*

I awoke in the middle of the night to find that Joe hadn't come to bed, and I realized it didn't bother me. I simply turned over as images swelled with my thoughts: Joe and Danny; Mary and Liz. I tried to still the questions in my mind: Do we ever really know our children? Can we hear their messages, told in half-truths and glances? Or, do we plug our ears and close our eyes for fear of what we'll find?

And I wondered: Are our children as afraid of us as we are of them? Afraid that we'll blame them? Afraid of our lies? "Trouble finds you if you go looking for it," Mary had told Liz.

I saw it then: I had been afraid of Danny. Afraid of his anger, afraid of the distance it could put between us. And Danny, I suppose, was afraid of me. Afraid I'd try to trap him in my world forever. Afraid I'd say no to his requests to grow up.

So Danny went to Joe the day of the accident because Joe wasn't afraid. "You've got to let him grow up," Joe said. And then Danny hugged me, and I couldn't say no. It was fear that had stopped me—a fear stronger even than concern for his safety. I feared confrontation would drive a wedge between Danny and me, and I'd lose him for a while. So I let Danny drive, and I lost him forever.

In the morning the rain came—a New England kind of rain, a curtain of water. Callie's car wasn't in the lot when I pulled in fifteen minutes later than usual, just as the bell rang for homeroom. I propped up my umbrella but didn't even take off my coat before I called Kate. I had to make sure I would reach her before homeroom ended.

"I've been waiting to hear from you," she said. "I was so concerned about you driving this morning."

I embraced the thought that someone other than my father worried about my safety. I no longer wondered why Kate cared for me so; I was just glad she did. "I'm fine, Kate," I answered. "A little wet, but fine." I wriggled out of my coat. "No. Actually, that's a lie. I'm not fine at all."

"What's the matter? Another rough night?"

"Yes, but I can't talk about it now. It's just that I asked Joe to see Dr. Goldstein with me, and he gave me a hard time."

"I'm so sorry. And I know you said you can't talk now. But listen. I've got to go out later, even in this awful weather. I have a dental appointment in that medical building on the boulevard, just around the corner from the high school. I should be finished by eleven-thirty or so. Why don't I pick you up then? We can have lunch at the Athena. I promise I won't take you away from work for too long."

"Thanks. I really do want to see you."

"It's a date then. I'll pick you up at eleven forty-five, if that's a good time for you."

"That's perfect. The end of fifth period. I shouldn't have any problem getting out then."

"Good. I'll pull up by the double doors near the bus platform. I know there's an overhang there, so you won't get wet even if this abominable rain doesn't stop."

It was still raining third period when Callie came by. "Hey, Beth. What an awful drive this morning! I was late for homeroom. Peter had Lucy Hershon cover for me, and she said he was really pissed. So I'm sneaking around like a mouse today, trying to stay out of his path." A smile played at her lips. "Hey, I just put another animal in our zoo."

"I was late too. And I worried when I didn't see your car." As I said that, I realized the rock that had settled in my stomach when I knew Callie hadn't gotten to school yet had disappeared by the time I walked to my office and phoned Kate.

"So lunch fifth period today. No excuses. Even if the rain stops, it'll still be too wet for lunch on Kate's patio."

"Cal, I'm sorry."

"No. Don't do this again. I know I said I understand your relationship with her. But come on. We've been friends for a long time. I can't believe you'd choose Kate over me on a day like this, when there's no way you'll be outside. I don't get it. Didn't we have a great time yesterday?"

"I don't know what to say, Cal. I love you. You and Tom and the girls are my family. Other than my father, you're my only family now. But I think you were right, what you said about Kate. She understands what I'm going through in a way that you can't. And thank God for that, because I'd never, ever want you to go through this."

"Yeah, well, remember something else I said: The serpent tempted Eve."

"What are you saying?"

"Seems clear to me. Kate's a snake. Plain and simple. A lonely old lady who's using you. And I'm not saying she doesn't truly like you, but that's not why she's latched on. Maybe she doesn't want to be alone next year when Zach leaves. Maybe she sees you as a daughter. Who knows? But in any event, she's using you."

"I don't see it that way."

"That's the problem. So remember Eve. The serpent tempted her, and nothing was ever the same." Callie opened the door.

"This isn't Sunday school, Cal. I didn't ask for a Bible lesson."

Callie left. I just sat for a while. Using me? Kate certainly wasn't using me.

The rain stopped before Kate picked me up. By fifth period, I wished I had earplugs to wear in the halls, where teens who thought they'd be trapped inside all day whooped it up as they ran out to

Burger King, Taco Bell, and Pizza Hut. It wasn't only the change in weather that raised the noise level, though. The countdown to the junior prom also created a buzz that grew louder as the big day approached.

I headed to the faculty room to make peace with Callie. Though I didn't recognize the truth in her words, I did see her jealousy. And I wanted to apologize to Denise and Joanne for deserting them too. But as I walked down the hall, I weighed the risk of my visit. If I ran into Peter and he saw where I was going, he'd expect me back in my office by the next period. Calling on Callie might mean having to give up my date with Kate. So I changed my mind and ducked into the ladies' room to comb my hair.

At eleven-forty I grabbed my coat and umbrella, in case the weather changed again, and told Sue I was off to lunch.

I spotted Kate's blue Honda as she rounded the corner of the parking lot. When she waved to me, I heard Tina call from the door by the gym: "Hey, Mrs. M." I turned and saw Jen slinking behind her, holding a carton of Burger King fries. "Jen, look who's going out. Where you heading, Mrs. M.?"

Kate pulled up as the girls approached. I smiled at her but didn't get in the car.

"Wait," Tina said. She turned to Jen. "Don't you remember who this lady is?" Tina knocked on Kate's window. "I know you. You're Zach's grandmother. We met at the Athena the night of the art show. You were there with Mrs. Maller. So, is this like your second date or something?"

"I don't know what you're talking about, young lady," Kate answered before I could say anything. "I'm simply having lunch with Mrs. Maller. She's a friend of mine. And I see *you're* with the same friend who was with you after the art show too." Then Kate called to me, "Come on, Mrs. Maller. I know you're on a tight schedule, and I'm hungry."

Tina followed me as I walked around the car to the passenger side. She reached for the handle. "Allow me, Mrs. M."

"No, thank you, Tina." I pushed her hand and opened the door.

"Have fun," Tina said. "And don't you two do anything naughty."

Chapter Twenty-One

The next day, I followed Kate's directions to Dr. Goldstein's. Though this was the first time I'd been in Glenwood, the main road looked familiar. Ubiquitous strip malls blended the town into a suburban landscape of CVS, Pay-Less, Yogurt and Such, and the Gap. Kate had told me to turn left at the second light after the King Kullen supermarket, and I was sure I had, as counting traffic lights—red lights, in particular—was an annoying practice I couldn't seem to shake now. And worse, I would decide before driving anywhere that if I got stuck at a certain number of lights, there would be some negative consequence—like running into Peter at school, or having an argument with Joe that night. Yet even though I was sure I had counted two lights after the supermarket, I didn't see Robin Lane, which Kate had said would jut in on the right. Instead, I passed Hummingbird Drive and Finch Court, where I circled around to backtrack. On the main street again, I forced myself to pay even closer attention to the traffic signals rather than to the image that popped up in my mind: Tina at Kate's car door. *Have fun. And don't you two do anything naughty.*

This time, when I counted two lights after King Kullen and then turned, I saw Robin Lane. I pulled up in front of Dr. Goldstein's house and remembered to take the path on the left, as Kate had instructed, to the office entrance around back. In the waiting room,

I studied two large paintings—their bold, acrylic colors jarring in the simple beige space. The canvases, like giant Rorschach blots in pink and purple and green, were signed R. Goldstein. Dr. Goldstein's wife, I figured, then thought about her name. How many female *R* names could I list? Rayanne, Ruth, Rachel, Rose, Rebecca, Ruby, Roberta, Roselle, Rosalie. I challenged myself by trying for ten. If I could come up with ten *R* names, I decided, then I'd know Dr. Goldstein would lift the fog that wrapped around me all the time now—except when I was with Kate. Everything looked clearer then, as if I'd put on glasses.

I repeated the names to myself, counting on my fingers as I stood in front of the second canvas: Rayanne, Ruth, Rachel, Rose, Rebecca, Ruby, Roberta, Roselle, Rosalie. Nine. Just nine. Could I add Rosie and still count Rose, I wondered, as I pictured Kate and me at the Athena the day before. After Kate had convinced me to forget about Tina, and after I told her what Joe had said about seeing Dr. Goldstein, Kate had talked about Zach's father. About how close she and her son, David, had been. About how after David died, Dr. Goldstein helped her become whole again.

"How do you ever get over it, Kate?" I had asked.

"Dr. Goldstein will help you, dear. I'm sure he will. What you're going through now is like trying to get your arms around an elephant. You think it's impossible. But you reach with whatever strength you've got. And then, one day, you wake up and your pillow isn't wet. That's when you know you're ready to heal. Your arms start to fit around your grief. You can pull it in. And though you'll still hold it forever, I'm afraid, it won't always push you down."

Looking at the paintings in Dr. Goldstein's waiting room, scrolling *R* names and searching for ten, I prayed Kate was right. Just one more possible name for his wife, and then maybe Dr. Goldstein would be able to help me shrink this elephant.

I didn't hear Dr. Goldstein come in and jumped at his hello. His appearance surprised me: he was short and lean—not the burly,

Tom-like guy I expected. If he'd have walked into the diner in the days when Joe and I played "guess the profession," I would have focused on his white shirt, khaki slacks, and wire-rim glasses. A professor, I would have said. Literature. The classics, perhaps.

"I hope you didn't have any trouble finding me," Dr. Goldstein said. "Robin Lane comes up so fast some people pass right by."

Robin, I thought. The tenth name. I shook Dr. Goldstein's hand, knowing now he would certainly help. In his office, he pointed to a brown leather couch with a tan, fabric cushion at one end. "Wherever you'd like. Feel free to sit if you want, though some people prefer to lie down. That pillow over there's pretty comfortable, Mrs. Maller. Or may I call you Beth?"

"Sure," I said as I sat in the center of the couch. "Beth is fine."

"Good. That's my wife's middle name, by the way," he said from his armchair, angled to face me.

"Could I ask you a question, Dr. Goldstein?"

"Of course." He leaned back a bit, in reaching distance of a spiral pad and pen on the small wooden table next to his chair.

"This is really none of my business, and you'll probably think it's a weird question—"

"There's no such thing as a weird question here. Ask anything, anything at all that comes up for you. I don't want you to censor your thoughts or your questions. Our time together will be much more valuable if you just say whatever's on your mind. So, what is it you want to ask?"

"Your wife's first name."

"It's Rhonda. Now, why did you want to know that?"

I told Dr. Goldstein about my name game. "Well, now I understand why you seemed so deep in thought," he said. "When I saw you studying Rhonda's work, I didn't know if you liked it or if you were trying to figure it out. But I never would have guessed you were focused on her name. I suppose we never know what another person's thinking unless we ask."

"I've been doing that a lot, Dr. Goldstein—listing things and inventing consequences, I mean." I would have been embarrassed to tell anyone else about these thoughts. I hadn't even told Kate about this crazy consequence game I couldn't stop playing. That I couldn't drive without counting: not only traffic lights, but stop signs, school buses, and particular types of cars. That I linked the number of objects to unrelated effects. I would decide that if I passed two buses before a stop sign, then I wouldn't dream about the accident. Or, if I saw four Camrys on the highway, then Joe would come home for dinner—though I wasn't always sure I wanted him to.

Dr. Goldstein crossed his legs. "And that's what you were doing with my wife's name—linking it to an outcome you want?"

I nodded. "I know that's crazy. But like I told you, I believed if I came up with ten *R* names, you'd be able to help me."

"And you've been doing this a lot, you say. At home and at work?"

"All the time now. Like at home, I'll tell myself that if I turn off the microwave before it beeps, then Joe and I won't argue. Or, on the way to school, I'll count the red lights. And I'll think that if I stop at fewer than six, I won't run into the assistant principal all day."

"Beth, did you do this before your son died?"

"No. It just started. I don't remember exactly when, but recently, some time in the last couple of weeks. And now I can't stop."

"How does that make you feel?"

"Scared. Like I'm going crazy, and I don't want anyone to find out. It doesn't make sense, Dr. Goldstein. I mean, even when I count the red lights, I know it doesn't matter. Traffic lights can't possibly affect what goes on at school. But even though it's crazy, sometimes I speed up when I shouldn't because I really believe I'll have a better day if I don't get stuck at a light."

"Where did you grow up?"

This change of subject startled me, but I answered without pause. "In Queens. Why?"

"Were there sidewalks in front of your house or apartment building?"

"Yes. And I lived in a house. But what does that have to do with my crazy thoughts?" I wanted a quick fix for this strange behavior. Then we could shift to the real problem: life without Danny.

"I'm sorry if it seems like I'm changing the subject. Sometimes my questions might sound unrelated to whatever we're talking about. But it's all part of the process. And if you trust me enough to answer, you'll always see the connection by the end of our session. Okay?" Dr. Goldstein kept on without my even nodding. "So, you said you grew up in a house in Queens. Did you ever play that game where you tried to avoid the lines in the sidewalk?"

"You mean *Step on a crack, break your mother's back. Step on a line, break your mother's spine?* Sure. Dori Berg, the girl who lived next door, said that all the time. But after my mother died, when we were in second grade, Dori stopped saying it. Though we still avoided those sidewalk lines."

"Maybe what you're doing now isn't so different from what you did then."

"But when I was a kid, I really did believe that something bad would happen to my mother if I stepped on a crack."

"I know. And now as an adult, you realize that where you walked had no connection to your mother. But back then, you believed it did, and that if you didn't follow the ridiculous rule, you'd be responsible for the negative consequence. So believing that silly rhyme made you fearful in a way. But it did something else too—something much more important. Believing that made you feel as if you had the power to effect change, and so it gave you the sense that you had some control over your universe."

"And you think that's what I'm doing again?"

"Yes. I think that's exactly what you're doing. I think you're trying to grab control like a little girl who'll believe anything that makes her feel as if she has some power over her destiny or the destiny of her family." When Dr. Goldstein said that, I thought of what my father had told me on my first day back at work: that kids have no power. And I pictured Tina, who squeezed all the power she could until she raged out of control, trying to dominate her world. And then Peter, who sacrificed his humanity to garner control over Meadow Brook.

"But going crazy isn't giving me control over anything."

"You're not going crazy, Beth. You're going through mourning. When did Danny die?"

"Three months ago."

"And you remember how you felt during the first few weeks?"

"Like I couldn't breathe. Like someone had smashed my chest with bricks. I felt that way till I went back to work, three weeks after the accident."

"And how do you feel now?"

"Tired. Really tired. By the end of the day, all I want to do is sleep. And angry. I'm so angry—at my husband, at people at work. Sometimes I feel angry at everyone but Kate."

"You're not going crazy, Beth," Dr. Goldstein told me again. "What you're describing is a very normal, very natural reaction to grief. You're struggling for control over what happens so you won't experience more catastrophes. You're not as numb as you were in those first couple of months after Danny died. So, maybe now you're starting to feel powerless in the face of tragedy. When bad things happen to us, we often feel like children, with little influence on our world. So even though you realize your consequence game can't really protect you, your mind's working overtime to give you a false sense of power over things you can't control. Perhaps if you understand that, you won't be so hard on yourself. You're not going crazy. You're just responding to grief."

I reached for the box of tissues Dr. Goldstein had placed on the couch. "Thank you. Kate was right. I should have come here sooner."

"Well, you're here now. And we have plenty to talk about. You went back to work really fast, you know. Probably too early, given the kind of work you do. It takes some people a couple of years to be reasonably functional after losing a child."

"But everyone told me it was time to go back. Joe went back after only a week. And now I think he really needs help too. I wish he'd be willing to see you. I don't think he talks to anyone."

"People grieve in different ways. You need to talk, but maybe Joe doesn't. Maybe he's not ready yet."

When I left Dr. Goldstein's, I didn't count trees or stop signs or traffic lights. I didn't get on the highway right away, either. Instead, I pulled into the King Kullen parking lot and headed for Baskin Robbins at the corner of the shopping center. I realized I was starving.

As I drove home, though, it was my thoughts, rather than the ice cream, that obliterated my hunger. Maybe Tina, Peter, and I weren't so different after all—all trying to grab power and seize control. But I needed to take control to help Liz; Tina and Peter were using whatever power they held to hurt her. Together, we had trapped Liz in our struggle. I wondered: Had Joe and I both trapped Danny? What if I had been strong enough to have snatched some of the power from Joe? If I would have spoken out, would Joe have backed down? And then would Danny have been home tonight?

Joe was in the den when I came in from Dr. Goldstein's—watching a *Seinfeld* rerun in which a college reporter assumes Jerry and George are gay. Jerry denies it. "Not that there's anything wrong with it," he adds.

After Joe and I first saw that episode, we tacked Jerry's line onto all conversations. "Anyone want more chicken?" I'd ask at dinner. "No thanks," Joe would answer. "Not that there's anything wrong with it."

"That's so dumb," Danny would say, laughing. "I can't believe you're my parents."

Now I wanted to tell Joe about Dr. Goldstein, not what he had said but how easy he was to talk to. I wanted to ask Joe to reconsider going. Even though I knew he'd say no, I wanted to hear it. *No*, I wanted him to say. *Not that there's anything wrong with it.*

But we didn't talk about Dr. Goldstein. "Your father called," Joe said when he looked up from the TV. "I told him you were out, but I didn't tell him where."

"Thanks. But it's no secret."

Joe focused again on the screen.

"Not that there's anything wrong with it," I said, my voice soft and tentative.

"What did you say?"

"I said, 'Not that there's anything wrong with it.'"

"What are you talking about?"

"Never mind. It's not important."

"Beth?" His voice caught me as I started to leave. "About tomorrow night. I know I said I'd go with you when you stop by the junior prom, but I can't."

"But you've always gone with me. And Tom's gonna be there with Callie."

"I can't. I just can't."

"Please, Joe. I know how painful it is. Don't you think it's agonizing for me? But I have to do this. Please come with me."

"I told you, I can't."

"Okay, I guess you have a choice. But I don't. I already told my students I'd be there, and Callie's worked really hard on the decorations. So I suppose I'm going by myself. I'm starting to get used to that." Credits scrolled on the TV. "Not that there's anything wrong with it," I whispered. Then I listened for Danny's laugh.

After ten junior proms I knew what to expect on the big day. Juniors came to school because they had to: if their names were on the absence list, they'd be barred from the prom.

Alison Thompson saw me third period. "Mrs. Maller, you have to come to the gym. You won't believe how great it looks already. Mrs. Harris has the whole decorating committee working all day. You're gonna be there tonight, right?"

"Sure, Ali. I wouldn't miss it."

"Great. 'Cause I want you to meet my boyfriend. He just finished his first year at Binghamton. I told you that already, didn't I?"

"I believe you did. His name's Eric, right?"

"Wow. You have a great memory. So anyhow, I'm glad you'll be there. And I have to get back to the gym, but Mrs. Harris said I should invite you to come and help."

On the way, Alison described her black dress so completely I saw every button, even the top one with a tiny satin rosebud. Peter blocked me at the gym door. "Go ahead, Alison," he said. "I need to talk to Mrs. Maller."

As Alison went in, I heard the pounding of a CD. "Yes, Peter?"

"What are you doing here?"

"Oh, the kids just wanted me to see how the room's shaping up for tonight."

"And the counseling center's closed at the moment?"

"Of course not. But I had a free minute, so I took Alison up on the invitation. I'll be back in the office in no time."

"You're right about that. I'm escorting you back right now."

I didn't see the decorations in the gym until that night, when I arrived a half hour after the prom started. Despite Callie's pleading for me to go with her and Tom, I had taken my own car. That way I'd be able to leave if the evening got too hard. If I pictured Danny in a tuxedo. If I started to cry.

Callie raced to the door when she saw me. "So whaddaya think?" she called over the music.

"Cal, this is incredible!" The volcano I had seen in the art room bubbled in the center of the gym. "How did you do that?"

"Pretty cool, huh? Kenny Roberts figured out how to hook up a pump to circulate that orange gunk." She pulled me into the room, where Susanna Smith, dressed in a red sheath with a too-high slit on the side, draped a lei around my neck. "Aloha. Welcome, Mrs. Maller. Glad you could come."

"Thanks, Susanna. This is wonderful. And look at you. You look gorgeous."

Callie walked me over to Tom, who stood by the palm trees propped against a wall. "Can you believe your wife did this?"

"Pretty amazing, isn't it?" Tom said as he hugged me. "Get a load of the waterfall."

I glanced around the room at barely recognizable teens, decked out in their finest, like tourists on a fancy Hawaiian vacation. A motorized waterfall stood in a corner, backed by a mural of blue-green sea.

"Don't look so shocked, Beth," Callie said. "You know the kids always do a great job for the prom. You've seen them all."

"But not like this. I can't imagine how you got that waterfall on your budget."

"Easy. Mark Bolton's father works at the K-Mart Garden Center. He got permission to take down a display so we could borrow the waterfall. It's going back in the morning."

Tom stepped between Callie and me. He put an arm around each of us. "Come on, ladies. Let me walk you to a table. Then I'll get us some drinks. What'll it be, Coke or ginger ale?"

He led us across the dance floor, to the far side of the room. A real pineapple, surrounded by paper ones, served as the table center-piece. Tiny toy ukuleles scattered on the blue paper tablecloth.

"See," Callie said, "that's what you do when you run out of money and the supermarket won't even donate pineapples and the music department can't get ukuleles. You mix and match, real and fake. And somehow it all comes together."

"Who did the hula dancers?" I asked. "They look so real." I stared at a painted lady and touched her pasted-on grass skirt.

"Oh, Susanna Smith and Alison Thompson did those. They're talented kids."

"They have a talented teacher," I said as Tom handed us soft drinks.

"Here's to another prom," he toasted, looking at Callie as her feet stamped a rhythm. "Great work, honey."

"Go ahead, you two." I said. "I know you want to dance. Don't let me stop you. You should be out there having fun with the kids."

"I'd rather stay here and talk with you," Tom answered. "I can dance with my wife any old time." He squeezed Callie's shoulder. "But I don't get to see you that much anymore."

"And you're not gonna have time with her now," Callie said. "Looks like the word's out you're here, Beth."

A parade of students marched toward our table. First Alison, in the black off-the-shoulder dress she had described so well. Alison introduced me to Eric, tall and handsome in a classic tuxedo. I told them they looked as if they'd stepped out of a fashion magazine. "See, Eric. I told you she's the nicest counselor."

"And I love the decorations, Ali. The room looks great."

"Thanks. I knew you'd like it. That's why I wanted to show you this morning."

Susanna Smith came next. "Sorry I didn't get to talk to you much when you came in, Mrs. Maller. I was kinda busy. But now I can relax."

"Well, you should," I said. "You've done an amazing job. I especially love the hula dancers. Mrs. Harris said you worked on them."

"Yeah. Ali and I did them together. It was fun. So anyhow, I've got to get back to Jason. I think he's ready to party. And when you see us on the dance floor, check out his tux."

There it was again: the tuxedo. Danny in a tuxedo. *Don't cry*, I warned myself. *Not tonight. Not here.*

Students came by in groups. Nervous girls with older guys. Juniors dating juniors. Mark Bolton with a girl who looked so young I imagined it was already past her bedtime.

"Go on, you two," I said again to Callie and Tom. "You don't have to stay with me. Go have fun. I'll see you later."

"Okay," Tom said. "I'm gonna get Callie out there now. But only if you promise me a dance."

"You're on. So go. Quit worrying about me."

Callie and Tom hit the dance floor as the DJ played music so loud I had to cover my ears. Students crowded the space, bouncing around with arms in the air. They shouted the words to the song and moved with the freedom of youth. Screams and laughter. Lives filled with possibilities.

Bob and his wife danced in the center of the room, stepping in half time to the music. He waved me over as I walked toward Kenny Roberts.

"Glad you were able to stop by," Bob yelled. "I know this must be especially hard for you, Beth."

I greeted Bob's wife. "Is your husband here?" she asked.

"Joe couldn't make it. But I promised the kids I'd come."

"It's nice that you did," Bob said. "It means a lot to them. And don't they look great all dressed up?"

"Sure do." I fixed on Bob's tie, black with a golden pineapple in the center. "Don't even try to guess," he said. "It's not a Beatles song. But it's perfect for a luau, don't you think?"

Before I could answer, Kenny Roberts introduced me to his date, who outweighed him by at least fifty pounds. I was saying hi to Kenny's Amazon gal when a tap on my shoulder made me jump. I turned and stared at Tina. Her hot pink dress looked glued to her body. "Hey, Mrs. M. How you doin'?"

"Fine," I shouted.

"Where's your husband?"

I started to walk off.

"Hold it, Mrs. M. Why aren't you answering me?"

"You want to talk? Then make an appointment in the counseling center."

"Come on, Mrs. M. I'm just being friendly. Let's dance." She grabbed my arm. I pulled away. She followed me across the floor, toward Callie and Tom. "Come on. One dance. We'll get Fred and Jen up here. And Fred's brother. He's Jen's date."

"No, Tina. I'm not in the mood for dancing."

Tom came over to me then. "Okay, Beth. Here's our chance." He put out his hand.

"Oh no," Tina said. "Mrs. Maller can't dance with you. She's not in the mood."

I took Tom's hand, and we moved away. "Wait, Mrs. M.," Tina yelled. "I'm sorry Ms. Richardson isn't here. She'd be a great date for you."

"Ignore her," I told Tom. "Just dance."

"And it's too bad Zach's grandmother isn't here, either." Tina's voice grew even louder. "Bet you'd love to be dancing with her." Why was Tina saying this? Had she sensed something other than friendship when she saw Kate and me together?

I stepped back from Tom. "Tina, stop it. Just stop!"

A chill zipped through the room. Everyone froze. I didn't know where Peter came from, but there he was, standing in front of me.

"It's okay, Mr. Stone," Tom said. "We're going back to our table."

"Mr. Harris, this doesn't concern you. And Mrs. Maller, you can take off this instant. I don't know what you and Tina were talking about, but leave it to you to spoil the prom."

Chapter Twenty-Two

After the prom, avoiding Peter became my game. I'd carry a thermos of coffee to work so I wouldn't chance seeing him by the cafeteria. And on the days I had lunch with Callie, I'd leave my office at the end of fourth period, hoping to fade into hallway traffic.

One drizzly Monday, when Kate and I decided I'd have lunch in the faculty room and visit with her after school instead, Denise came in without Mr. Rat. "Where's your furry friend?" Joanne asked.

"He's not well," Denise said, her voice thick with tears.

"Whaddaya mean?" Callie asked.

"He was fine when I took him home for the weekend, but yesterday he was kind of quiet. And this morning, he squealed when I picked him up to clean the cage. Not his usual squeak, but sort of a cry."

Joanne removed tomatoes from her salad. "I didn't know you could differentiate squeaks. Since when do you speak Rat?"

"Come on, Joanne." Callie looked at me and rolled her eyes. "Give her a break. Can't you see she's upset?"

Denise opened a bag of potato chips and offered them around. "I left him home today. The vet said I should bring him over after school."

Callie put down her sandwich. "I didn't know vets treated rats."

"The one in Plainfield does. But I'm nervous. Mr. Rat's the best one I've had. I'm not ready to lose him."

"Maybe it's just a virus," Callie suggested. "He'll probably be better by the time you get home."

Denise forced a smile. "Thanks, Callie. I hope so."

"Or, maybe," Joanne said, "your pet's beyond the vet." She winked at me.

"Give it a rest," Callie said. "That's not funny."

Denise popped the top of a Diet Coke. It fizzed onto the table. She dabbed at the spill as she spoke. "I know you think of him as nothing but snake food, Joanne. All you see is he's a rat, and that disgusts you. It's like you put a sticker on him: RAT RAT RAT." She raised her voice and looked up. "But he's not just a rat. He's my pet."

"You're right," Joanne said. "I'm sorry."

We all pretended to focus on lunch until Joanne spoke again. "Did I ever tell you about the extra credit assignment I gave my global studies class?"

"I don't think so." Denise's voice softened.

"Good thing," Callie said, "'cause you're about to hear it now."

Joanne ignored her. "When we studied China, I gave the kids a chance to raise their grades by doing a report on the Chinese calendar. Several kids wrote about the sign of the rat. You sure I never told you this?"

"Would it matter?" Callie asked. I elbowed her.

"So, what'd they find out?" Denise asked.

"That people born in the Year of the Rat are known for honesty and loyalty. And also, the sign of the rat's associated with charm and talent."

"Thanks, Joanne," Denise said. "I'll consider that a full apology."

"It is. You know I only give you a hard time because . . . because . . . well, that's just what I always do."

"And you do it so well," Callie said.

"Enough, Cal," I cut in. "I suppose in China, you wouldn't call someone a dirty rat."

"That's scary," Callie said.

"What?" I asked.

"That sounded like something Joanne would say."

"Give it a rest, Callie." Joanne barely got the words out without laughing. "Hey, I just thought of the perfect snake food, and it's not rodents."

"Spare us," Callie said.

"No, really. The perfect food for snakes: broccoli." Joanne got up to go to the ladies' room. "If the odor wouldn't kill them, the gas might."

Denise smiled at Callie and me. "I love you guys."

"I really hope Mr. Rat's okay," I said as the bell rang.

"Me too," Callie added.

But when Denise got home, we found out the next day, Mr. Rat was dead.

When I heard, I thought about that one time I touched him, the surprising softness of his fur. Yet I ran to wash my hands, unable to rid my mind of what I'd been taught: All rats are dirty; they carry germs.

By the time I left Meadow Brook High the day Mr. Rat died, the rain had stopped. Teenagers strolled through the neighborhood—some in groups of two or three, others in packs. Girls headed toward the card shop, where Mr. Fenton sold them cigarettes without asking their ages. Boys met at the 7-Eleven, where they'd hang out, leaning against Eddy Olsen's orange Mustang. I passed them on my way to Kate's.

She waved as I turned onto Pebble Lane. *Step on a crack, break your mother's back*, I said to myself when I saw her standing on the sidewalk in front of the cherry tree. She gave me a fierce hug—one that made me feel safe and protected—when I got out of the car. Then Kate ushered me in with an arm around my shoulder. We walked through the living room and into the kitchen, where spring flowers filled a vase on the table and a basket brimmed with muffins.

"This is so special. Thank you."

She motioned to a chair. "My pleasure, dear."

"You'll spoil me, you know. I could make a habit of coming here after work."

"I hope you will. Getting this ready made me remember how I used to fuss when Zach's father was little. And then I did the same for Zach. But these last few years, why, he's hardly home after school. He's so busy, you know. Sports and friends. And this year especially, he's just so tied up as editor of the yearbook that . . . well, sometimes he barely has time to talk to me at all." Kate stirred her coffee, looking down as if memories floated in her cup. "And next year—it's so hard to believe—he'll be away at college. Then I'll really be alone. I'm not ready to face that. Not after raising two generations. And now, without Carl . . ."

"You won't be alone." Caught in Kate's spell, I forgot Callie's warning. "I'll come to visit. Often. I promise."

Kate reached for my hand. "I really hope so."

"Of course I will. Nothing will keep me away."

"You never can tell, dear. You just can't know what tomorrow will bring. But right now, we need each other."

"That's what you said the first time we spoke. 'Please keep my number,' you said, 'because people like us need each other.'"

"That's right. I believe we do. We come into each other's lives for a reason. And I'm delighted you've come into mine. Especially now." Kate sighed and shook her head. "Two generations of children." She looked away for a moment. "And maybe I've come into your life for a reason too—to help you through grief, I suppose. But once you get beyond it, heaven only knows how you'll feel about hanging out with an old lady ready for a rocking chair."

"I know exactly how I'll feel. I'll come and rock next to you." I welcomed the mysterious pull Kate had on me, this web of affection.

After my second cup of coffee, she suggested we take a walk. We stepped outside, into the heavy dampness that hung in the air. "Oh my, you're chilly," Kate commented when I shivered. She went inside and came back with a sea blue sweater. Kate held it around me until my hands pushed through the sleeves. Then she buttoned it up to the neck, as if I were a child. The cotton yarn felt soft against my skin.

"This is lovely, Kate. Did you make it?"

"Yes. For Helen, my daughter-in-law. Zach's mother." She put her arm around my waist. We started walking. "You remind me of her."

I hesitated before paralleling Kate's gesture as Tina flashed in my mind. *Don't you two do anything naughty.* "You haven't told me about Helen."

"Oh, she was a wonderful gal. David met her in freshman English right here in Meadow Brook. They were inseparable from ninth grade on." We turned onto Acorn Drive. "From the time David and Helen started going together, Helen spent most of her time at our house."

"She was lucky to have you."

"Carl and I felt lucky to have her. Helen was the daughter we never had."

I unbuttoned the sweater as we walked, the air still heavy but not quite as moist.

"I made that sweater for Helen just before she went away to college," Kate said. "She wore that old thing for years."

I pulled it tighter around me. "It's beautiful."

We crossed Pine Lane, which horseshoed around to Meadow Brook Avenue, where the 7-Eleven angled on the corner. "I want you to keep it, dear."

"No. I couldn't."

"Of course you could. It would mean so much to me to see you wear it."

I didn't notice the boys still huddled by the orange Mustang as we walked across the street from the 7-Eleven. I didn't hear them when we stopped and I hugged Kate to thank her for the sweater. I didn't see them watching as Kate linked her arm around my waist again and we walked on. But I did hear someone call to me in a voice that made me shudder. "Yo, Mrs. Maller. How goes it?"

Kate stopped. She dropped her arm and looked over at the boys. "Just keep walking," I said as I moved in front of her. Fred Morris called again, louder this time, daring me to go on. "Yo, Mrs. Maller. I said how goes it?"

"Answer him, Beth. He sounds like he'll make trouble if you don't."

I turned and waved at the group.

"How goes it, Mrs. Maller?"

"Fine, Fred," I called. "Come on, Kate. Let's walk."

"How 'bout another show?" Fred yelled as we moved on.

Kate seemed to understand, leaving her arms at her sides and distance between us. The boys whistled. "Come on, ladies, another hug. And how 'bout a little kiss? Go ahead, Mrs. Maller. Plant one on her."

As Kate and I circled back onto Pine Lane, I imagined the buzz in the phone lines that night: Fred reporting to Tina and Tina telling Jen, like the telephone game I had played as a child. One girl would say to another: *My brothers eat stew, and then they play with friends.* In a chain of whispers, the secret would travel until the last girl said it aloud: *My brothers meet at the zoo, and then they play with hens.* We'd laugh, and I'd want to start the next message.

I wondered how Fred would start his. Would he say *Mrs. Maller hugged Zach's grandmother across from the 7-Eleven?* Or, *Zach's grandmother had her arm around Mrs. Maller. Then they hugged.* Or maybe, *Mrs. Maller and Zach's grandmother were outside by the 7-Eleven. And they hugged. And it looked like they were ready to kiss.* And if it started that way, how would it sound when Tina told Jen and Jen passed it on? How would it end after snaking around Meadow Brook?

During the last two weeks of classes, I tried to avoid Fred and Tina and Jen. When I passed Tina in the hall, I pretended not to hear as she called, "Hey, Mrs. M. How you doin'?" And I ignored the stares of students who might have been linked in the chain of whispers I was sure had spread throughout the school.

I ran into Zach once in the main corridor by the ladies' room. "Hey," he said as he raced past me. No boisterous greeting. No Danny-like smile. Was Zach caught in the rumor too? *Your grandmother and Mrs. Maller. Are they like a couple, or what?*

Kate told me not to worry. "You know how kids are—always looking to start trouble. But we haven't done anything. Goodness gracious, dear, I've spent my life here in Meadow Brook. Everyone knows who I am. And Zach tells me he's fine. He's a popular boy. Silly rumors don't bother him."

Peter scheduled the senior yearbook assembly, as usual, during the last week of classes before exams. Steve told me I had to attend. "Why?" I asked, at the end of the day before the assembly, when he came into my office and sunk into a chair.

"Who knows? Peter just said he wants a counselor there. Maybe he feels someone from guidance should be at the last senior gathering before graduation."

"That's crazy, Steve. In all my years in Meadow Brook, I don't think Peter's ever invited us to a yearbook assembly."

"But he did this time." Steve smiled. "And you're gonna be our representative."

"Please don't make me do this."

"I thought you'd be glad to go. Don't tell me you're worried about those stupid rumors that were flying around."

"You know about that?"

"Sure. But it's not a big deal. I haven't heard any talk about you in days, which means the kids have gotten all the mileage out of this that they can. Right now the rumor mill's probably grinding up someone else. So it's not even worth talking about." Steve picked up a pen from my desk and played with the cap, pulling it off, clamping it on. "Unless . . . unless there's some truth to it, which of course I assume there isn't."

I disregarded the hidden question. "So, I have to show up at the assembly tomorrow?"

"Yep, you do." Steve looked at me. "And remember, it's not the seniors who started those rumors. Everyone knows it was Tina Roland's little group. And no one with half a brain pays much attention to those kids."

The next morning Callie came by my office before homeroom. "Congratulations!" She closed the door, tossed a Tootsie Roll onto my desk, and hugged me.

"On what? What are you talking about?"

She sat. "Oh my God. You don't know. I can't believe I blew it."

"Know what, Cal?" I took two Styrofoam cups from my desk, opened my thermos, and poured.

"Shit! Now I have to tell you. I just assumed you heard, what with Zach being yearbook editor."

"Oh no. Please tell me they're not dedicating the yearbook to me. And how do you know?"

"Big ears, I guess. And now I've got a big mouth to go with them. Some of the seniors with lockers by the art room were talking about it when I came in a few minutes ago."

"Cal, I can't go up on stage and have Peter congratulate me. Not with everything that's been happening."

"Sure you can. You're a terrific counselor. I'm glad the kids recognize that." She raised her coffee cup. "So here's to you. Congratulations! And by the way, what lame excuse did they use to rope you into the assembly?"

"Steve just said Peter needed a representative from the counseling center."

"And you didn't know why?"

"Uh-uh. Guess I've been trying so hard to tune everything out I didn't even pick up the clue."

"Well, just enjoy the honor. No one deserves it more." Callie put down her cup, still full, and got up to leave. "The next time I spill the beans, though, I'll bring milk and sugar. How can you drink this stuff?"

Hours later, seniors raced into the auditorium like unsupervised sixth-graders. Bob stood by a microphone at the front of the stage. "People, people. Settle down, people. The sooner you get quiet, the faster you'll get your yearbooks." Girls filled in the seats toward the front of the room, leaving the first six or seven rows empty. Boys scattered in groups toward the back and sides. I chose a seat in the third row next to Alice Hansen, retiring from the science department. "Guess it's your year, Beth," she said. "Congratulations. Well deserved."

Bob tapped the mic. "Come on now, people. Settle down or you'll be the first graduates without yearbooks."

"No way, Mr. Andrews," Brian McKenny called from the back. "We already paid for those yearbooks. They're ours."

Laughter spread through the room. "You're right, Brian," someone shouted. "You tell him, man!"

"They'll be yours in a few minutes if you listen up." Bob talked over the noise. "Now, Mr. Stone's going to give instructions for graduation, and then we'll turn the program over to Zach Stanish, your yearbook editor. Mr. Stone?"

Peter, who'd been leaning against the wall in the back of the auditorium, ambled up the aisle and onto the stage. When Peter got to the mic, Brian yelled again, "Just give us the fuckin' books!"

"What's the rush, Brian?" Peter said, his voice filling the room. "You're not getting yours today anyway. When you behave like a graduate, you'll get your yearbook."

"Fuck you!" Brian stormed from the auditorium. Bob followed him out as boys applauded and cheered.

Peter ignored the disruption. "I need to go over a few things about graduation. So listen up." He gave directions for cap and gown distribution and announced two rehearsals. "There'll be reminders on the back of the exam schedule. So no excuses for not knowing where you're supposed to be."

When Peter called for Zach, boys from the baseball team shouted: Sta-nish! Sta-nish! Sta-nish! Their chant took me back to the night Danny won Bay View's Athletic Leadership Award. Maller! Mal-ler! Mal-ler! Danny at the front of the auditorium. Joe and I seated together, hands lightly touching as Danny accepted his plaque.

A deep voice slashed the memory. "Shut the fuck up and let him speak!" a boy yelled when Zach took the mic. Zach looked down for a second, then slowly raised his head and thanked the editorial staff and the yearbook adviser. Next, he asked Alice Hansen to come up. "In keeping with Meadow Brook tradition," Zach said, "the senior class acknowledges teachers who will retire when we graduate." He took a yearbook from the carton on the floor by his feet, opened to a page in the front, and read a message of appreciation to Alice.

When she sat down, yearbook in hand, Zach called me forward. Peter, in the first row now, turned and stared as I came up. Avoiding Peter's gaze, I looked out at the students about to honor me. I longed for Danny and Joe—the Joe from the first years of our marriage, the one who would have lifted me off the ground in a hug. Of course, I couldn't have anticipated what was going to happen.

Zach picked up a yearbook, opened to the dedication, and read:

The graduating class of Meadow Brook High School dedicates this yearbook to Beth Maller, a counselor who knows the true meaning of guidance. Throughout our four years here, Mrs. Maller has championed our right to a well-rounded education and has cheered for our personal growth. Her door has been open to all of us, even those who are not her students.

Mrs. Maller knows our performance in the classrooms and on the playing fields, and our skill on the stage and behind the scenes. She has applauded our efforts by attending concerts, plays, exhibits, and athletic events. Mrs. Maller has encouraged us to look at our abilities and to work hard to develop our potential. By example, she has motivated us to overcome hardships and to meet life's challenges.

Therefore, it is with great pleasure that we dedicate this yearbook to our friend, Beth Maller. As we leave Meadow Brook and head out into the world, Mrs. Maller's lessons of compassion and caring will continue to touch our lives.

Zach passed me the yearbook and shook my hand. And as he did, a male voice, one I didn't recognize, called from the back of the room: "You've got that touching part right, Zach. We all know what she does with your grandmother."

Laughter erupted like a tidal wave, growing louder as it rolled through the auditorium. My eyes caught Peter, who grinned from his seat.

Zach didn't move. I ran from the stage.

Chapter Twenty-Three

That voice stayed with me as I drove home: *You've got that touching part right, Zach. We all know what she does with your grandmother.*

I wasn't surprised to see Joe's car in the garage. He had said he'd be home early to go for a run. I found him seated at the kitchen table, an open beer bottle in one hand, the phone in the other. "Don't call here again, you punk!" Joe yelled.

"Who was that?"

Joe looked at me, confusion tightening his face as if I were one of his masonry suppliers showing up for a meeting on the wrong day. "You tell me."

"I don't understand."

"I don't either, Beth." Sweat ran down Joe's neck, soaking the top of his T-shirt. He took a long swallow of beer, then swiped the back of his hand across his forehead. "But I'm sure you can explain it. That was the third call already, and I only came in a few minutes ago."

The phone rang. "Hello?" Joe answered, his voice chilled with anger. "Tell her yourself, you pervert!"

"Hello?" I said softly.

"Dykes should die!" the caller whispered. "That means you, Mrs. Maller."

How could this be happening? And how could I tell Joe what had been going on in Meadow Brook? I hadn't even told him about

Kate. I had kept my time with her a secret. It hung like a curtain between Joe and me.

"Wait," Joe said as I turned to leave the kitchen. "You're not going anywhere till you explain these calls. And who the hell is Kate?"

"What do you know about Kate?" I kept my voice even, hoping to hide my alarm.

"Who is she?"

"Not now, Joe. I don't want to talk about it."

"Well, why don't you listen to the message on the answering machine. Then maybe you'll feel like talking. And you'll tell me what the hell's going on."

I pushed the button. "Beth, it's Kate." I stiffened at her harsh sound. "Zach's quite upset about the assembly. How could you have left him standing there while his classmates laughed at him? How could you let them ridicule him like that? And now these threatening calls. Horrible things they're saying. Awful things. I don't even want to pick up the phone. Why didn't you tell me how bad it had gotten in school?

"I can't believe you didn't do anything to stop this gossip about us. You should have stopped it before it came to this—if not for yourself, then for Zach, for me. Meadow Brook's our home. I've always felt safe here. But this . . . this changes everything, Beth." Silence settled in the kitchen before Kate's last words broke through. "You got us into this by not stopping those rumors. So now you'd better think about getting us out."

Why was Kate blaming me? I wanted to feel angry so losing her wouldn't hurt so much. But sadness pushed me down.

I reached for the phone. Joe grabbed my arm. "You're not calling anyone. You're not talking to anyone until you talk to me."

"I have to call her."

"Who is she?" He tightened his grip.

"Give me the phone."

"Not till you tell me who she is."

I pulled away. "No! Give me the phone. I have to talk to Kate." The threat of tears filled my voice.

"No, you don't. Why would you even want to? Why would you call anyone who speaks to you like that?"

"You don't know who she is. You don't know what's going on. So just give me the phone."

"Not until you answer me. Who the hell is she?"

I left the kitchen and headed for the stairs, for the phone in the bedroom. Joe followed. "You can't keep running away from me."

"Who's running from whom? You're the one who's never home anymore." I raced up the steps. "Maybe that's why I've been spending so much time with Kate. At least she cares about me."

"Oh, yeah. That message sure sounds like it's from someone who really cares about you."

Joe's sarcasm released my anger. "Fuck you, Joe!" I screamed.

He took the stairs behind me, the cordless phone from the kitchen still in his hand. It rang as I passed Danny's room. Joe answered in an icy voice. I looked back as he slumped on the top step, as if socked in the stomach. "You've got it wrong, you pervert. The only one who should die is you, you fuckin' creep. And if you call here again, I swear I'll make that happen."

I ran for the phone on the bedroom nightstand. Joe came up behind me and slammed it down. "Who is she, Beth?"

"It's none of your business, dammit!" I squirmed from his hold and moved toward the dresser, took off my earrings. They clinked in the porcelain dish as the voice from the assembly came again. *You've got that touching part right, Zach. We all know what she does with your grandmother.*

Joe sat on the edge of the bed. His sneakered feet jiggled on the floor. "Oh, you think this is none of my business? Well, let me tell you something. This is *my* house, *our* house. And you're my wife, for

Christ's sake. So how can you tell me this is none of my business? And just look at you. You look like you've had the living daylights punched out of you. You have to tell me what's going on."

"No. I don't have to tell you anything. I have to make a call."

"Not until we talk. We need to talk now! What's going on, Beth? You have to tell me."

"You won't understand."

"How do you know if you don't even try?"

"I can't tell you. I haven't been able to tell you anything in a long time 'cause you don't listen, Joe. You didn't even listen when I said it wasn't safe for Danny to drive."

"Jesus, it was an accident! It wasn't my fault. And the only reason we can't talk anymore is 'cause you won't. First you beg me to go to some shrink with you, to work things out, you say. And now you won't even tell me what's going on. We don't stand a chance if you won't talk to me. We don't stand a chance if calling this Kate person is more important than talking to me. So, who the hell is she?"

Silence filled the room, amplifying outdoor sounds: the whir of a sprinkler in a neighbor's yard; the bouncing of a basketball. I looked at Joe, hunched like an old man, and kept my distance as I spoke. "She's the grandmother of one of the Meadow Brook kids. I met her at the art fair. Remember, that night you refused to go with me?"

"And?"

"And nothing. She's a friend, that's all. A good friend."

"Well, let me tell you something. I have a good friend too. Mike. But no one calls here accusing me of anything because Mike and I are friends."

"It's different. Kate and I are really close. Maybe some of the kids misinterpreted our relationship."

"Those phone calls aren't the result of any fuckin' *maybe*, Beth."

"I told you, you wouldn't understand."

The phone rang again. Joe grabbed the receiver on the nightstand, though the cordless lay on the bed. He listened to the caller for a moment and then said, "What the hell do you want with my wife, lady?"

I jumped to take the phone from Joe. "Yes, she got your message, and she can't talk now." Joe slammed down the handset before I could snatch it, before I thought of reaching for the other phone.

"How dare you, Joe!"

"Who is she?"

"I told you. Her name's Kate. And you can't keep me from talking to her."

Joe held my wrists and looked at me hard. His face reddened. "And what do you do when you're together? Tell me, Beth. What is it the Meadow Brook kids know about you?"

I tried to free myself. "I don't have to answer your questions, dammit! And get your hands off me."

"So Kate Whoever-She-Is can touch you, but I can't?"

I pulled until Joe loosened his grip. "It's not like that."

"Then what *is* it like? I'm asking you one more time. What's going on?"

I couldn't find words for my relationship with Kate. Truth is, I didn't know what we had become to each other. Had we been playing mother-daughter? Best friends and confidantes? Or, had we tapped into a longing I had chosen to ignore? Is that what the Meadow Brook kids had picked up? What Callie had sensed from the beginning?

Anything I'd tell Joe would make my time with Kate sound wrong to him, dirty somehow. I couldn't define it. I wouldn't discuss it. "Nothing's going on. But I know you won't believe that."

I turned to leave, to go downstairs to call Kate. I had to explain what had happened—that when I had tried to tell her things were heating up, she dismissed my concerns. "Zach's a popular boy," she reminded me. "Silly rumors don't bother him." And now I had to tell

Kate that, despite everything—despite the rumors and the assembly, despite her anger and her blame—I still needed her in my life.

"So, you're really not gonna tell me?" Joe's voice grew louder as I left the bedroom. "Okay. Then go run away again. That's what you always do. It's you who runs from me, you know—not the other way around. So run downstairs and call your precious girlfriend, the one you think cares about you. And then just keep running. Run all the way to the city, to Rayanne's apartment, if that's what you want. And don't you worry, I won't try to stop you. But look who's throwing away our history now. Throwing it away like garbage. Garbage! Isn't that what you once said? So here's what I have to say." Joe's fury filled the house. "Good riddance to bad rubbish! Good riddance to bad rubbish, Beth!"

"Fuck you, Joe! It's your fault. All of this. Everything," I shouted as I took the stairs. "You were the one who let Danny drive!"

At the bottom step, I heard the bathroom door slam. I raced for the phone in the den and called Kate. She didn't pick up. Neither did Zach.

I tried many times that night. No answer. No machine. And with each attempt to reach Kate, my anger grew, slowly crushing my need for her. How dare Kate blame me for what happened.

Chapter Twenty-Four

I awoke in a pool of sweat and replayed the dream I just had. Peter leads a mob of students. They attack Kate and me at the beach. "Dykes should die!" the kids shout, pushing us toward the ocean. Kate reaches for me. A snake twists in her hand. I stumble into the sea as she drapes it around my shoulders. Peter laughs. "Serves you right, Mrs. Maller," he calls when I fight to free myself from the serpent coiling around my neck. "You didn't even protect your own son. So how can you help other people's children?"

Although I hadn't been aware of Joe during the night, the turned down sheet told me he had come to bed. As I drove to school that morning, I wondered how much longer I could stay in a house where grief strangled intimacy. And how much longer could I stay in Meadow Brook, where laughter and ridicule heaped on me like garbage? I trembled as I pulled into the parking lot.

Sue jumped when I walked into the counseling center. "Liz Grant's in your office, Beth. I couldn't stop her. She's real upset."

I didn't want to see Liz. Especially not then. But something had to be wrong or she wouldn't have been waiting for me. Yet, how could I help her when I couldn't even help myself?

I took a deep breath and opened the door. Liz sat on the edge of a chair, her back rigid, feet planted squarely on the floor. She jerked when I placed a hand on her shoulder. "Hi, Liz. What's going on?"

She didn't answer. I moved behind my desk and sat facing her. "What's the problem, Liz?" She looked straight ahead, eyes slightly off focus, hands clutching paper rolled up on her lap. "What do you have there?"

Liz lowered her head. "They'll kill me if they find out I have this," she said. "They'll kill me for tearing it down."

"What is it? And what can I do to help you?"

"I don't want you to do anything, Mrs. Maller, because if you tell anyone I brought this to you, they'll be after me. But I can't stand the way everyone's laughing at you, so I ripped this down without even thinking, and I was about to throw it away, but then I thought you should see it so you know what everyone's saying."

"So, let's see it."

"It just made me so angry. It was taped on the custodian's closet right across from my locker, and I don't even care if it's true, but this is what they're saying. They're saying Ms. Richardson converted you. That's what they were saying yesterday after the senior assembly, that Ms. Richardson converted you and now you'll get to Mrs. Harris, like it's some contagious disease and you're infecting the school. And then yesterday in the hall, Tina said now she knows why I spend so much time with you, that they're on to me too, that they know why I don't have a boyfriend." Liz looked at me then. Her shoulders rounded as tears started.

I pushed the box of tissues across my desk. I wanted to hold her. But for the first time, I realized my touch could be dangerous. What if someone walked in and found me hugging Liz? What if Peter saw us? So all I said was, "It'll be okay. Why don't you show me what's on that paper now."

Liz rolled it back and forth across her lap. "They said if I ever did anything wrong again they'd kill me for real." She raised her voice and spoke even faster. "But I couldn't help it, Mrs. Maller. I didn't want everyone to see this and to keep talking about you the way they do about Ms. Richardson, 'cause it's so mean and I hate them so much and I wish they were dead!"

As I watched Liz ball a tissue in one hand and grasp the paper tighter in the other, I heard Peter's voice from my dream: *You didn't even protect your own son. So how can you help other people's children?*

I had to help Liz; I had to protect her. "I don't want you to get hurt, sweetie," I said. "You can't defend yourself against kids like Tina. I want to help you, but I just don't know how."

"Promise you won't tell anyone I came here. Promise you won't tell anyone I talked to you about this."

"Okay," I said, implying secrecy. "Now, let's see what's on that paper."

Slowly, Liz unrolled the newsprint. She turned it around. I read the edict: DYKES SHOULD DIE! THAT MEANS YOU, MRS. MALLER. READ THE BIBLE.

I grabbed the sign, knowing the writers would, indeed, kill the messenger if they knew Liz had ripped down their work and brought it to me. I shivered as my fingers crushed their words.

Liz didn't seem to notice Fred Morris when she walked out of my office. He stood by the shelves of college catalogs, his back to my door. "Yo, Mrs. Maller! How goes it?" he called, turning toward me as Liz left.

"Go to homeroom, Fred. The bell's about to ring."

When it did, I longed to call Kate. But the old Kate didn't exist anymore. So while Peter's voice blared the morning announcements, I headed for the ladies' room, where I pulled down the notice taped to that door: DYKES SHOULD DIE! READ THE BIBLE, MRS. MALLER.

At the first period bell, I went to the art room, walking the long way around to avoid Peter. He would be in the cafeteria buying breakfast or heading back to the main office with a bagel. Fred bumped into me in the hall before I barged in on the photo class. Callie's students stopped everything, like children playing freeze tag. Girls, suspended in year-end cleanup, stood by open cabinets while boys, holding playing cards, sat perfectly still at the back tables.

Callie turned from the bulletin board. I motioned to the door. No one said a word as she followed me out.

I told her about the phone calls the night before and about my meeting with Liz. Callie said signs were plastered all over the school. One of her homeroom students had seen Tina and Jen tape them to the walls.

"How could I have been so naive, Cal?"

"Kate seduced you. Though I did try to warn you. But that's not important now." She touched my arm. I backed away. "Don't, Cal. What if someone sees us? I don't want them to start in on you now."

"I'm not worried."

"But I am." Tears stung my eyes. "I can't do this anymore."

"Do what?"

"Work in a place where I'm always looking over my shoulder. I used to love this school. I used to feel good about what I do. But now I sneak around like a criminal. I don't even know how to do my job anymore."

"Just do what you always did."

"I can't. I didn't even know what to say to Liz. And I'm scared— scared she'll get hurt—and it'll be my fault."

"Come on, Beth. You've tried to help, and Peter's blocked you every time. It's what I told you before: The gorilla always wins."

"You're right. You've always been right, Cal." I tried to breathe, to force stale Meadow Brook air into my lungs. "I'm sorry I spent so much time with Kate. I'm sorry I didn't listen to you. I don't know why you even bother with me anymore."

"Because I'm your friend." Callie hugged me then, and I didn't resist. "And I don't give a rat's ass if anyone sees us."

I went straight from the art room to the gym. If Tina was planning to attack Liz, she'd do so in the locker room. I had to talk to Ann.

Girls congregated on the gym bleachers. A group of boys huddled in a corner. Others played basketball. "They just did locker clean out," Ann explained as she came toward me. "It's such a waste, this last week of classes." She opened the door to the hallway. "Let's talk out there. I don't want to give the kids any more ammunition. I know about the posters, Beth. I can handle that kind of hate. I've had lots of practice. But you? I'm so sorry you have to go through this." I sensed she was about to pat me on the back. But instead, she moved away. "And if anyone sees us together, things'll get even worse for you."

"But I have to tell you about Liz." I told Ann I was sure Tina had set Liz up, posting the message on the custodial closet across from Liz's locker, then sending Fred to spy on her.

"That group has their last gym class tomorrow," Ann said. "I'll make sure Tina's nowhere near Liz. I can send Liz to the library. I'll tell her to empty her locker after school. No one'll bother her then. Tina and Jen surely leave the building the second the bell rings. They'd never hang around."

I wasn't thinking about Peter on the way back to my office. I didn't even notice him standing outside the counseling center as I rounded the corridor. "Mrs. Maller," he said with a chuckle. "Now I understand why you wanted to start a sensitivity program when that first sign went up about Ann Richardson. Dr. Sullivan will sure get a kick out of this, all right. Guess the truth always comes out, doesn't it?"

Chapter Twenty-Five

I'd been in Meadow Brook long enough to know how the school explodes at the end of the year, when students empty lockers, tossing papers and candy wrappers and notebooks into overflowing trash bins in the hallways. The last week of classes, Bob leans against a table in the main corridor, where he sips orange juice and gives the kids a pep talk as they come in: "Study hard. Do well. We've had a good year. Let's not blow it now, gang."

Unlike Bob, Peter sticks to the main office, where he checks exam schedules, assigns proctors, bundles tests. Too busy to mingle with students. No time for that. No sir. No way.

Tina's busy too, I imagine. I see her in my mind, guarding the hall before school, watching Jen hang that sign on the custodial closet across from Liz's locker. *Rip it down*, Tina must think when she sees Liz. *Then run to Mrs. Maller like you always do, even though all we were doing was having a little fun.*

The day after Liz came to me with that sign, she ran to my office once more—this time a half hour after dismissal. And this time, what Liz shared was far worse than homophobic slurs. Tina and Jen had attacked her, Liz told me through sobs, in the deserted locker room right after school when she went to empty her gym locker. She cried with embarrassment and fear as she whispered that Fred Morris had pulled down his pants after Tina and Jen had stripped off Liz's clothes, after they had forced her down on the cold hard floor that scraped her spine, which Liz said really hurt now. They pinned her arms back and told her they would kill her for sure if she screamed. And when the custodian cracked open the door and called in to see if anyone was there, Tina had stuffed a smelly sock into Liz's mouth before they all raced off.

"So I just need to hide here for a little while," Liz said in a voice barely audible, "in case they're out there waiting for me. But you can't tell anyone what I told you, especially my mother. If she finds out, she'll be really mad at me."

Liz's soft voice trembled. I strained to hear her swallowed words. "My mother will say it was my fault. She'll say I went look-ing for trouble. But I didn't, Mrs. Maller. Honest, I didn't." Liz melted into my arms and sobbed.

Suddenly, though, she pulled away and stood rigid, staring at me as if I were a stranger. "Wait. You told Ms. Richardson." The words caught in Liz's throat. "Now I understand. You told her I came to you yesterday, didn't you?"

Her voice grew louder as she backed toward the door. "How could you, Mrs. Maller! You promised you wouldn't tell anyone! And that's why Ms. Richardson wanted to keep me away from Tina and Jen. That's why she sent me upstairs to help the librarian while everyone else cleaned out their lockers. But Tina must have heard Ms. Richardson tell me to clean mine out after school. That's how Tina knew I was in the locker room. Why did you do that, Mrs. Maller?" Liz asked. "I trusted you!"

Liz flew out of my office and crashed into Peter. "What the hell's going on?" he screamed. Liz squeezed by him. "You come back here," Peter ordered as Liz pushed open the counseling center's door and rushed into the hall. "I'm talking to you, missy. You come back here this instant!"

"Please, Peter. Leave her alone," I begged.

He faced me for a second, hatred sparking in his eyes. "Don't you tell me how to do my job!" he yelled as he took off after Liz.

He hauled her back as if she were a dog that had messed on the floor. They stood in my doorway, Peter's fingers collaring Liz's twig-like arm. "When I talk to you, missy, I expect you to listen."

Liz stayed still, silent. When I looked at her, I sensed she had evaporated. Only a shell of pale skin remained. An image flashed in my mind: Danny in the Buick, snow coating the windshield.

"It's okay, Liz," I said, a forced calm in my voice. "No one's going to hurt you."

"What in the world are you talking about?" Peter asked. "You think I'm hurting her?"

"Please, Peter, let her go. She's had a horrible day."

"Is that true, Liz? You've had a bad day?"

The mocking playfulness in Peter's voice fueled my anger. "Yes," I answered for her. "Now let her go!"

Peter's fingers tightened around Liz's arm. "She has a mouth, Mrs. Maller. She can speak for herself."

"Tell him, Liz," I said. "You have to tell him what happened."

Liz didn't look up. She didn't speak. I tried to take a deep breath, but the air had thinned, as if all the oxygen had been sucked from my office.

"Jesus Christ!" Peter said. "We've been through this before. And I told you then, Liz. It's time to grow up and act your age."

"Let her go, Peter!"

His neck reddened, the color rising to his chin. "Don't you tell me what to do!"

"She's been hurt." I softened my voice, struggling to shed the anger. "Please, let her go."

Peter pushed Liz into a chair. "You're not going anywhere, missy. Not until you tell me what Mrs. Maller's talking about."

"Tell him, Liz. Then we'll make sure no one hurts you again."

Peter stood over Liz, his hands crushing her shoulders. "Okay, Liz, I'll make this real easy for you." He enunciated each word as if talking to a toddler. "Did anyone hurt you?"

I had to speak out. I couldn't let them hurt Liz again. "Tell him, Liz. You have to."

Peter took his hands off Liz and pounded my desk. "Christ almighty! I haven't got all day here. I've got far more important things to do than play kindergarten games. I'm trying to run a high school. I've got exam envelopes to check."

Liz stared at the floor. Her lips pressed together.

"I'm tired of repeating myself, missy. So, you tell me right now. Did anyone hurt you?"

Liz looked up, her eyes vacant as they met mine. "No," she said softly.

"Speak up," Peter said. "I want to make sure Mrs. Maller and I both hear you. Did anyone hurt you?"

Liz stood. "No!" she shouted, then bolted from my office.

My spine tingled. Guarding Liz's secrets hadn't protected her, and now she was denying the truth. How could I possibly keep her safe?

Peter grinned. "I'll see you in two minutes in Bob's office, Mrs. Maller. And don't be late. We've wasted enough time with your nonsense this semester."

Anger boiled in my gut. I couldn't control the tears. I didn't even try. I would have to tell Bob and Peter what Liz had told me. I would have to betray Liz's confidence to save her. Finally, I was thinking clearly—something I hadn't been doing since returning to Meadow Brook. My silence had been as harmful as Bob's ignorance, as deadly as Peter's spite.

This had to stop. It had to stop now.

I entered the principal's office from the hall so I wouldn't pass Mary's desk. If I saw her, I'd have to tell her Liz had been abused, and I wouldn't know how much to say. I couldn't predict Mary's reaction. Maybe she wouldn't believe Liz's story. *My God, Beth. Don't you think Lizzie would have come to me if they had tried to rape her?* Or maybe Liz had been right: Mary might blame her. *I've been telling Lizzie all semester to just stay away from those kids. If she would have listened to me, she wouldn't have gotten herself in trouble.* As I pulled myself together to meet Bob and Peter, I understood why Liz shielded herself from her mother. Blame the victim. Kill the messenger.

But what if Mary believed Liz had been attacked and hadn't asked for it? Then would Mary confront the attackers? And would she confront me for not having pushed her to see the truth earlier? Or would she attack Bob and Peter for the gaping hole in school security, that pit into which Liz had plunged?

Bob pointed to a chair at the conference table. "Okay, Beth," he said as I sat. "I'm told there's been a little problem with Liz Grant."

"It's not a little problem. It's possible Liz was raped. She was stripped and abused after school today in the locker room. I'm not exactly sure how far they got. And Tina Roland might still be after her. We have to protect Liz so they don't get her again."

"Just a second, Mrs. Maller," Peter said. "You say you're not exactly sure what happened? Then how can you accuse anyone? And what was Liz doing in the locker room after school anyhow?"

Bob jumped in before I could answer. "Hold on, Pete," he said. "I need to know what happened this afternoon."

"But Mrs. Maller already told us she's not sure exactly what happened," Peter said. "And I need to know what Liz was doing in the locker room after school."

"Emptying her gym locker," I said quickly, refusing to meet Peter's eyes.

"Which she was supposed to do during gym class," Peter added.

"Forget that, Pete!" Bob said. "Beth, what happened this afternoon?"

Peter stood up and leaned against the table, bracing himself with his sausage fingers. "Just give me a minute here, Bob." He stared at me till my eyes met his. "Tell me, Mrs. Maller, since you seem to be the expert on what goes on around here: Why didn't Liz empty her locker during gym class, when she was supposed to?"

"I don't believe this!" I answered. "A student's been attacked, and what's important to you is why she emptied her locker after school?"

"You know what Bob says about rules, Mrs. Maller. We run a tight ship in Meadow Brook. It's the rules that keep us afloat. But you don't seem to care about that, do you? Because every time you let Liz hang out in your office when she's supposed to be in class, you break the rules. Every time you refuse to send her to Debra, you break the rules. And when Ms. Richardson breaks the rules . . . well, look at what you say happened because Liz didn't clean out her locker when she was supposed to. But you know, I'm not really surprised. I mean, it's your kind, people like you and Ms. Richardson, who always break the rules and mess things up. Don't you agree, Bob?"

"That's enough, Pete! For God's sake, sit down, and let Beth tell us what happened. I need to know."

"But she doesn't know what happened. She already said that."

"That's not true!" Anger and frustration rolled in my chest. "I know Liz was stripped after school in the locker room. This wasn't the first time those kids got her."

"What kids?" Bob asked.

"Tina Roland, Jen Scotto, and Fred Morris. I know Tina and Jen stripped her once before. We have to stop them now. We have to find Liz and make sure she's okay. They could be waiting outside for her."

"I don't believe this," Peter cut in. "It's not enough you want to take over in school? Now you want to take over outside too?" He shook his head and looked at Bob. "Don't you see what's happening here? Word's out that Tina was the ringleader in yesterday's little sign-posting, though there's no proof, so we can't accuse her, of course. And we're not going to make a big deal out of this. But you know the signs I'm talking about, the ones that said—"

"Enough!" Bob held him back. "We all know what those signs said."

"But don't you see what Mrs. Maller's doing? She's making these allegations to get even with Tina for telling us what we should have guessed months ago. I mean, come on, Bob. I know you see what's been happening. Mrs. Maller wanted to start some stupid sensitivity program after the word was out about Richardson. Do you honestly think Mrs. Maller would have cared one whit if not for her own sexuality? And now she wants to punish Tina for making her the Meadow Brook laughingstock. But accusing Tina and her friends of raping Liz? Well, that's . . . that's just taking it too damn far. I can't believe even Mrs. Maller would stoop that low, especially when Liz herself denied it. She told me nobody hurt her."

"Listen to me, Bob!" I ripped my shroud of silence. "Liz needs our help. We can't allow Tina to hurt her anymore. That's what this is about. That's all this is about. Please, Bob, believe me. They're going to get her again. And they threatened to kill her if anyone found out what they did. But you can stop them. You're the only one who can protect Liz. You can't let Tina hurt her anymore!"

"Hang on here, Mrs. Maller." Peter stroked his cheek as if thoughts sprouted on his skin. He spoke slowly now, his words deliberate. "You said Tina and Jen attacked her before. Did you know about that, Bob?"

"It doesn't matter," I said, not listening for Bob's answer. "The only thing that matters is protecting Liz." I had to speak out. There wasn't a choice. I hadn't saved Danny. I had to save Liz. This time I would make a difference. And if doing the right thing meant risking my job, if Joe had been right about that, so what? What had mattered was Danny. What mattered now was Liz.

Maybe it wasn't a gorilla I was up against after all. Maybe I was battling my old self—the Beth who cared about year-end evaluations and pleasing Bob with a Beatles tune. The Beth who would let Peter chew her like a piece of Tina's gum. It was time to let go of that Beth. I said goodbye to her that afternoon Liz was attacked, as I glared at Peter and fought for Liz. "The only thing that matters is making sure Liz isn't hurt."

"Now you just hold it right there!" Peter struck the table. "You're saying it doesn't matter that Bob and I didn't know about the first attack? Let me get this straight. You claim a student was abused in our school, and you say it's not important that you never reported it?"

I looked at Bob. "We can't let them hurt her again. That's why Ann kept Liz out of gym today—to protect her. Tina's been threatening Liz all year. And now it's up to you, Bob. You have to stop those kids before they get her again. You have to do something!"

Bob nodded. "Had you heard anything about this, Pete? Anything at all before now?"

"Hell no! And that alone's grounds for dismissal, wouldn't you say? Not reporting a threat against a student? Sounds to me like Mrs. Maller's guilty of endangering the welfare of a child."

"You want to talk about endangering the welfare of a child, Peter?" The sound of my voice, firm and strong, surprised me. "This is how you endanger the welfare of a child: You close your eyes when a student's in pain; you refuse to listen when she cries for help. Liz begged you to change her gym class at the beginning of the year, but you wouldn't budge. And you yanked her from my office after the first attack in the locker room. Even when you saw how upset she was, you told her she couldn't talk to me. You sent her back to class."

A fireball of anger swept through me. "This is how you endanger the welfare of a child, Peter: You steamroll a student who needs to be heard. You crush her with your power and stamp on anyone who gets in your way. You're so freakin' busy enforcing your stupid rules, you have absolutely no idea what goes on around here. And you endanger the welfare of everyone in Meadow Brook when you ignore signs of harassment and hate. You didn't do anything when that poster went up about Ann. You didn't care that homophobia would fester—and it did. And its eruption in the senior assembly led to this attack on Liz."

Peter spread his fingers and flexed his hands on the table. He looked at Bob, who nodded at me to continue.

"You're right about one thing, though. I should have told you about the threats against Liz on the outside chance that maybe, just maybe, you would have done something to ensure her safety. But you probably wouldn't have believed me. And even if you had, my guess is you wouldn't have done anything to help her, because you care more about rules than about students. Your tight ship is more important to you than anyone on it. And all you're interested in is keeping everything nice and quiet so parents don't give you a hard time and so Dr. Sullivan doesn't get on your case.

"I'm just sorry he didn't see how you dragged Liz back to the center a little while ago, Peter, when she may have been a rape victim. But you don't care about that. All you care about is making sure no one finds out what really goes on in this school. Because if anyone did, you'd have to handle it. You'd have to do something. And you'd have to face the facts: You don't run a tight ship at all. Because your ship's sprung a big leak, and the sad thing is, you don't even care about the students who are going down with it. The only thing you care about is that no one knows it's sinking.

"So don't you dare accuse me of endangering the welfare of a child when it's you who calls the shots. I'm not the captain here. You've made that perfectly clear. But I'm telling you: Meadow Brook is sinking, and when kids get hurt—and believe me, they will—everyone will know it was you who brought us down."

Bob spoke first. "Are you finished?"

I nodded.

"Good," Peter said, "because now that you've gotten that off your chest, let me tell you something. You're not going to have to worry about what goes on around here much longer. Your little tirade there just clinched it." He smiled at Bob. "I'd say we've got her on three charges: conduct unbecoming a teacher; insubordination; and endangering the welfare of a child. What do you say, Bob?"

I stood, not waiting for his answer. "Please don't let them hurt Liz again," I said. Then I walked out of Meadow Brook.

Chapter Twenty-Six

In the end, I could see it started long before last winter. I sit in Starbucks now, in Manhattan, and I wonder: If Danny hadn't died, would I have fought so hard for Liz?

Dr. Goldstein says I've traded my consequence game for *What if*. What if Danny hadn't written about Matthew Shepard's murder? Would I have pushed for a sensitivity program in Meadow Brook? Would I have met with Tina and Jen? And what if I would have spoken out sooner? Would Peter and Bob have listened? Could I have prevented the abuse? Or would Liz have been hurt no matter what?

Liz doesn't go to Meadow Brook anymore; she transferred to St. Francis. I hear she's doing well.

"I saw a recent photo of her," Callie told me in one of her almost daily phone calls. "It's on Mary's desk, next to the picture of Mary and her new husband. And Liz looks pretty good. Not as skinny as last year."

Dr. Goldstein says I play *What if* to make sense of situations I can't control. "But life doesn't always make sense, Beth," he said a few months ago. "So you can't control it any more than you could have controlled whether your mother broke her back if you stepped on a crack."

I remember that particular therapy session well. I took the train from Manhattan to Glenwood, and Joe met me at the station. We saw Dr. Goldstein together. Then Dad insisted on treating us to dinner at the steakhouse. "I won big at the poker game at Saul's, honey. And it makes me feel good to take my children out." He winked at Joe. "Better than Chinese food. Right, son?"

I stayed in Bay View that night. Moose hunkered down by my side of the bed, and Joe chuckled. "That's the first time he's slept in here. Guess he really misses you, Red."

I fell asleep next to Joe and dreamed I was a little girl, standing on my father's feet as he danced me around the living room. When I shared that dream with Dr. Goldstein, I realized it has taken me a lifetime to hop off of Dad's shoes and move around on my own. Dr. Goldstein has helped me to see that with Joe, too, I've been fearful of taking my own steps.

I sit alone now and think about Joe. And I wonder: When did we stop loving enough? Was it when I became Danny's mom— when my focus tunneled to my child? Or did our love evaporate slowly, as Danny grew and Joe worked harder and the "us" of Joe and Beth slipped away?

Do it right the first time so you won't have to tear it down and start again. That's what Joe always said. He and I hadn't built our relationship right. I see that now. A storm far less powerful than grief could have ripped it apart. I wonder about building it back. I know that's what Joe wants. He calls every night. And last week he came into the city twice, though he says he's not comfortable seeing me in Rayanne and Andy's apartment, surrounded by their furniture and using all their things.

There is one item that's mine, though. Just last week, I wandered into a store to pick up a greeting card for Callie, who, in addition to calling, sends me a funny card with a note every few days. Her misspelled words don't bother me at all now. At the store, in the card aisle, I saw a rack of coffee mugs—all simple white china, each with a letter of the alphabet. I reached for a *B. B* for Beth. Just Beth. That mug now sits on the kitchen counter in Rayanne and Andy's apartment.

Joe thinks I should look for my own place, "unless you're ready to come back to Bay View," he said on his last visit. I told Joe the truth then: I don't know if I am coming back. So he wants me to use some of the college fund for a temporary sublet or a short-term lease. Nothing fancy. Just a place of my own for the time being, because we can't ever know what the future will bring.

Kate was right about that—about the unpredictability of life. Sometimes I still hear her voice: *You just can't know what tomorrow will bring.* Last spring I'd have guessed that Kate would have been in my life forever. Yet, I've spoken with her only once since the senior assembly. I called when I sent in my letter of resignation. Maybe I felt the need to tie up loose ends, to define our relationship before shelving it in my mind. Or, maybe I was finally angry enough to lash out at Kate for having blamed me for the explosion at school. But when she picked up the phone, I didn't say much—just told her I was leaving. Kate wished me luck. "And let me know when you're settled, dear. Perhaps we can get together then." *No way*, I said to myself. *Find someone else to fill you up when you're lonely.* "Maybe we could visit in the city," Kate went on, "away from Meadow Brook."

I still dream about Meadow Brook High School. Dr. Goldstein says my dreams help me sort out the anger and sadness that have shadowed me since Danny died. He says that trying to make sense of my emotions guides me toward the future, while playing *What if* tethers me to the past. Two of my dreams recur. In one, Tina drags me to the gym, where Liz hangs by the neck from a rope. In the other, Peter chases me until I fall into a hole at the end of a hall.

Callie tells me she hears Peter's in the running for a job as principal of Garden Grove High School. Rumor has it that when Peter and Bob disagreed on the candidate to replace me, Peter got his resumé in order.

Callie tells me about Tina too. She's in Callie's photo class now. "What's up, Mrs. Harris?" Tina said at the beginning of second semester. "And how's your girlfriend, Mrs. M., doin'?"

Callie told me that every time Tina asked, Callie gave the same answer: "She's doing fine. Thanks for asking. And lose the gum, please." Tina stopped asking about me, but she continued coming to class with a purple wad in her mouth. All that cracking and bubble popping drove Callie mad. So, after a couple of weeks, Callie finally said, "You can't chew gum in here, Tina. And if you don't like that rule, drop this class. I wouldn't miss you."

I certainly don't miss Tina, but I do miss working with students. Last Sunday I saw an ad for a part-time counselor at a private school on the Upper West Side. When I stopped at the post office on my way to Starbucks this morning, I heard Danny's voice as I sent off my letter of application: *Way to go, Mom! Way to go!*

Acknowledgments

Heartfelt thanks to family and friends who read early drafts of this book and cheered me on—and to those who cheered from the sidelines. How lucky I am to have you on my team.

Special thanks to my agent, Jennifer Lyons, who got the ball rolling; and to my wonderful editor, Julie Matysik, who not only "gets" my novels but also "gets" me. What a pleasure it is to work with you and the dedicated folks at Skyhorse.

And belated thanks to my former students, who were, actually, my best teachers. You are still in my thoughts—these many years later.

Without you all, there would be no book. I am filled with love and gratitude.

Discussion Questions for *Danny's Mom*

1. Blame and guilt are significant issues in *Danny's Mom*. Why does Beth feel the need to blame Joe for Danny's death? Does blaming Joe serve a purpose for Beth? Why do you think she initially absolves herself of guilt? And what causes Beth to realize that she shares responsibility for the accident?

2. Beth seems to think of Danny as her son only, not as Joe's son. Why does she feel that way? How, in general, do you think the mother-child relationship differs from the father-child relationship?

3. The characters in *Danny's Mom* face many conflicts. Discuss the conflict between Beth and Joe. What causes the tension in their relationship? And what causes the conflict between Joe and Al, Beth's father? Why does Joe seem at odds with him?

4. Throughout the novel, the tension between Beth and Peter is palpable. In fact, Beth says, "Peter and I were allergic to each other." Discuss the tension in their relationship. Is Peter solely to blame for their antagonism? And is Peter alone to blame for what happens at Meadow Brook High School?

5. When characters are well drawn, readers gain insight into what motivates them. Discuss what motivates Joe. What motivates Beth? What motivates Peter?

6. Several reviewers call *Danny's Mom* "a story about relationships." Discuss the relationship between Beth and her father. Talk about the relationship between Beth and Callie. Contrast Beth and Joe's relationship with the relationship between Callie and her husband, Tom.

7. In thinking about Joe, Beth recognizes that "Danny had glued [them] together, even when [they] argued about him. And now [they] were peeling apart." Do you think Beth's realization applies to most marriages that have to incorporate tragedy or hard times? Discuss the difference in how Beth and Joe each respond to grief.

8. Some reviewers say that the book is primarily about bullying. Who are the bullies in this novel? How does each one grab power and hold on to it?

9. Other reviewers call *Danny's Mom* a book about motherhood. Although we don't experience the relationship between Beth and Danny firsthand, we know a lot about it. Do you think Beth was a good mother? Discuss Beth's thought that "maybe [she] didn't have enough love for a husband and a child. Or maybe [she] didn't know how to divide it." Compare Beth as a mother to Liz's mother, Mary Grant.

10. Many of the characters in the book make poor decisions. Talk about the decisions and/or choices made by Beth, Liz, Bob and Peter, Joe, and Ann Richardson. What, if anything, do you think Beth should have done differently at school and at home? What do you think Liz should have done?

11. Why doesn't Liz speak out? Why doesn't Beth speak out sooner?

12. Although Beth makes poor choices as she fights to help Liz, Beth is passionate about trying to do what she feels is best for Liz. Beth's motivation extends beyond simply being a counselor. Why does Beth feel compelled to rescue Liz?

13. Discuss Kate Stanish. What is her motivation? Talk about the relationship between Beth and Kate. Beth trusted Kate immediately;

Beth "embraced Kate's words like a kind of religion." Why? And why does Beth obsess about Kate? What does that obsession offer Beth?

14. Discuss the symbolism of Beth's reading *To Kill a Mockingbird*. Similarly, discuss the black and white clown that Zach Stanish drew.

15. Beth lies a lot. Why? What benefit does lying give her? And what harm does it do?

16. Discuss Beth's crazy consequence game—the way she lists or counts things and invents consequences. Why does she do that?

17. Beth realizes that, maybe, parents can never fully know their children. ("Do we ever really know our children? Can we hear their messages, told in half-truths and glances? Or, do we plug our ears and close our eyes for fear of what we'll find?") Beth wonders if parents and children are afraid of each other. ("Are our children as afraid of us as we are of them? Afraid that we'll blame them? Afraid of our lies?") What do you think? Can parents fully know their children? And do you agree with Beth that parents and children are afraid of each other?

18. *Danny's Mom* has been called a coming-of-age story for adults. How does Beth grow and change and find her voice? What lessons does she learn? What have you learned as a reader, or what thoughts do you have after reading the book?

19. Discuss the cover: the image of a sinking school. Why do you think that picture was chosen?

20. There are two epigraphs at the beginning of the novel. One is attributed to Kiran Desai: "The present changes the past. Looking back you do not find what you left behind." The other is from Anne Morrow Lindbergh: "Woman must come of age by herself. She must find her true center alone." Discuss these quotes as they relate to *Danny's Mom*.

A Conversation with Elaine Wolf

Q: What inspires your writing? And, specifically, what inspired you to write *Danny's Mom*?

A: In general, my novels stem from my work as a high school teacher, school district program director, and camp counselor. I love teenagers, and I'm troubled by some school and camp cultures in which our teens learn to navigate their worlds. I'm angry that the adults we charge with keeping our children safe sometimes turn their backs on the victims and ignore the bullies. And, as a parent and grandparent, I'm haunted by the knowledge that danger can be present when we're not around to protect our children, and, sometimes, even when we are.

Here's the story behind the story—what brought me to *Danny's Mom*. It started many years before I wrote the novel, when my son, Adam, received his early decision college acceptance letter. It arrived on a wintry day, and Adam begged to borrow my car so he could deliver the good news to his girlfriend in person. I knew I should say no, that it wasn't safe for him to drive because snow was starting to fall, and the forecast was bad. But Adam persisted, and he was so happy, and he promised to be extra careful. Stupidly, I gave in.

Adam arrived at his girlfriend's house without incident. But then he and his girlfriend decided to drive to the local pizzeria to celebrate. You can imagine what happened next. The car spun out, slid across the icy road, and crashed into a tree. Fortunately, the kids walked away with no injuries. But for years after that accident, I played the "what if" game. And I beat myself up for having let my son take the car. That event morphed into the opening scene of *Danny's Mom*.

Still another story about Adam played a role in leading me to this novel. When he was a young teen at a sleep-away camp, Adam's group went on a camping trip. I found out after the fact that the counselors took off, leaving the kids alone "in the middle of nowhere" all night. When Adam finally told me about this, he admitted that the boys were frightened. They didn't know where they were, or when—or if—their counselors would return. When I heard that, I started to think about the people to whom we entrust our children's safety. They often fall short, and we probably don't know about some of the times our children are in peril. Keeping our children safe is something I think about a lot. It's a big theme in *Danny's Mom*.

Lastly, I started writing this book shortly after I retired from my job as a high school teacher and district reading/language arts director. In that position, I occasionally battled with administrators whose opinions of what was in the best interests of students sometimes conflicted with mine. The struggle and power plays between teachers and administrators permeate *Danny's Mom*. Like Beth Maller in the novel, I found that it's not always easy to do the right things for our kids.

Q: What inspired the book's cover?

A: I was pleased that my editor asked for my input when the designer was working on the cover for *Danny's Mom*. I had been thinking about Beth's final run-in with Peter, the assistant principal, and how the administrators of the fictitious Meadow Brook High School pride themselves on having rules which, they claim, keep the school afloat. Beth believes Meadow Brook is sinking, and she fears for the students who, she imagines, will go down with it. So I shared my vision of a turbulent ocean with a sinking school building in the center. I believe the designer captured the essence of my vision, and I think the cover works well.

Q: What goes on in the high school you created is horrible. The administrators seem incompetent and uncaring. Do schools like the fictitious Meadow Brook really exist?

A: Fortunately, most schools are so much better than the fictitious high school in the novel. But, sadly, what happens in Meadow

Brook could actually happen. Although most school administrators truly care about the well-being of students, some don't. As in any workplace, some administrators become jaded and power hungry—and when they do, their schools can turn into dysfunctional communities in which students and teachers are victimized.

I think parents believe (or want to believe) that everyone who works in their children's schools are compassionate, knowledgeable adults who always look out for the students' best interests. And most of the time, most of the adults to whom we entrust our children's safety do a good job. But sometimes they don't. I think of *Danny's Mom* as a book of admonition: know what goes on in your children's schools; stay involved—even when your children are older, when they're in high school; speak up and speak out; and always be a fierce advocate for your children. When parents act like Mary Grant in *Danny's Mom*, who ignores the warning signs of problems and refuses to acknowledge the difficulties her child faces, then, yes, schools like Meadow Brook can really exist.

Q: What inspired your crusade against bullying?

A: I didn't intend to become an anti-bullying crusader; I started by writing what I hoped would be good, compelling novels. But because my first young adult book, *Camp*, is set in a sleep-away camp, and *Danny's Mom* is set in a high school, it was impossible not to write about bullying.

Early reviewers stated that I had created "really believable bullying scenes" and that "the mean girl voices are pitch perfect." The more I heard that, the more I realized that my novels could serve as springboards for conversations about bullying, and the more eager I became to use my books to make a difference: to keep anti-bullying conversations going so that, in concert with professionals in our communities, we will make our camps and schools kinder, gentler, more inclusive places for everyone. I never imagined my books would lead me to this mission, but I'm really glad they have!

Q: What do you hope readers take away from *Danny's Mom*?

A: I hope readers find the book to be a gripping story, one that they're eager to share with friends and book groups. When they do, I really hope *Danny's Mom* will be a springboard for lots of conversations about what actually can go on when school doors shut. Although, as I said, most schools are good places, and most teachers and administrators really care about the education, welfare, and safety of students, not all schools are good. The sad reality is that schools are businesses, and not all teachers and administrators are "in it" for the right reasons. As in all places of business, there are power struggles in schools, and bullies lurk in the halls. In some schools, like the fictitious school in the book, mean girls (and boys) practice bullying as if it were a sport. And sometimes the biggest bullies in our schools are the administrators we entrust with the sacred responsibility of keeping our children safe.

I believe that if we're aware of what goes on in schools, of what it's like for some of our kids who wish they could fade into the walls, then we'll work harder to make our schools kinder, gentler, and safer places for everyone. I feel honored that my novels have given me a platform, a literal bully pulpit, from which to carry on this movement. I hope that readers take away from *Danny's Mom* the importance of joining this mission to make our schools better communities for our children and grandchildren. I hope, too, that readers take away from this novel the necessity of maintaining honest, open communication with our children, whose cries for help should never be ignored.

**For additional interviews, information,
and anti-bullying resources,
please visit the author at www.authorelainewolf.com.**